SEISMIC DRIFT

SEISMIC DRIFT

SHADOW ZONE BROTHERHOOD
BOOK 2

DALIA DAVIES

ISBN: 9798322643401

Cover Art & Interior Illustration by Sophie Zuckerman (@dextrose.png)

Editing by Meg at Amethyst Dragon LLC (@opalescent4026)

www.daliadavies.com

SEISMIC DRIFT

Love isn't finite.
Grief only fades.
Danger is inescapable.
Is a second chance is worth the risk?

Dancing is my life. I love it more than anything on this planet.

Maybe that's a lie I tell myself to keep the longing at bay.

On Isia, the women who work at Margot's can do as much or as little as they like with the Sian men who come in to learn how to please their future human mate. I'm the only exception to that rule.

The Agency is careful to tiptoe around the risks with traveling to Isia for alien mate. I've been here long enough, I thought I knew them all.

My first bondmate was murdered—an event I almost didn't survive. Bonding again... that's a risk I don't think I'm willing to take. But I am tempted.

D is the only man I've let get close enough to touch me since my bondmate died. And I count the days between his visits. He's the only one who has ever tempted me. The only one who gets my time.

And all he wants to do is talk, and sleep.

I've learned as little as I can about him, because longing is as close as I'll let myself get to losing him.

But keeping myself in the dark, where only he can see me with his strange crystal ball eyes, puts me directly in the path of men who want him dead.

They want me to do it, and they know enough of my past to be dangerous.

For E

Who loves me in spite of all of my flaws

WANT TO SKIP STRAIGHT TO THE SPICY BITS?

If you're just here to bang an alien, I totally respect that.

There is a secondary table of contents at the end of the book (a menu, if you will) that will get you to each of the spicy scenes. Just flip to the back and you can skip ahead.

I'd recommend reading the book through chronologically first, but I'm biased.

Enjoy this book however you want.

AUTHOR'S NOTE

A much shorter version of this book was published in 2020 as "Alien Obsession" when I was writing under the pen name Elise Jae. The novel in your hands has been completely rewritten, reedited, and reshaped into a story that has similar bones, but is otherwise brand new.

Kimba & Drift's romance always felt like it had more to tell. Finding the right version of their story has been an act of love and I hope you feel that in the following pages.

GLOSSARY/ PRONUNCIATION GUIDE

Azhibka *(ah-zeeb-ka)* mistake

Bakat *(bak-aht)* virtual board game similar to sudoku and chess

Cavrinskh *(kav-rins-k)* monsters inside the Shadow Zone

Dajzha *(dah-\zha)* an archaic Sian honorific for "lady"

Keruun (Cay-roon) Jewel

Kisimb (Key-seemb) fate

Lasap *(Lah-sahp)* a military grade metal composite

Nyac telum *(Knee-ack Tey-loom)* I can't lose you

Nawt melum *(Not meh-loom)* you won't lose me

Ojuin (Oh-joo-in) love nest

Sian *(Sigh-an)* alien race galaxies away

Susre *(Soos-rey)* Soulmate

Weeun *(Ween)* baby / small child

Zurgle *(Zoor-gul)* a domesticated, cat-like creature

TRIGGER & CONTENT WARNINGS

SOME ELEMENTS of this book may be triggering to readers. Please see the following list of CWs to ensure that you are comfortable reading this book before you continue.

Blackmail
Breeding
Explicit Human/Non-Human sex (bipedal aliens.)
Fluid Kink
Gender Essentialism
Kidnapping/Abduction (of tertiary characters)
Mentions of Femicide (historic, extinction-level & recent, singular. Off page.)
Hunting Animals (invasive population, not food.)
Pregnancy (Planned, primary and secondary characters.)
Murder/Death

If you feel something was missed in this list, please contact Dalia at authordaliadavies@gmail.com

CHAPTER
ONE

KIMBA

"HE'S BACK!" Hannah slips past me, scooting close to the mirror to check her flawlessly winged eyeliner.

The redhead looks at me in the reflection with a smile that tells me it's not one of *her* regulars.

The date is wrong for it to be mine, but she wouldn't be acting like this for nothing.

"Who?" I ask, pretending at cluelessness as she rolls her eyes at me.

I know who she's talking about... even if I don't actually *know* who she's talking about.

"*Big* D." Hannah sticks her tongue out at me.

At Margot's, the clients don't *have* to use their real names with us. Margot knows *exactly* who they are. We don't need to.

The women who work here call them whatever they ask to be called. Hannah and the others are the ones who added "big" to his "D".

I wouldn't know.

That's not a service I provide.

3

Of all the women on Margot's payroll, I'm the only one who couldn't. Even when my resolve falters and I let myself follow that temptation my imagination has played with too many times, D's big D isn't for me... even if we both want it.

And I'm not even certain he does.

I hum, smoothing a brush over my cheekbone and continue to feign innocence. "Who do you think he's going to ask for tonight?"

Rolling her eyes, Hannah gives me a shove. If I hadn't been braced for it, I'd have fallen out of my chair—she's used to Sian men, and she can throw her whole weight into *them*.

"You're such a tease." She laughs as she says it, sweeping her gorgeous red hair up into a ponytail. "Save that for him."

I almost mention the bite mark on her neck. If that's not gone by the time her favorite regular comes in, the man might hunt down the biter and remove all his teeth for bruising her.

Hazard isn't her bondmate, but he certainly acts like it. He doesn't mind sharing her—in fact, he seems to relish it —but he won't tolerate anyone hurting her.

D hasn't said as much, but I imagine a bite mark like that wouldn't end well for whoever gave it to me.

The door to the back hall opens and lets in the heavy beat of the club's music. We use them to wind our way through the club without being seen or distracted by patrons. On this level, the electronic beat is fairly subdued, but it still rushes in in a wave that ebbs as soon as the door closes behind Margot.

She doesn't yell for me across the room. She walks casually to me through the empty sofas of the lounge area where the girls take their breaks, over to the

4

makeup tables, where we do our quick changes after cleaning up.

"Your biggest fan is here," Margot says, when she stops beside me, glancing at Hannah, "but I imagine someone beat me to that announcement."

"You move fast, but the whispers move faster." Hannah winks at her and then looks at me with an apologetic smile. "The other girls are waiting for you to give in, so they can hear all about that big D."

Her smile goes a little tight, but she doesn't reveal what she knows.

She, Margot and D are the only ones at the club who know why I can't fall into the temptation he poses.

Because you have to be bonded to work here, and I'm not.

They can't send widows back to Earth—it would make the Agency look bad—and bonding again... that comes with risks most women in this building have never considered.

But I like D, and he's never crossed a single boundary, even if he makes me want to break the rules.

I twist and the shimmer of my bra reflects in the mirror.

I love that vibrant blue, but if he'd warned me he was coming, I would have changed from my post-dance outfit into something more appropriate, something black and soft.

Something that wouldn't hurt his eyes.

Changing now would take too much time, and that's something I never want to waste with him.

Margot drags my robe off the back of my chair as I stand.

"Why are you scowling," she asks. "This is your favorite part of the job."

5

That's not exactly true, but I'm not going to argue.

Margot helps me slip the robe on and skims her hands over the soft velvet flowers on my shoulders.

"Everything still hunky dory with him?" She asks, meeting my eyes in the mirror.

"Completely."

Because Margot's not here to make money. She's here to keep us safe... and also make money.

If I wasn't sure I wanted to step into that room, she wouldn't let me.

But she knows who he really is. She's the one who told me I'd be safe.

I trusted her then.

I trust him now.

"You," Hannah says as she hands me the clasp that holds the robe closed, "are the only one in this place with a client who asks you to put clothes back on."

"I'm the only one who *can't* take them off." I remind her.

"You could give him a blowjob and at least sate the others' curiosity."

"You mean I could sate your curiosity?"

The women who work here love to share notes on the men they sleep with—the men they are essentially *training* until they are given a mate by the Agency.

I lean forward and kiss her forehead. "The stage is the only place I take my clothes off for them, love. And it has to stay that way."

"I think he could make you happy." Hannah says it quietly... like she knows she shouldn't say it at all.

I turn away from the mirror so she doesn't see my face. Maybe she's right, but, "That assumes I'm not happy already."

"Are you?" Margot hasn't asked me that question for a *very* long time, but the lie comes easily enough.

"Of course." I squeeze her hand. She's my friend, even if she's also my boss. "How could I be sad when the two of you do everything in your power to make sure I'm not?"

I kiss her on the cheek and leave before they can poke holes through that logic.

I leave so the dim hallways hide the tears pricking at my eyes.

Happiness died with Edan. Finding it again… that feels like betrayal.

D gets me close—I'll never deny that—but contentment is the best I can hope for.

Pushing through the doors and into the dark, pulsating beat of the club's public play room on this level, I feel a dozen eyes track me.

Margot stopped telling me about the requests for my company in specific numbers, but they never stop coming.

Men—even on this planet—are more inclined to lust after what they can't have.

I don't normally venture into these rooms.

The only time I use them is on nights like this, when I want to get to D faster—the back halls take twice as long.

The stage is where I *work*.

These spaces are meant for getting ready to disappear into the private rooms… or the men who like to be watched and the women who love performing with an audience.

I don't need to weave through the chairs and tables looking for a man who catches my eye and vice versa.

The faces that turn my way are immediately turned back by a finger of the woman on their laps.

Everyone who works here knows me. They can guess where I'm headed, if they don't actually know. And they know Margot will give them hell if they let someone *accidentally* get in my way.

I have to walk all the way through to get to the elevator that will take me to the right level. It's a gauntlet, but the rules are strict here. If a man was to approach me on his own, he'd be banned. And no one's willing to risk that.

In the neon glow of the descending lift, I take deep breaths, settling myself. And when the doors open again, those threatening tears and anxious fidgets are gone.

I can be sad at home. No one's paying me to cry here.

The third floor is the quietest, which is why he always comes here.

The path into the neon arches of the mirrored hallway is a familiar one.

A woman slips out of a door ringed in orange and offers me a little smile and wave. She doesn't know the private rooms that line these walls are the last place I should be.

Everyone else who works here is bonded. Their mates consent to their choice and men who aren't bonded—either because they haven't done their year's membership or they're waiting for their match—get the chance to learn how to treat their mates when they finally get them… or find out they don't want a permanent partner, after all.

Only a few of the doorways are ringed in red—currently in use. Fewer still are lined in orange—waiting for the cleaners to slip in and finish up with what the automated systems can't manage.

Other floors will be completely full at this time of night. The louder, more boisterous crowd likes to fill the public play rooms and then migrate off on their own when they've had enough of just watching.

The Agency pays Margot a lot of money to keep Sian

men interested in finding their bondmate—it's not a bad return on investment. I've seen the numbers.

I pull open a door marked with a black light number seven and slip inside, swiping my hand over the lock before I turn to him.

Unbonded men who come to Margot's are eighty-three percent more likely to pay the Agency to find them a bondmate. They *have* to be a member of a city's club for at least a year before they can even apply, though. This is a place to figure out what they liked—so they can fill out the questionnaire honestly, so their matches are approved.

But D's not here for that.

He's never asked for anyone else.

He's never asked me to do anything the others would do as standard.

D knows I'm not bonded anymore.

He knows what happened when Edan died—in theory.

That's why I keep coming back to this room. Because he understands I can't be the lover—the bondmate—anyone else in his position would want me to be.

And I'll keep telling myself that until it's the truth.

It takes me a moment to find him in the darkness of the room, and it's the sound of water that helps me get there in the end.

He stands at the vanity across the room, his back to me as he washes his hands.

I don't need more light to know it's him.

They're all tall. Impossibly so, it seems at times, but D *is* big.

I've been around so many Sian men, I know that there's actually an inch of leeway in either direction—only one man who comes into this club defies that norm.

D is at the high end of the spectrum, but he's broader than most, and his eyes...

9

They're a faint glow in the mirror when he looks up at me. Like a zurgle's caught by headlights.

"It's been a few days," I tease. *He's early*. "I thought maybe something had happened to you."

He smiles. It's a flash of bright teeth that disappears quickly. "Something did, but I survived it."

The words are tense. But then... D's always tense.

He barely relaxes in his sleep.

I watch him as he moves into the center of the room, shrugging out of his coat and shirt and tossing them onto the chair I can't see, but I know is there.

My eyes have adjusted to the dim light that rings the floor, just enough to see the long scars turned shiny with age. They cross over the dark skin and banded muscles of his chest, extending up his arms and down his back.

I assume his legs are riddled with the same, but he's never taken his pants off.

There are only two professions that would leave a person with that many marks.

And I can't ask if it's one... because I don't want to know it's the other.

There are a dozen questions I've kept tight to my chest because I'm afraid of the answers.

"Did you dance tonight?" he asks, trailing his hand down the sleeve of my robe and then lacing his fingers in mine.

"I did." I look down at the bright blue bra designed to catch the light and wince at the way it glitters, even in the dimness, even under the robe's flowers. "If I'd known you were coming, I would have changed."

"It's my fault. I should have sent the reservation on my way here, but I was distracted."

I'm easily able to track his glowing gaze as it travels

down to the offending fabric. I see them narrow and can imagine him wincing.

"I'm sorry I missed your show," he says.

That's the usual routine. I dance, he watches from the back of the room with his dark glasses on, and then I change and come to him.

"I could dance for you now." I offer it, even if he never takes me up on it.

There's space and equipment in the room for it.

"I'm not here to make you work." He toes off his boots and goes to the bed, leaving me standing there—making me make the decision—again. Always.

D is here for one thing and one thing only.

He's here to sleep. And for whatever reason, he wants me with him.

The first time we did this, I'd spent hours laying beside him with my eyes wide open, watching for any shift in the mirror over us.

There are people—on Earth, if not here as well—who get off on that sort of thing, and I didn't know him then.

But now...

Turning away from him, I do the quick gymnastics required to wiggle my bra off and I stuff it under his coat —after a series of fumbling pats at the chair and fabric.

It would have reflected back at him, and I don't want to do anything that might disturb his sleep.

The bed is enormous—custom made for four—and he's settled at the center of it, dragging pillows down the way I like them.

He doesn't say anything about my barely veiled breasts as I crawl next to him—he's seen them dozens, if not hundreds, of times before.

When I settle down next to him, his arm wraps around me and he holds me close.

11

The room is silent, but even as we lay in the darkness, his silver-white eyes reflect back to me from the dark mirror above.

"Do you want to tell me about it?"

There's a long pause and I feel his breathing change.

But he doesn't tell me.

He pulls me closer, pressing his lips to my forehead. "Go to sleep Kimba. Everything will be better when we wake."

I put my head on his shoulder and wrap my arm around his chest—as far as I can anyway—and with a deep breath, I close my eyes and try to do what he needs me to.

Someday he'll answer the questions I'm willing to ask...

Maybe someday, I'll be brave enough to ask the ones I'm not.

DRIFT

Kimba babbles in a fitful slumber, only stilling when I murmur her name and tell her I'm here. A faint little sigh slips from her lips and she hugs me closer as I wrap my arms more tightly around her, always wanting her near.

She falls asleep so easily now, and that trust does more for my peace than anything else ever could.

I watch her and remind myself she's mine for the next few hours.

I got here late enough that she's taken out the extensions she weaves into her chin-length black hair. She told me once that the tips are higher when she wears them. The tips are higher when she wears more clothes.

Clothes like the glittering blue top she hid away in deference to my eyes. She's always so careful about that...

which is why I know she's unaware of the way her makeup sparkles for me.

I draw my finger along her cheek and her dark lashes flutter, but she doesn't wake.

These nights I steal with her are secret and sacred.

And I know more than one of the brotherhood would tell me I'm an absolute fool for falling in love with her.

I'd give her everything, but Kimba doesn't want anything from me, not even my name.

If Margot wasn't in charge of the monetary side of this exchange, I don't know that she'd even take my money.

After all, with or without her fake hair, the tips for each dance are high. Kimba commands attention. There are a few women who work here who get requests because they vaguely resemble her.

But Kimba doesn't fuck anyone.

It's one of the secrets a very few of us know, hidden away like her real name.

She's a soft weight in my arms. Breath fluttering across my chest, I tuck my chin against her hair, using the gentle thump of her heartbeat to ground me.

Her robe is sheer where it isn't covered by soft, velvety flowers, and her body heat seeps through it, leaching into my skin.

Usually, I can sleep here, like this.

As long as I have her.

But tonight...

Tonight I have too many questions and too few answers.

Tonight, a man was killed by a monster that should never have made it into the city. A monster *I* should have stopped.

That monster is why I'm here when I shouldn't be. I've

spent years keeping the people in this city—the women and children, specifically—safe.

She was safe here as long as the brotherhood and I kept the cavrinskh inside the caldera walls. But if one can slip through… how many more could?

I've been content with these stolen nights because I thought she was safer here than she would be with me.

And bringing her into my home—into my *life*—means bonding her.

That's the secret she keeps almost as well as her real name. Her bondmate died five years ago.

It's a secret I assume she keeps to ward off the unending offers she'd receive from unbonded men, but also, I suspect, so that she doesn't have to hear misguided opinions.

There is a cruel idea that surviving your bondmate's death somehow means you didn't love them enough.

I know for a fact that isn't true.

Kimba has told me dozens of stories while sitting cross-legged on this bed. It's why I know that she misses Earth wine and that she broke her toe when she was seven years old, kicking a ballerina who was picking on another kid in their class. It's why I know that she's always loved to dance and has always hated bullies.

She's told me half her life's story in the two years that I've been coming to her and every time she says her late bondmate's name, her voice still cracks. Tears still shimmer in her eyes, even though she tries to hide it.

I would give anything to be loved the way she loved him.

And I have no intention of competing with Edan. She loves him still and I would never ask her to stop. But love isn't finite. I believe with my whole being that she could love me too if I give her enough of a chance to get used to the idea.

There may not be time for that anymore.

With three of the brotherhood bonded—and all three of their mates pregnant—even ignoring the anomaly of the cavrinskh I had to kill tonight, the monsters are getting bolder. They're making their way out of the inner caldera more and more, and it is only going to get worse.

But being here with Kimba, knowing she's safe… helps calm me.

The ceiling is a dark abyss, reflecting the low lights back at me.

Darkness suddenly broken by scrolling blue from the lenses that sting at my eyes. The lenses that are the only way I can function without the opaque shields others think are darkly tinted glass.

There's a perimeter warning, but Trench has already flagged it and is on his way out to deal with the problem.

Before tonight, I would have said Kimba was safer here, miles from the icy caldera, far beyond the cavrinskhs' reach… even if she's also far beyond mine.

"You're not asleep." She says from beside me before burying her face against my side to yawn. "Tell me why you came tonight?"

"I'm here to be with you."

"Your schedule doesn't change." Her words are sleepy. "Tonight it did."

"A friend was in trouble…" The Continental Security Service asked me to keep the details to myself. "It reminded me that we're all living on borrowed time, and all my best memories are with you, here in this bed."

I see a flicker of panic in her eyes and I know, before she even opens her mouth, that she's going to deflect with a joke.

"Said by a man who won't even let me suck his cock."

"You're not ready for that yet."

She chuckles, "I think I'm more than capable of determining what I'm ready for."

"Fine, you're not ready for what it would mean for me."

She swallows, the delicate lines of her throat moving in a nervous flicker, and she doesn't say anything else.

"Do you need to go?" I ask, loosening my hold on her.

I shouldn't have said it.

But I can't even kiss her until I know she's *mine.*

She's never left me early before, but I've never let something like that slip before either…

"No." She shakes her head and then drops it back to my shoulder. "I'll stay."

The relief that washes through me escapes in a shaky breath.

I can't keep her yet, but I won't let her go, either.

CHAPTER
TWO

KIMBA

SOMETHING about last night almost made me expect him to show up again tonight. But Margot let me know he confirmed his usual reservation... which means I definitely won't be getting another surprise visit.

I've never seen D that unsettled before. It makes me feel jumpy.

But there's one sure-fire way to get rid of that nervous energy.

And that's to do my job.

I picked three slots from the line up on the stage availability board. There are a lot of girls who don't like the main stage, preferring the tiny stages in the various levels' small public areas, or even private dances only.

Too many eyes, too much attention. What pricks at other women's nerves is what I love. It turns them all into a sea of indistinguishable observers. I don't care about the many. The more the merrier.

Snapping on the last of the light rings—the fun little Sian tech that makes it so I set the monetary threshold and the "clothes" come off on their own as soon as I've been paid. I get to put all my focus and energy into the dance.

"Margot is marketing the absolute *hell* out of this surprise dance," Hannah says, coming in to brush edible glitter over her cleavage.

"It's not a surprise. It's been on the schedule for hours."

"Sure, but how often do you dance three times in one night?" She blows me a kiss before reapplying her makeup and adjusting her fake-emerald-crusted bra. "It leaves them wondering what other habits you might break tonight."

"None. They should know that by now."

"I'm sorry I'm going to miss it." She says, not looking sorry at all. "Hazard's on his way."

"I could have guessed."

Hannah has perfected her professional smile. You could have told her her mother had broken her hip and it wouldn't falter, but when she talks about Hazard… that one's real.

And she's wearing it right now.

It's not uncommon for the women who work here to have favorites, but Margot usually cuts things off before they get to where Hannah and Hazard are.

It's not my job to tell her how to do hers. And if the little things Hannah has let slip about her bondmate are true…

I shake that away. Hannah knows Margot and I will help if she needs it. I can't ask anymore.

There are a hundred different ways to get onto the main stage. Coming up from below or sliding down from the platform hidden in the top of the dome are fun and eye-catching, and there's numerous other acrobatic ways, but I picked a song that doesn't allow for that, a dance that starts slow and will probably confuse more than a few of them before the beat drops and the tempo hits.

Applause, whistling, and shouts echo across the room as the woman's voice filters through the speakers, and then their voices die away when I take hold of the pole.

I've heard men talk about that pole as if it's an analog for their cocks, and I have to laugh as I turn around it, the metal spinning with my hand.

We'd all be dead.

I've done this routine a hundred times… but not for a few years. Most of them have never seen it before, but they *all* get excited when I start to climb.

The higher up I am, the more animated they get.

I listen for the timing cues, waiting for the piano in the recording to flutter one last time…

The beat drops. So do I.

There's movement and sound from beneath me, but I've only fallen a few feet before I catch myself, swinging into the next position.

The thump of the bass is a heartbeat that centers me. It pulls me into the moment and lets everything else fall away.

The music and dull murmurs are the only thing I hear. The fluctuating spectrum of light is the only thing I see.

They watch me, wanting all the things I won't give, but they don't know I'm not dancing for them. I never dance for them anymore.

Every time I step on this stage, my mind is with D, wherever he is.

I know he's not in the crowd tonight, but a small part of me hopes he snuck away.

Every twist and turn of this dance, every move I make is a part of the fantasies that swirl around that man whose real name I don't even know.

The audience loves what I do for him. Around me, neon holograms of dollar signs burst against the faint, smokey haze. Those digital tips tick higher and higher, thrown at me by hopeful men, both young and old.

I don't even notice when the first layer of ring-controlled "clothing" bursts away, or the second, or the third…

When the music ends, delicious exhaustion weighs down my bones and I spin on the pole for a few moments until the stage opens up and I drop, letting it swallow me whole.

That move is met by gasps and sounds of disappointment, but part of the reason they like me is because they can't have me.

It's why they come back.

It's why they spend the money they do.

They want to be the one I choose… but they're too late.

Margot is waiting when I pull myself from the soft cushions placed perfectly for that kind of an exit.

She offers me real clothes, instead of the digital ones and my robe. "Three dances in one night, and one from the first year you worked here. What's going on?"

If anyone else had asked me that, I would have blown them off, deflected… done *something*, anything other than tell them the truth, but this is Margot.

I'm still *here* because of Margot.

We came to this planet on the same transport almost fifteen years ago. We've been here longer than almost anyone else.

Margot knows everything that's happened. She's the one who helped me pick up the pieces and find myself again.

She's the only person I tell everything to.

"Last night was weird. He wasn't supposed to be here.

D's never broken his schedule without warning. And he didn't sleep. Something was wrong, but he didn't want to tell me what it was."

Her mouth scrunches, neon orange lipstick emphasizing her scowl. "I don't know what happened, but I can find out. I wouldn't worry about that too much. His job is…" she trails off because I've told her not to tell me.

And maybe I shouldn't worry, but saying it out loud…

"I think breaking the routine has jarred some things loose, or made them more noticeable, maybe."

"Do you want to get to the meat and potatoes of whatever's going on in your pretty head, or am I going to have to call someone in to cover my place at the bar?"

"I like him."

Margot stares at me for a moment and then she laughs, twisting her fingers in my long ponytail. "Well, I should hope so!"

"No, I mean…" I shake my head because I don't know how to explain, I just know, "I should probably stop seeing him."

Saying it feels like I've just flushed my veins with ice water, like my skin doesn't belong to me anymore. And I can't look up at her. I don't want to know how she's looking at me.

"Is that what you want?" she asks, softly.

"No."

"Then why do you think you *should* stop when you don't want to?"

"I dream about him."

Margot wraps her arm around my waist and drops her head to my shoulder. "No one is asking you to bond again, Kimba. You know *I* would never push you into that. I just want you to be happy and he does that."

Her voice wavers as she says it and I know if I looked,

21

I'd see too much sparkle in her eyes as she fought back the tears. Because she remembers the woman I was after Edan died better than I do.

And that's why I trusted her when she said she wasn't setting me up with D as a matchmaker in the first place.

It's why I know that if I tell her I never want to see him again, she'll make sure I never do.

But I *don't* want that.

Even if I *should*.

We walk back to the main lounge for the women who work here. It's furthest away from the private rooms and it's not meant for quick changes. This is where you set up for your shift, where you tear down.

I'm surprised to see Hannah sitting in the enormous velvet chair she loves—it matches that emerald bra she's still wearing.

"What happened to Hazard?" I ask, because her professional smile is back in place.

"False alarm. Problems at work he couldn't get away from."

This time, she doesn't try to disguise her frown.

In this place, we can just be ourselves. We don't have to be anyone to anyone.

Hannah holds up the tablet in her hand, shaking it at me, and the flexible surface wobbles. "Luthiel is asking about you again. He offered to pay triple your normal rate, to 'just have dinner and talk.'"

"You don't have to worry about that." Margot leads me to a sofa and then sits in the chair opposite before she smooths her nail polish. "I told him you weren't available this week. He's going to ask for a private dance next week. He hasn't yet, but I've learned his patterns."

"You can tell him the answer is no, indefinitely." Luthiel is one of the patrons who likes to march straight up to the edge of the rules and show just how well he can walk a tightrope.

He's probably kept track of every cent he's tipped me in a little ledger to claim some kind of ownership over my body.

I could ask Margot. I *know* she has those figures and statistics. I just receive a per-dance breakdown.

Stretching out my back, I remind myself that Sian men aren't like human men… not like that. Rejecting Luthiel doesn't fill me with anything like the ugly feeling that had taken over me when I told my high school boyfriend "no" for the first time.

"I'll tell him that he's been banned from requesting you and if he puts in another, he'll get a penalty. Most of them are better at taking the hint."

The three of us stay there, running through the week's schedule, and I listen as they compare stories about the weird interactions they've had, or been witness to, in the past week.

Earlier tonight, a man had come in for his first visit to the club as a member. "And you know me," Hannah winks at me, "I love first timers."

Margot leans over. "She did *not* love this one."

"Oh no." There are so many ways it could go wrong.

"Oh no is right, but also, probably not the kind of 'oh no' you're thinking." Hannah chuckles and takes a drink of her pale purple lemonade. "He was more nervous than I've ever seen *anyone* before, and that probably should have been a warning."

"Did he bolt?" I ask.

"Nope. He stayed put and the second I touched him, he puked."

"What?"

"All over me." She waves her hand over her chest and stomach.

Hannah is laughing now, but I would not have been.

"I told him it happens all the time, got him cleaned up, switched rooms, and then sent Anna Maria to him. He had a hard time looking at me after that. I didn't think it would be a good time for him if I stuck around." She chuckles again. "I let him down easy."

Margot pulls a folding tablet from the pocket on her thigh and lets it fall open. I watch the lights shift on her face and I know she's in the security feeds.

All the rooms have cameras. It's a safety precaution.

And I see when she gets to the footage she's looking for. "Oh," she says, brows high, and then, "Oh no."

Hannah giggles into her drink. "He's already reserved another room next week, with a request for Anna Maria, so I don't think he had a bad time in the end."

"Speaking of bad times, I know neither of you saw it, but that last dance caused an injury." Margot looks at me with a sidelong glance as she closes the tablet and puts it away. "That first drop no one was expecting? Two men lurched from their chairs—I assume to rescue you—and another fell out of his and bashed his head on one of the tables."

"I'd say I was sorry, but you know I love giving them a good jolt." I smile as I wander to my locker and grab out my water bottle, taking a long drink.

"Do you think it's a universal constant that men get flustered simply by looking at a pretty woman?" Hannah asks.

"Do you remember the guy…" I can't remember his name, or the rhyming nickname the girls had given him. "I want to say it was two years ago by now. He saw Sherry

24

dance once and then begged her to take him home with her… like he was some sort of pet."

Margot snorts. "I remember her bondmate coming in that night and the guy suddenly had a change of heart."

"Self preservation is a stronger force than lust." Hannah says.

Margot nods. "I set him up with Carrie. She's good at pet play and I think he wound up putting that in his special requests for his Agency application."

Hannah chuckles. "He's not a member anymore, so he must have found who he was looking for."

"He did. She's a sweet woman too."

"Do you remember everyone who's been a member here?" Hannah asks, turning in her chair so she's half upside down.

"Just the fun ones like him, or the weird or bad ones."

I listen as they bandy those stories back and forth, but I can't stop myself from yawning.

Hannah and Margot are almost fully nocturnal at this point… I'm not.

"I think I'm going to go home and try to go to sleep."

"Probably a good idea." Hannah stands, stretching and picking up her empty glass. "I'm going to go see if anybody's lonely."

She pauses and drops a kiss to my forehead before she goes.

"Let me know you got home safe, okay?" Margot squeezes my shoulder. "I've got to get back up there to make sure they're all on their best behavior."

As if anyone would jeopardize their membership.

My end-of-night routine takes about twenty minutes to complete.

Extensions: out.

Makeup: off.

Clothes: changed.

Bag: packed.

After one last look in the mirror, I head for the door.

There's a private elevator for employees and a separate parking lot that has enough security.

None of us have to worry about walking out alone in the middle of the night.

I don't even look around before walking straight to my car.

I don't need to.

And when I've crossed the city and pulled into the garage that spirals down beneath the high rise I live in... I don't check that I'm alone before I get out of the car either.

I *shouldn't* need to.

The garage has a passcode entry. There are cameras everywhere...

I don't see them until it's too late.

They were waiting for me.

Surrounding me as they step out from behind my neighbors' parked cars, they move in a way that's mechanical, almost like it's rehearsed.

The unspoken ceremony of the action scares me more than the fact they've ambushed me.

Eight of them surround me... keeping their distance.

Seven of them look bored.

The last man is the only one who isn't perfectly aligned in their little circle. He's the only one who looks like he wants to be here.

He takes a step forward, a smirk on his lips. "Hello Nadine."

That makes my heart stutter and my skin go cold.

No one has called me that for years. It's not who I am anymore.

"We've been waiting to talk to you for hours. Your work schedule is highly inconvenient."

The absurdity of that knocks some of my flee-freeze reflex loose.

"It's easier to find me at the club," I say, glancing at the cameras and seeing no lights indicating they're operating.

"And we both know I wouldn't get within twenty feet of you there."

Which means he tried. "Stalking is a crime on this planet too—"

He laughs and I take an involuntary step back.

"Crimes are funny things, aren't they? Punishments are subjective... the right person could even get away with *murder*."

I swallow back the ugly slither of a memory. "What do you want?"

"I want to hire you."

I know he doesn't mean for a dance or the night, but still, I say, "You'll have to go through Margot for that."

He laughs again and I already hate the sound of it. "I don't want to sleep with you. Pretty as you are, I have a better use for you."

I almost tell him no, outright, but there are still eight of them and only one of me...

"How much did you make tonight?" he asks.

I give him the ballpark number because I want to be done with this as fast as possible.

He looks at the man beside him. "Triple that, and give me a yearly?"

The man spits out a ridiculously large number.

"How does that sound?" The man doing all the talking asks.

"It sounds like a lot of money."

"It's yours, plus a seat on a ship back to Earth."

I don't want the money, and I've never wanted to go back to Earth. But a ticket back to Earth is impossible, rumors say it's worth more money than I'd earn in a lifetime.

What could be worth that? "What is it, *exactly*, that you expect me to do?"

"You have an appointment tomorrow night. Keep it."

D.

This is about him.

"Next time Drift comes in… you're going to inject him with this."

It's the first time I've heard D's real name, but the syringe in the man's hand captures my attention and I can't focus on anything else.

"No," I shake my head.

"Would you prefer a blade? The familiarity of the weapon might help, but it's harder to clean up."

"I'm not killing anyone."

"This isn't a request." His smile seems to slide off of his mouth. "You do it and get paid, or… you'll deal with the consequences. And believe me, you don't want to suffer through that."

I don't tell him I've already suffered through the worst thing I can imagine.

He can probably imagine far worse.

"Your life has been full of choices, hasn't it? This is the most important choice you'll ever make. Choose wisely and you'll step off that ship and return to the loving arms of your family. Choose poorly…"

The syringe in his hand catches the light and he holds it up and out to me again.

I take it. What other choice do I have?

"Good girl." The smile he gives me now is smaller… softer. It sends a shiver down my spine.

My stomach writhes with coils of dread.

"I have a feeling it will be a pleasure to do business with you." He bows in the old-fashioned way men from this province do sometimes and turns.

The others file past me and I stay perfectly still as they crowd into a car that was built for nine.

I don't move until after I've heard the tires screech on the final corner and hit the metal plate that leads out of the garage exit.

Then, my panic finally catches up to me and I run.

DRIFT

I'm starting to feel like a junky.

I went a full day without seeing her and now my skin itches. Pulling into the parking lot, some of that tension eases, but I know it won't go away until I see her.

The elevator entrance to Margot's makes no concessions for my eyes. The ride is a riot of color and I have to pinch my lids tightly closed, even while wearing the opaque glasses that block out ninety-nine percent of that light.

Getting through the main room of the club is always the worst part though. When I step out of the elevator and into the room I can see without having to see it, light slips through in the slots at the periphery of the glasses.

I scan the space through those and the night's guests as well as the woman on the stage assault my vision—but only half as much as they would if I looked at them head on.

I catch grumbles of discontent from the crowded bar.

She didn't dance tonight.

She wasn't scheduled to dance tonight.

That's not like her.

I ignore the chatter from those who think she owes them her time, especially the ones who ignore the other women trying to distract them.

The rules at Margot's are strict, and she's already letting me bend one. If I break someone's face, I'm out of here.

"Hey there, bright eyes." Margot says, her voice syrupy sweet. "She thought she'd change things up tonight. Second floor, look for the door without any markings."

Something is definitely off.

She's never changed rooms before. But the way Margot says it… she's not going to let me ask any questions.

"I'm sure I'll find it."

"I'm sure you will." She glances to either side before leaning close. "If she gets hurt, I don't care about our connection, I will find my way up that mountain and I will destroy everything you love."

I don't know what connection she's referencing, but I do know where her logic is flawed. "If she gets hurt, everything I love will already be destroyed."

With a curt nod, she leaves me and I watch her go, wondering… but there's no point in tracking her down to ask. Kimba should have all the answers I need.

I pause before I push through to the public room and study the man who's been watching me since I arrived.

His face is turned toward the stage, but he's definitely following my movements.

There's another one at the bar…

On any other night, I'd turn around and go find out what the fuck they want, but that itch has turned to a burn that courses across my shoulders.

I need to *see* Kimba. I need to know she's safe.

I've never been to the second floor before. Most of the

levels have vaguely connected themes or uses for the rooms. And I have no idea what this floor holds.

When I step out into it, the place is deserted.

And as I walk the ring-like hall, dread seeps into my skin.

Margot didn't need to tell me which room to go to. Every door on this level is ringed in red, save for one.

Like a green halo, the available room shines a little brighter. It hurts a little more. But inside, the room is completely dark. Not even the lights that line the floor are on this time.

I don't need them.

Slipping off my glasses, the room shifts and outlines form in gray lines.

Kimba waits for me on the bed... fully clothed.

Her shoulders are hunched and even though I know she can't see it, her eyes are locked on the syringe in her hand.

A syringe that provides a glow so faint, no one with normal eyes could tell.

"What's wrong, Kimba?"

She looks up and her eyes meet mine. She *can* see their glow.

"Someone asked me to kill you." She holds the syringe up to me in the flat of her palm. "Or maybe they just want me to sedate you so they can do it themselves. I don't know."

Her hand trembles.

I'd thought I'd seen every emotion painted on Kimba's face, but this is new. This is panic.

And thank the saints she's not afraid of me.

But I don't want to see her like that. I need to distract her. If I can make her laugh...

"I didn't realize murder required street clothes."

It doesn't work.

That fear is replaced with frustration.

"Do you think this is funny? Someone wants you *dead*."

She's scared, and I'm being an asshole.

"I'm sorry." Dropping to my knees in front of her, I push her hair back from her face.

She leans into my hand, her eyes closed, her brows knit, and I want to kiss her, so badly.

"I think this is the first time I've seen you wear shoes."

"When they find out I haven't done it... I think I'm going to have to run."

"I'll carry you if it comes to that."

She shoots me a skeptical look and then takes a deep breath as she shakes her head, mumbling, "You could certainly manage it."

I could be half dead and I'd find a way to get her out of harm's way.

"They called you Drift."

"That's my name."

"Who are you and why do they want you dead?"

She could have asked Margot.

"There are a few reasons they might... but I can't guess which it is until I know who they are."

"I can't help with that." Her voice is shaky, like she's mad at herself and I want to strangle whoever taught her to feel like any part of this situation is her fault.

"Let's turn the lights up, okay?"

She nods and I go to the panel beside the door, punching it to the minimum level that she can actually see me, and my eyes shift back to what most would call "normal" vision.

"You're a part of the brotherhood, aren't you?" She looks up at me, eyes so clear, they look molten.

"Yes."

"I'd hoped it was that." She winces as if she hadn't meant to say it. "There are only two ways I can think of that would get you those scars. I didn't want to believe you could be... well, the kind of person who ambushes a woman in her garage and hands her a syringe full of poison."

I pluck that syringe from her hand. I should keep it for testing, but I don't trust it enough to hang onto it long enough for that. Margot's has an incinerator, and every room has a chute for biohazard waste that can't go down a drain. This room is unfamiliar to me, but the oddity in the wall's density will make it darker. Scanning the room, I find it half-hidden in the vanity.

I throw it away before either of us can think too hard about what might have happened if she used it.

"Why do they want you dead, D?"

I turn back to her, searching her face as I lean against the textured wallpaper. "Would you be willing to put this off until we get someplace safer?"

She shakes her head. "I'm not going anywhere until I have more information."

Closing my eyes, I drop my head back against the wall and search for any other option... "Best guess?"

She doesn't say a thing, but she's waiting.

"There are some, as you know, who don't want you here." Some hate them, some think we deserve to go extinct, the reasons are numerous.

"What does a group of extremists want with you?"

"Say you want to paint humans as dangerous... Say you've found out that the head of the group that guards against the monsters has a human woman who is not bonded to him, that has ready access to him. What sort of picture can you paint if she kills him?"

She snorts and I agree. It sounds ridiculous.

"That humans are conspiring to hurt you all?" Kimba shakes her head, a scowl twisting her unpainted lips. "One instance isn't going to be enough."

"No, but it's a start, and a high-profile one." I don't like how conceited that makes me sound, but… "And you're famous. They probably thought you'd be easy enough to convince. Did they threaten you? Or offer to pay you?"

"Little bit of both." She grimaces as if the admission is a foul taste in her mouth.

"Tell me."

"It was a 'your life or mine' offer… and they'd send me back to Earth." She smiles ruefully and looks at the ceiling. "But we both know they weren't going to let me leave. I assumed they planned to kill me once I'd done what they wanted, but if what you say is true, they'd probably have found a way to put me on display, make an example of me."

"And they'd pull your past out to add to your sins."

She flinches and for the first time, that concern writ on her face is actually directed at me.

"Did they blackmail you with it?"

"Not in so many words. Was that your plan eventually?"

"I've known who you are—who you were—from the beginning. There's nothing to hold against you. And if I was that person, it would have already happened."

She nods and glances at the door. "I know."

I can't tell her the real sentence she'd face. Isia has one single prison, and they'd never send a human woman there. They'd have to come up with something new.

"They probably have people watching the exits," she says.

"Oh, I have no doubt of that." I scowl at the door too, but I wipe it from my face before I turn back to her.

"You said you wanted to take me somewhere safer... where?" She wrings her hands. "I can't go home. That's where they approached me. And I've already checked, the security systems went offline when they were there and the building management can't explain it, which means they can't stop it from happening again."

And I have no intention of letting her go anywhere alone. "Unless you can promise me you have somewhere that's safer... do you have a coat?"

Her brows pinch together, and then clear, almost immediately. "You want to take me home with you."

"Margot can keep you safer than the security at your home, but people come in and out of here in a constant flow. My outpost is designed to keep monsters out. It can handle mere men." I've put her in this position—somehow —and I have to get her out of it.

She's watching me, as if unsure of what to say, then, "Is this the part where you say 'come with me if you want to live'?"

"If you tell me you won't come with me, I will find another way."

But she takes my hand when I hold it out to her and she lets me draw her to her feet.

I brush my thumb along the line of her jaw. "I will do anything to keep you safe."

"And there's nowhere that would be safer than with you." She says it with a sadness that squeezes at my heart.

"We should go. They probably already know something's gone wrong with their plan."

She nods and lets me go to the door first.

"I need you to stay behind me, and stay close. If they want to do what you didn't for them, they'll only be able to get to one of us before security takes them down."

"Not that way." She grabs my arm as soon as I head for

35

the elevator. "Margot shut off access to the floor as soon as you got down here. They have people up there, waiting."

"I saw them." And part of me wants to deal with this problem head on, but if she gets hurt because of it… Get her home, and *then* deal with these bastards.

I let her lead the way, because I trust her and I trust Margot. But I don't let her go through any of the doors first.

"Where did you park?"

"Against the building, close to the employee lot." I'll never tell her, but I *always* waited for her to leave first after the nights I spent here.

I never followed her home. I just needed to know that she was okay after I left her.

"Good, that'll make this easier." She grabs a bag stashed by the next door and looks up at me. "I assume you want to take your car… they probably have a tracker on mine by now. In case I went to the CSS or something."

Continental security wouldn't do much for her. With no proof, they'd be more likely to detain her for whatever was in that vial.

"What's in the bag?"

"The things I can't live without."

I won't fit in her bag, but I want to be included on that list.

"This elevator goes directly to the employee lot and the lights will cut out. Margot will tell anyone who notices that it was a fuse issue."

Nodding, I take her hand and pull her behind me again.

"I won't be able to see, so I'm not going to let go of your hand until we're at your car."

"I understand." I slip my neural link on and trigger the prestart program on the car.

We get into the empty lift—so peaceful compared to the one I came in on—and descend.

"The lights are going to go off as soon as we reach the ground floor."

And they do.

Everything is exactly the way she said it would be. Except letting go of me when we get to my car.

I pop it open as soon as it's in sight and scoop her up, tossing her bag into the passenger seat and holding her close to my chest as I back out, the roof snapping closed a moment before we pull out of the lot.

There are shadows behind us, but I don't know if they belong to random bystanders or the men who tried to use her as a weapon.

She thought our escape through. "You were thorough."

"I didn't want you to die."

"Do you miss it?" I ask as I turn the car onto the long straight that leads away from the city, toward the mountains.

If not for the current situation, I wouldn't have mentioned it.

"Do I miss planning escape routes and extraction missions?" She asks, a bitter note in her words. "No. Not even a little bit."

Because that's who she *was*. Not who she is.

"Hopefully, you never have to do it again."

Some might think she was the perfect mate for me *because* of what she'd done on Earth. But that's not why she came here. And that's not what I would ever ask of her.

I want to give her everything she desires. And painful memories don't fit into that.

CHAPTER
THREE

KIMBA

D DRIVES out of the city without any lights on.

I look behind us at every turn, but there's no one following us.

I don't even see any drones in the sky.

Then again... they knew who I was. They probably know exactly where D lives.

"They won't bother us until they've got their next plan in place." D explains it like he knows what I'm thinking.

But he can't feel my anxieties that way. We're not bonded.

"If they wanted you to kill me, they wanted it done a certain way. There's a narrative they need to follow. Coming after us guns blazing doesn't fit into that."

"I hope you're right."

We're deep into the mountains before I ask another of the questions I was too afraid to before. "Are you bonded?"

There's a pause, but it feels like confusion, not deceit. "No."

I nod. Swallowing back the bile that had threatened in my throat. "Okay." It would have been okay if he was. "I just didn't want to walk into her house and blindside her."

He looks at me. The faint blue of the neural implant glows silver in his eyes. "You are the only woman in my life. And I have no intention of changing that."

Warmth spreads through my chest and I swallow back a lump of sadness that snags in my throat and makes me ache.

I told myself I could live without the connection Edan and I had.

I think I lied.

I turn to look out at the snow, but what greets me isn't the vast expanse of yellow crags jutting out of blue powder. We turned a corner when I wasn't paying attention and D's home—he called it an outpost—pulls my focus away from everything else. Bathed in the light of four moons, it doesn't look real.

Perched on top of a ridge, it juts out over the caldera I can't see like an enormous cantilever.

It looks like a fortress meant for weathering a siege, not a *home*.

The car slows, and we pass through large automatic gates into an underground parking structure fit for a small convoy.

"Your house is enormous."

"It was built to hold an army for small amounts of time."

He gets out and offers to take my bag, but I don't let him. I don't want to hand *that* part of myself over to him yet.

He doesn't try to make me.

The door from the garage opens into a living room

that's more of a conference center than some place meant for daily life.

No, that's not right. It's too similar to a place I spent too much time on Earth.

This is a high-tech war room.

Screens are marked with red points of light, and it doesn't take long to figure out what they are.

"I didn't think the cavrinskh problem was this bad." The monsters that killed off the female half of the population were supposed to have been dealt with. They barely seem contained.

"It isn't… Those are the sightings for the last six months."

I look at the board again. "Four a month feels like a lot."

"Sadly, no. But don't worry. The house is set up so they can't get in—not without a fight that will make them toothless. I wouldn't have brought you here if I wasn't prepared."

There's something in that statement. Something that makes me think he's been planning to bring me here all along.

"Nothing, and no one, can get to you here."

I trust him, so I don't ask what it is that's keeping them out. I don't ask him if *he's* safe here too.

Instead, I take a long, slow turn about the room, just cataloging the basics. The map on the far wall, lit with a pulsing glow, shows the patrol zones.

D's isn't small.

"So, who keeps watch while you're with me?"

"The system's automated. If something had come up while I was gone, I would have known immediately and sent one of the brotherhood to deal with it, or been notified that they'd already headed out to do so. We all know when we're off for the night."

He's standing so close to me now, I barely have to shift, and I'm touching him. Hip to leg, shoulder to biceps.

And for the first time since I've known him, when his eyes travel from mine down to my lips, I feel that tiny lace of fear.

Not of him... not really, but of the possibilities he holds.

Good, and bad.

But risk is another part of life, one I can't hide from.

This time, I press up on my toes, the invitation for him to bend down.

"Kimba..."

He says my name like it's a warning as I reach up and lace my fingers behind his neck. "Let me kiss you, D. Please."

"You don't need to thank me for this."

"I'm not thanking you. I want—" I take a deep breath and meet his strange and beautiful crystal clear eyes. "Kiss me or tell me I can't have this and I won't ask for it again."

"You can have anything you want, Kimba."

He dips his head and as soon as I can reach his lips, I kiss him.

Instantly, I wonder if it was a mistake.

Heat blooms through me and my body reacts to his like I've been starving.

He wraps an arm around my waist, lifts me, pulling me close.

His lips are soft and warm. His free hand travels up my neck cupping my jaw, tilting my face, just so.

When I open to him, he doesn't surge, rather his tongue dips in, a gentle caress.

I've been nearly naked with him a dozen times and this is the most intimate thing we've ever done.

It makes me want all the things I can't have... even though I'm certain he would give them to me.

It makes me want to laugh and cry all at once.

It makes me want to break my vow to myself and make him truly mine.

But I can't.

When he pulls away, his eyes are closed, and something akin to pain is written across his brow ridges.

"I'm sorry," I say. Because taking what I want—what he'll give me—could be torture for him.

"Don't be." His words are soft. "I've wanted to kiss you like that for so long..."

I ask the question, even though I know the answer. "Why haven't you?"

His smile is sad and his tongue peeks out to lick his lips, one fork for each.

"It had to be your choice." He lowers his forehead to mine. "It all has to be your choice."

He pulls away, kissing my nose before he takes a step back and takes my hand.

"Come on. I don't want to be up here. Not with you. Not right now."

He gently tugs, and I follow as he leads me down a wide, curved staircase.

The exterior wall is glass and that floor to ceiling expanse continues on until it hits the rough rock wall the outpost's supports are driven into.

The moon reflecting off the snow below floods the room with a soft light.

He's not wearing his glasses here.

Every surface is soft, or dull. Even the windows don't reflect anything from their surface.

This is where he lives.

There's an enormous couch, the kind that's meant for laying down more than it is for sitting on.

D watches me as I look around. It's a fairly spartan space. And there are no screens here.

I sit on the couch, not at all surprised that it's the most comfortable thing I've felt in years, and look up at him. "What do we do now, D?"

"You can call me Drift, if you prefer."

I'd rather call him something more personal, but I can't say that, not right now. "I think you'll always be D to me... and I'm not actually Kimba, so, it only seems fair that neither of us use our *real* names with each other."

He pauses, looking out into the night. "Who we were at Margot's was as real as anything I've ever experienced. Changing where we are on the planet doesn't change *that*."

Scowling at the pale expanse beyond the windows, D crosses his arms, closing up. "I have to bring the brotherhood in on this." He twists his neck to the side and it lets out a half dozen pops and cracks. "If they're after me, they might be after others."

"Of course."

"Would you be willing to talk to them? Help describe the man who asked, give any details you can think of?"

When I hesitate, he takes my hand. "If you'd rather not be seen in my home, you can stay down here. They won't leave the main floor and I won't tell them you're here."

I don't understand why he'd offer, unless...

"If I was going to let the world think I'd chosen someone..." I take a deep breath. "It would be you. I'm not worried about your brothers spreading rumors. Though, I don't think they would."

"Arc might. He loves gossip." He looks back at me and the skin around his eyes crinkles. "You're going to need more clothes than what's in your bag. I don't think you're going home anytime soon."

That's when I realize this is the first time he's seen me fully dressed. Even when I was "covered" at the club, I was still in the equivalent of lingerie.

"I have things in my car, in case I needed to disappear on my own."

I hadn't been concerned about the state of my wardrobe when we'd bolted from Margot's because I don't like wearing clothes around him.

"If you give me your neural link, I'll have one of my guys go get it. They'll sweep it for anything dangerous before they bring it to us."

I pull it from the zippered pouch on the side of my bag and hand it to him, but I catch his wrist and don't let him pull away. Dragging him down to his knees in front of me instead. "How long do we have before we have visitors?"

"Not long. I sent the message on the way over here and Trench has a response time of about fifteen minutes which will be up right... now."

He winces, looking up, and I wonder what he sees.

"Neither of us are fans of wasting time." I meet his eyes —eyes others have said they could *feel* on them.

But it doesn't feel like he's looking through me the way so many others have complained when they've seen him— oh, so briefly—at Margot's without those glasses on.

"Do you want them to know I'm here?"

His lips quirk and I have a feeling "I do" isn't what he actually meant to say. But it's what he does.

Standing, he twists his hand and takes mine to pull me up with him.

I don't make him lead me upstairs, but I do hang back by the wall while he goes to the first brother, standing at the consoles. I'm used to keeping space between me and strange men. I prefer it that way.

Six more of them pile through the door, exchanging japes and, occasionally, fists.

That all stops when they see me.

They freeze and they stare. Confusion written on their faces... well, except for one of them.

Hazard just smirks at me and goes to the enormous refrigerator to grab a drink.

D positions himself between me and the other five.

Whether he's guessed I want to bolt, or is feeling particularly possessive, I have no idea. Life is easier with a bond... easier with a partner who always has your back. It feels like D is trying to be that partner, even though he hasn't asked for the bond.

I wish he could feel my gratitude.

"Sit down, and everything will be explained."

With curious smiles and looks shot between them, they move away, to the round seating area on the other side of the enormous room.

D lets them go in silence, casting me a glance before he follows, letting me choose where I want to be for this discussion.

And there are certainly options.

The circular couch, sunken down like it's straight out of the nineteen seventies could fit twenty-five.

But I don't want space right now.

When D sits, I sit beside him, not quite as close as I want to, but close enough that eyebrows raise.

I don't know them.

I can only guess at what they're thinking.

But I'm used to staring. And only one of them is doing it rudely.

"I had assumed," The rude one says, "That your

45

reasoning for calling us in was related to the cavrinskh. Maybe you'd figured out how that one got all the way into the city. And then I thought it was to show off your lady, but you would have had those two bring theirs if that was the case."

"And," Hazard says, a narrow-eyed smile trained on D. "We all know that we don't get to take Margot's dancers home, so something is wrong."

I hear a trace of bitterness in his tone, and honestly, some days, I wish he would kidnap Hannah.

But his words make the others look at me more closely —the unbonded ones, at least.

"Holy shit."

There's a general mumble before D says, *"Enough."*

"It's fine," I say, lowly, noting a few of them look concerned when I speak their language. "I'm used to people being weird when they find out who I am."

"And that's fine, but right now, it doesn't do us any good to waste time with their gawking." He turns back to them and answers some of their hushed questions before he goes around the room introducing them.

"Yes, this is Kimba. Yes, she is *the* Kimba. No, she is not my bondmate."

I know I'm not the only one who hears the faint flicker of disappointment when he says it.

"These are most of the brothers on this side of the caldera. Trench," he nods to the brother closest to us and the emerald green Sian man gives me a quick salute.

"The two over there who look antsy to leave are Strike and Core, they are bonded and don't like leaving their women home alone."

I nod and offer them a little wave.

"Those three are Arc, Shock, and Risk." I look at the three men who are... the palest Sian men I've ever seen who aren't actually white or gray. They look like they've been covered in frost.

"It's a *pleasure*," Arc—the rude one, and if D is right, the gossip—says, in a way that is *far* from pleasurable.

"And you know Hazard."

"By reputation only." I speak quickly, so the others don't mistake his meaning.

He offers me a wide smile for the clarification and Arc makes a mocking sound. "*Reputation.*"

"Don't worry, kid." Hazard says, winking at him. "Someday, a woman will like you enough to talk about you too."

"And I'm Kilo."

We *all* turn to the man standing near the windows, and I'm pretty sure I'm not the only one who's just noticed him.

Moreso when Trench asks, "Where did you come from?"

"I was here first. Not my problem you guys don't pay enough attention." He hops over the back of the couch, getting an irritated growl from Arc, but Risk hooks his arm around the mint-green man's neck and pulls him away from the other brother.

"The rest of the brotherhood are either too far away, or unable to come for… other reasons."

"Laurel and Richter are still recovering from the whole 'attempted murder' thing," Core says quietly, and all humor drains from the room.

"She's fine," Core says quickly, to me. "But he's not going to leave her side unless it's an emergency, or the cavrinskh come out to play."

"And Fault is probably at Margot's already," Arc says, looking straight at me. "He likes the morning crowd. Something about sloppy seconds."

47

I don't know if he's trying to shock me, or if that's just how he always is. But the fact that he doesn't react when I don't react makes me think it's the latter.

"If it's not monster or bondmate related, why are we here?" The one D called Shock asks.

"Someone wants me dead."

"This is news?" Arc asks. "Pretty sure there are a dozen people I could name on that list. And now that we know about this…" He waves his hand at me. "Whatever *this* is. I'd add half the men who go to watch her dance. They get you out of the way, they're one step closer to her."

"Our arrangement is discreet." I say, before anyone else can suggest something equally as ridiculous.

"Hazard knew about it." Trench points out.

Hazard snorts. "That's because I have friends in the right places."

"And she wouldn't tell anyone else," I agree with him.

"The other factor that makes it clear, to me at least," D says, "Is that they tried to pay Kimba to do it. And when she didn't agree outright, they threatened her."

"That's weird." Core says. "They'd have had to know you were… whatever you two are and then they would have had to be reasonably sure their money or threats would persuade you. They were clearly wrong."

"What about the *Company*?" Trench asks, and I don't like the way the others grimace.

Whatever the Company is, there isn't a Sian word for it and the English one sounds jarring at the end of the question.

"I can't think of any reason they would want to remove me, or harm Kimba." D's response is so quick, I don't have a chance to ask what it is.

"Could be the *other* group of men who go to watch her." Kilo says, looking pensively at me.

There's a general murmur, agreeing to the possibility.

"What group is that?" I ask.

"The ones that think you're a stuck-up bitch who's toying with everyone until you can sling your hooks into the biggest fish you can find." Arc says. "They're jealous, self-loathing pricks. Nothing more."

I almost ask if it takes one to know one. Something about Arc makes me think he'd hate me if I gave him half a chance.

"There's nothing to say they were targeting me, specifically." D says. "There are plenty of people who don't like us."

The list is long. All of them offer up possible people and groups that might want the brotherhood gone. It makes my skin crawl that they don't seem to have any end to suspects in sight.

D finally gets them to be quiet.

"Kimba and I will work on figuring out who the guy was," but he doesn't ask me to describe him. "I want you all to be careful. Especially those of you who aren't bonded... it's clear they'll use underhanded methods to distance themselves."

The others stand and start to leave. Some of them stop to speak to each other. But the two who left their bond-mates home are out the door without even saying goodbye.

I'm a little surprised at how quickly they move.

But I suppose I shouldn't be. They're here to keep monsters from getting out of the caldera.

D is the only one who doesn't shift. He stays perfectly still, like a rock in a stream.

And I'm holding onto him—mentally—to keep myself from swaying into motion.

49

There's an anxious energy flowing all around us, and he's the sole calm.

When only Hazard and Trench are left, he stands.

"Thanks for staying back. I need to speak to both of you, for different reasons."

"I know why I'm still here, and you can save the lecture." Hazard angles himself like he's prepared for a fight. "If you think for a second I am not going to make sure Hannah is the safest woman on this planet, you have another thing coming."

"They won't be able to get to her."

Both of them look at me when I say it. "She lives in Shiga Heights. No one gets into that community unless they live there or have been cleared ahead of time."

"And if *they* live there too?" D asks.

"You shouldn't have told me where she lives." Hazard says, casting a sharp gaze at me. "Even if I already knew, that information isn't something any of her clients *should* know." He's right, of course.

"I'm sorry, I'm tired and I wasn't thinking."

Hazard dips his head, acknowledging, but not accepting the apology.

"She'll be safe at home. Her bondmate's job doesn't allow him to skimp on his security."

I hadn't known that Hazard knew who Noa was either.

Then again, I've told D things I never should have... and Hazard makes her happy. Noa seems to try really hard not to.

"I'm just going to warn her and make sure she takes it seriously." Hazard looks at me. "Do you want me to let her know you're safe here?"

"Yes, thank you."

"Trench will go with you to Margot's, don't leave yet."

They both cast confused glances at each other, and then Hazard nods. "I'll be waiting in the car."

He goes and takes some of the nervous energy with him.

"I don't think there's an order you could give that would keep him away from her," Trench says.

"Good."

They both look at me.

"Hazard is the only one who makes her happy. If he's hellbent on protecting her, I'm going to help him, not stand in his way."

Trench dips his head in acknowledgement. "That is very sound reasoning. But *I* am not going to run off after another man's mate, so why am I still here?"

D drops my car's neural link into his hand.

"I need you to go get her car, but make sure you sweep it for everything and anything before you move it even an inch. Trackers, bugs, explosives... everything."

"You think they wanted her to kill you and then were going to get rid of her too?"

D shrugs and, not for the first time, I wish I could feel what he's feeling.

"Maybe. I don't want to risk it."

"I'll have it back to you as soon as I can."

He, too, heads to the garage, and a moment later the outpost is empty again.

Beside me, D is tense.

"Can we go back downstairs?" I ask.

There's too much light up here. Bright and blinking, they can't be good for his eyes.

He nods and I slip my hand into his. "We were interrupted by this whole affair, but... I would like to sleep. The problem will still be here in the morning."

We walk down the staircase and he pauses long

enough that he can pick up my bag before he leads the way down a long, dark hallway.

I almost try to take the bag from him again. But I don't need to run, here.

I'm safe.

It's safe.

The house wakes up as we reach each room. Low lights blossoming to life, only to sleep again as we pass by each doorway. Like a watchdog, raising one lid to ensure that its master is the one whose presence is disturbing their sleep.

When we stop, it's in front of the only doorway that doesn't come to life.

"There are no lights in my room. We can use another, if you'd prefer."

"If you promise there's not a bear or some other creature waiting to gobble me up in there, I'll sleep in your cave."

He nods, but turns away from the door anyway. "You can use this room for all the things you need light for."

The room directly across the hall has windows all the way across one wall, but they're covered by heavy curtains, even though I have a feeling they're tinted.

There's a bed and dressers built into the walls and most importantly, a bathroom.

"Get ready for bed. When you're comfortable, come to the door. I'll carry you so you don't bump your toes."

"Thank you." I catch his hand before he can leave me. "I really mean that. Thank you… for everything."

He smiles and raises my fingers to his lips. "Thank you for not killing me."

"Are you sure I won't change my mind and murder you in your sleep?"

He pauses and for a moment, I worry he thinks I

52

might. "You won't. But if you do... well, I wouldn't want to be alive in a world where you'd be willing to do that. So, either way, I want you with me."

He presses a kiss to my forehead and leaves.

I drag my bag into the bathroom with me—there are no curtains here—and unzip it. On top of everything else, Edan's picture looks up at me. A ghost with a smile that always makes my heart ache.

He would have liked D.

I set him on the bathroom counter. It's not a proper place for his shrine, even if it is a temporary one, but I pull out the pieces I grabbed in my mad dash out the door.

This is a good place for it. D doesn't need to see it. I don't want it to hurt him. And I don't think he'll come in here.

I didn't bring any of my work clothes with me, and even though I know I could go to him completely naked and nothing would happen, I'm not going to tempt myself like that.

But this is the bag of things I couldn't leave behind. The only thing in it that was actually made for sleeping wasn't made for sleeping at all. It was made for a bonding.

I shift the things back over to hide that nightgown and instead, I unlace my shoes and kick them off, wiggling out of my pants and unhook my bra.

That's as good as it's going to get.

But flurries swirl outside the window behind me and I look at them in the mirror instead of turning around.

Anxiety coils in my stomach.

Not for myself... for D.

There are things beyond these walls that want to kill him.

Before I knew who he was, the scars beneath my palms, beneath my cheek, made it clear that D didn't lead a gentle life. Monsters and men both want him dead. And I'm going to have to find a way to ensure neither of them manage it.

I hurry out of the bathroom, letting the lights fade behind me, and slide to a stop—socks finding little traction on this floor—in front of the dark rectangle that opens to his room.

DRIFT

My room is pitch dark to her, I know. But with the light from the doorway that halos her, I can see every corner.

Her skin always sparkles, even when she doesn't mean for it to.

I step out of my boots, kicking them into the corner and go to her... knowing she can't see me makes me feel like I'm stalking her.

"Ready?" I ask, needing her to know I'm close before I "appear" from the nothing inside this room.

"Yes." She looks toward me and the tiny smile on her lips makes my heart ache.

That it widens when she can finally see me makes my heart want to burst.

She reaches for me, and I pick her up to carry her through the darkness to the bed.

When I set her down, I watch her stretch out on the mattress, testing the size of it, finding the pillows and the edges of the sheets.

I pull off my shirt as I walk to the other side, but... like every time I've gone to her at Margot's, I keep my pants on.

When she snuggles close to me, she frowns in the darkness. "Take off your pants."

I almost laugh, because she sounds so stern.

"It's fine." I say resting my hand on her stomach. "I'm fine."

"This is your bed, D. I'm going to be uncomfortable if I think you're uncomfortable." Her fingers hook in my waistband. "I know you. I trust you."

Her hand quests up my chest until she finds my face and her fingertips brush the ridge along my jaw. "I know you'll never hurt me. *Especially* not like that."

My jaw tenses, and I know she can feel it.

"Either take off your pants, or take me back to the hall. I'll sleep in the other room if you refuse to be comfortable."

"What if I normally sleep naked?" I ask.

"We could *both* be naked and you wouldn't do anything I didn't ask you to." She glares at me, even though I know she can't be sure I can see her. "Do you?"

Do I…?

Sleep naked. Right. It takes a moment for my mind to catch up.

"Yes."

Her stomach moves under my hand and I clench my teeth again.

"But I'm not going to do that while you're in my bed, unbonded." Being with her that way is a dream. Waking up to find I'd taken that choice away from her *while* dreaming would be a nightmare.

"Do you at least have something softer?" She rubs at the fabric, mouth twisted in a scowl.

I roll away from her and go to the drawers built into the wall on the other side of the room. It takes me less than a minute to swap out what I had been wearing for the pants I would throw on if I had an unexpected visitor in the middle of the night.

"Much better." She snuggles close to me, her legs wrapping around mine, and I settle into the familiar rhythm of our time together.

As always, time falls away and she dozes off in my arms.

I hope the stress she's carried since I first found her waiting for me has melted away.

I hope that sleep means she feels safe here.

Time ticks away, and I breathe in the scent of her, letting her fill my lungs the way she's filled my mind and my heart.

A tone peals and she flinches, startling awake. I hug her closer to me while I scan the dim readout projected on the ceiling.

"There's been a breach in the trio's sector." I say, rubbing my hand over her back. "Arc's already on his way to handle it."

I'm not sure the man sleeps—it would explain why he's such an asshole.

"Do you need to go?" she asks. Her words are thick and sleepy.

"No." I kiss her forehead and breathe in the scent of her hair. "I'll reconfigure the system in the morning so it doesn't wake you."

She shakes her head against my chest. "It's important that you know what's going on. You can't rearrange your life around me."

I almost laugh. I'd rearrange *both* our galaxies around her if I needed to.

"I'll lower the tone… and I'm going to reconnect the lights so you can move around if you need to."

"D…"

But whatever she was going to say, whatever argument she was going to make, she clamps her mouth shut and presses her cheek to my chest.

"Just don't do anything permanent."

Because she isn't staying.

I can't even ask her to stay, I just have to hope she'll change her mind.

Her breath stills as she falls asleep beside me, and I let the rise and fall of her chest soothe me to sleep as well.

But like most nights, sleep is just a black void. My eyes snap open hours later, as if time has skipped forward.

The room is still completely dark, but it is after midday outside, and she stirs against me, eyes fluttering open.

"Good morning," I say, softly against her hair.

"Good morning." She stretches and the movement presses her flush against me. "Oh!"

Her eyes go wide and she freezes.

This is why I should have kept the thicker pants on.

My cock strains against the too-thin fabric. "Sorry."

She swallows, still not moving and then looks up at my face she can't see. "I could... help with that."

Saints.

The throb turns to pure torture at the idea of what her "help" could entail.

But her being here isn't transactional.

"You don't need to do that."

She opens her mouth to say something, but on the breath she takes to say it, I see her change her mind. "Okay."

I get out of bed and pick her up, holding her high enough up my morning erection doesn't... disturb her while I walk her to the door. It slides open when we get close enough and I pause, blinking away the brightness of the hallway beyond. When I set her down, she turns back to me and I see her force herself not to look down.

"I'm going to take a shower." She swallows and licks her lips. "If you need some time."

57

I take that time and a shower of my own to *deal* with it.

And when I'm done, I still hear her shower running through the walls.

I pull on my clothes and the lens I'd taken out before I went to her last night. The data shuffles across any surface my gaze lands on, spewing out the reports from last night and this morning.

The sound of Kimba in the bathroom is soothing in a way I hadn't expected.

Other people in my space feels wrong.

Out of place.

But my skin doesn't crawl at the idea of her in a position to dig through all of my secrets.

Maybe I'm a fool for that.

I go to the kitchen as soon as I've got all my clothes on again. It's been years since I disconnected the lighting in the living spaces of my outpost, but they connect back up easily.

The lights in my kitchen flicker on as Kimba joins me and she looks up at them like she's offended. "Don't hook up anything else."

"You need to be able to see." My eyes trace over her, gaze stuttering over her bare legs and the shorts that barely peek out from under her shirt.

"In here, with the knives, yes. In the bathroom I'm using, also yes. But the living room gets enough light through the windows, and your bedroom... you need it to be completely dark in order to sleep. Don't sacrifice that for me."

I nod, not wanting to acquiesce to that, but I'll do what she wants unless I have to do what she needs.

"I did not anticipate needing to feed you."

"Do you have a weird diet?" she asks, tipping her head to the side to look behind me.

"No."

"Then I should be fine. Show me what you've got." She climbs up to sit on my counter as I run through the options.

I don't have any of the Earth food the Agency imports, but she's been here long enough, she doesn't blink at any of the options.

"I'll get an order in today and restock. Just let me know what you want."

She shakes her head. "Give me your address code and I'll order my own. I'm already taking too much from you."

"You saved my life, remember? I owe you."

"You don't owe me anything, D." She takes a deep breath and plucks a packet out of my hand, looking at it, she laughs and then scowls. "And of course, I grab the *one* thing I'm allergic to."

She hands it back to me. "I cross two galaxies and still can't get away from a peanut allergy."

I look at the packet and she points to the ingredients.

"Marbaroo root is called peanut on Earth?"

"No, they don't have marbaroo there, but the allergen is chemically the same." She wrinkles her nose. "Margot won't let the stuff through the door."

"I will remember that."

In the end, she eats what she calls a sandwich and her expression fades from those soft smiles. A little crease forms beneath her dark eyebrows.

"You're still worried." I want her to say no, but I already know she won't.

Her brows pinch tighter as she looks up at me. "Of course I am."

"You're safe here." From everything. "I won't let them anywhere near you."

59

Her face goes blank and she blinks at me and then, it clears.

She sets her sandwich down and walks around the table to me. "You silly man. I'm not worried about them trying to do something to me."

"I won't let them."

"I know." She kisses my forehead and hugs me close to her. "Someone out there is trying to kill you. Now that they know I'm not going to do it for them... I'm afraid of who they'll send next."

"No one on this planet or any other could get as close as you."

I see the muscles in her arm tense, I feel her swallow...

"Good," she finally says, taking a step back. "But that just means they're going to get more creative."

Taking a deep breath, she doesn't go back to her seat with the last of her meal. She nudges me until I move back and she sits on my thigh, her legs dangling between mine.

"Why didn't you let me help?" She studies my face and her fingers tighten in my shirt. "You never let me dance for you, but you say things that make me think..."

Her words die away and I imagine it's because she doesn't know how to finish her sentence.

But I understand what she's asking. "I can't do more than what we have done, without knowing that it will mean the same thing to you that it does to me."

"What does it mean?"

This is the kind of conversation I would rather have without the threat hanging over us... but we're in the Shadow Zone. There will always be a threat.

"I know we set down rules when this started."

She presses her lips together and looks at me, wide-eyed. "But the situation has changed."

"In more ways than you know." I look at her hand as I

lace my fingers in hers. "The other night, when I showed up unexpectedly, one of the cavrinskh had gotten out of the caldera."

She stares at me, eyes too wide, skin paling. Her breath hitches and I see her pulse jump in her neck. "But you tracked it down."

"Not exactly. We'd gone to Isagma Valley to deal with a different problem and the man we were after... the cavrinskh killed him."

"That's strange." She scowls at me, but I know it's not meant for me. "It bypassed hundreds of women and children to go after a man?"

She would have heard if it had killed anyone else. There's no way the CSS could have covered that up.

"Yes."

I watch her face shift through a half dozen emotions. "That's a huge deviation from previous behavior."

"I know."

Her face screws up and then she looks at me, even more confused than she was before. "What does that have to do with me... with us."

There's a lack of surety in the way she says that last word, but I ignore it. I can't afford self doubt right now.

"You've been safer in the city than you would have been here, so I never asked." I take a deep breath and say the first terrifying thing I have to get off my chest. "I want you to stay."

"Of course I'm going to—"

"Even after we figure out who's trying to kill me."

She freezes, eyes locked on mine. "D, I—"

She's about to pull away from me. "I know you loved Edan, that you still do."

I have a feeling the shock of hearing someone else say his name is the only thing keeping her planted in my lap.

61

"I know that when he died, it almost killed you."

"It should have." The words are a whisper.

"No." I respond reflexively. "I refuse to believe the saints are so cruel that they would punish true love and devotion with death."

Bonded pairs die together too often, but I will not accept the idea that someone like Kimba didn't love her mate enough to die with him.

And I hate the look on her face, because *she* has accepted it. And it's wrong.

"You love him too much to let him go. I understand that. I don't plan to fight it."

"I'm broken, D. You don't deserve that. You deserve someone who loves you and you alone."

"I don't want anyone else, and I don't need to eclipse him. I would never ask you to set his memory aside in favor of me... But I have to believe there's room left in your heart."

I brush my thumbs over her cheeks. She isn't crying, but she looks like she might.

"We'll talk about this later. Just... think about it."

She slides off my lap and stands on unsteady legs.

"And if this is all too much, if you don't want to be *here* anymore, I will find a safe place for you."

Because I spoke too soon and I'm going to lose her already.

CHAPTER FOUR

KIMBA

"DO YOU WANT ME TO LEAVE?"

I watch his face, looking for any sign that the "Of course not" of his reply isn't a lie.

But it's not.

He wants me here, even if I can't give him what he wants.

And I don't want to go anywhere.

"You know more about me than a normal person should." I laugh as I hear myself say it. The unsteady sound makes my chest hurt. "But you're not a normal person, are you?"

"What gave it away?" He quirks one of his brow ridges in an expression that's so human...

"So you know about Edan, I assume you know he was murdered." He has to know *everything*.

D stares at me, unmoving.

"When he died..." I've spent so long *not* saying it, the words are leaden in my mouth. "When the bond breaks, every ounce of emotion in your mate pours through the

63

connection into you. Pain, fear... rage. It's like they're metal stakes, driven through you, and all you can do is stand and take it."

Silence settles between us and I look up to meet his eerie eyes. Eyes that trace over me before he says, "You're cold."

I shiver when he says it. As if his saying it makes it true.

"Can I hold you? Or do you want your space?"

I go to him, curling myself into a ball in his arms. It will be easier to tell him the rest if I *can't* look him in those eyes that see too much.

Closing mine, I press my cheek to his chest, stealing the warmth from him.

His hand draws soft circles over my back. "I didn't know he'd been murdered."

"They kept it very quiet..." but not quiet enough, apparently. "Maybe that's why your would-be killers picked me. Means and opportunity, all they had to do was supply the motivation."

"What are you talking about?"

I try to keep the sigh quiet, but I know he feels the full movement of it. "I killed him. The man who murdered Edan. They knew."

He's quiet and I don't know what he's thinking. I don't know what I want him to think.

"I didn't do it on purpose. The moment Edan died, I turned into this... this rage monster and... I don't know if the man even knew I was there before he was dead."

"That's a normal response." D brushes his fingers along my cheek and tips my head up, forcing me to meet his eyes. "Just because it's a response that has happened more often when the female of the pair has been killed, doesn't make it an oddity that it happened to you. If you'd done something wrong, the CSS would have penalized you for it."

"I don't even know how I did it. I was consumed by this... feeling of death, and when I finally clawed my way out of the void of despair and rage... there were two dead men in my home."

D nods and says, "And you think that's why they went to you, because you had access to me and you've killed before."

I nod. I can't bring myself to agree with that out loud because it feels like I'm agreeing with them.

"I could have told them they were wrong to pick you," he says. "You're not a killer."

"How can you be so sure?"

"It takes one to know one."

I deflate a little. It's different. "You kill monsters, not people."

"We both know people can be monsters too." Pressing his thumb to my lips, he doesn't quite look at me. "What kind of monster I hunt doesn't change that."

"It does."

He looks away from me for a moment and I hear the words he mutters under his breath as if they're a curse. "I've already said too much, might as well dig my grave deeper."

"D—" I say his name, but I'm not sure if I want to stop him or...

"I would kill anyone who tried to hurt you. I would kill anyone you asked me to. I am a killer and at the end of the day, my reasons don't matter."

"I don't believe you." I don't know if I'm lying or not.

"You don't have to."

When he meets my eyes, it's not the physical manifestation of his mutation that scares me. There's an intensity within them that's terrifying.

It thrills me.

I want him. And I want him to want me.

It's an admission I've spent so much time shoving to the periphery, that even acknowledging it now makes me ache in all the parts of me that have been empty for too long.

When I didn't know what he did to get them, those scars scared me, because I knew what they meant.

The way that losing your bondmate tears out your very soul and then feeds it back to you is an experience I almost didn't survive. I can't imagine going through that again.

It's not simply that his job is dangerous. The fact that someone actually asked me to kill him is just more proof.

But still... I want him. I've wanted him for too long to deny it.

Now that we're here... maybe I can have him.

Just a little bit.

But I need to know...

"Why don't you have an Agency contract yet?"

His brow ridges quirk. "You know why."

"Tell me anyway."

I wait, and my breath feels too loud in my head. I need to know... I hope I'm wrong, even if being wrong will gut me.

"I considered it. Several times," he says. "The Agency sent me plenty of their marketing material but I always ran into the same problem... you'd never be one of the faces that popped up on that screen.

"They could have offered me every woman in the universe and none of them would be right, because they wouldn't be you."

I kiss him as though it's the only way to get my bearings. As though *not* kissing him would send me spinning off into oblivion.

He's my anchor. I don't know when that became true. All I know is that it is.

D kisses me back and it's so sweet, I want to cry.

It's been years since… but I still remember what it felt like to kiss Edan.

The surety of the emotion coming back across the bond had made everything easy. I knew what he wanted, how he liked it without even asking, and I knew what he was willing to give and how much he could take.

Kissing D has none of that.

Every angle of my mouth is a question, when I open myself to him, it's an offering I don't know if he'll accept.

We are disconnected… but I can feel the physical manifestation of his desire.

And I can feel his restraint.

His hands are firm at my waist, he doesn't move them.

He pulls back from me—just an inch—with a groan that rumbles through me. "I am a patient man, Kimba. We don't need to rush into anything."

That makes me laugh. There's nothing about him and me that could be considered "rushing."

Edan had collected me from the Agency spaceship and whisked me away to a hotel room in the city center. The door had barely closed behind us before our clothes were off. He was inside me before I'd been on the planet for a full hour.

D lifts me off of him, moving me—again—so that his erection doesn't touch me.

His muscles are clenched tight as he lets go of me. I can see the tightness in his shoulders. D has more control than anyone I've ever met.

67

"You've never let me do any of the things I offered at the club."

"I couldn't… Because I hadn't told you what I wanted."

"And now that I know?"

"I'm yours," he says with a tightness to his jaw that looks painful. "Completely. And I'll be content with as much or as little of yourself as you can share with me."

He looks out the window, but I don't know if he sees any of the landscape. His eyes have taken on that strange green cast from the contact lenses he wears.

"Your car's here."

DRIFT

I don't want to do this right now, but Trench has already come through the door and the last thing I want is for him to come looking for me and find *her*.

So I get myself back in order and head up the stairs.

The brotherhood have free rein of the top level of my outpost. I would never take that away from them. And I can't imagine Trench invading my private spaces, but I'm also not willing to risk it.

"Find anything?" I ask as he tosses her neural link back to me.

"A neatly packaged little bomb that would have killed her and made it look like a freak accident. Even though we all know there's no way that high-end of a vehicle would ever spontaneously fail like that."

Kimba can afford the best and she didn't settle for anything less with her car. "Nothing else, no trackers?"

"Nothing." He looks toward the stairs behind me. "I know it's not my place, but… this feels like something we should let the CSS handle."

"We both know the CSS has its uses, but I'm not willing to trust them with her." I look back toward the stairs. "I'll let my friend in their offices know what's going on, but at least five of the names on my list of possible suspects wear a CSS clearance badge."

"Which ones?"

"The pro-bomb squad, who else?"

Trench grimaces, but nods. And then he too looks down the stairs. "What about her bondmate? They could take him to hurt her. They'd probably be safer together."

"She's not bonded." I wouldn't have told any of the others. "But let's keep that between us."

Trench is good at keeping secrets.

He blinks at me, looking a little stunned and then shakes it away like he does everything.

"That makes sense. Well, more sense than the alternative, I guess."

"What's the alternative?"

Trench gives me a look. "That her bondmate gave her to you for safe keeping."

"It's not unthinkable."

"Would you hand her over to another man?"

"If she would be safer with him."

He snorts and looks away as he shakes his head. "Well, at least now I know what you look like when you lie."

"It's not a lie... but I know there isn't anyone safer, so it's a non-issue."

"Sure. Let me know when you have more news and whatever you do, don't go anywhere without one of us with you."

"I can take care of myself."

"No one doubts that. But you don't have to do this alone. You have us."

"I'll consider it."

He turns for the door and then stops, turning back to me and pausing. "Do yourself a favor. If you love her, don't let her leave without being certain she knows."

I stare at the closed door between us just a little too long, because that's always been the question... how do I convince Kimba that this is love... not just an obsession, like the other men who drool over her.

CHAPTER
FIVE

KIMBA

D HAS COME BACK DOWNSTAIRS. I heard him descend the spiraled steps and my gaze moves back and forth between my face in the mirror, and the bottle of vitamins on the counter. Vitamins I've been taking out of some weird habit since Edan died... vitamins that make human female anatomy work with Sian male anatomy.

It's no secret that the more you take, the more you *can* take... there was a woman at Margot's who took five of them twice a day, solely so she could use her acrobatic skills to take three Sian men at once without tearing herself apart.

I would have called it an exaggeration, except she showed anyone who asked the security footage from the room.

They're vitamins I shouldn't have. The *point* is to facilitate breeding. They're meant to make us easier to fuck, and I'm not fucking anyone anymore.

But I could be.

I look back toward the living space and my pussy

clenches on air at the idea of having him in every way, not just the ones I've allowed myself so far.

Maybe not today... but someday soon, I may need these.

I pour two out into my hand and swallow them down with a long drink of water.

It doesn't mean I *have* to give into the way I feel about him. It just means that if I do, I might not get hurt.

Taking a deep breath, I go to him, bare feet padding on the oddly warm floors.

Snow swirls outside and he sets aside the tablet he'd been reading from. As soon as he lets go of it, it retracts into its compact form.

Good. No distractions.

Stepping into the space between his knees, I say, "I have a request."

When he looks up at me, it's with that soft smile I've begun to crave.

But it vanishes as I sink to my knees between his, hands resting on his thighs.

He says my name in a warning tone, one I've heard before...

"I have been asking to suck your cock for too long. You just got rid of your last excuse, are you really going to disappoint us both by manufacturing another one?"

"You don't have to—"

I cut him off. "I don't ask for things I don't want."

He nods and looks... just a little terrified.

His muscles are clenched tight, but I ignore that as I weave the fabric of his waistband through the buckle, and run my finger along the seal that holds the flap closed.

The move drags my finger along the bulge there, and his cock twitches against my touch.

Sian men—if Edan and all of the ones who go to

Margot's are the rule, not the exception—*crave* physical touch. Sex is an outlet for that that I'd grown to crave as well.

And I'd be lying if I said I didn't imagine D when I use my toys at home.

Having him in front of me now... heat coils between my legs, and I lick my lips, looking up to see his jaw locked, eyes narrowed in concentration.

His cock literally pops out as soon as it can get free. And my eyes go wide.

It's been a very long time since I've seen a Sian cock in person—I've learned how to avoid them in the public play rooms—D's is a surprise, not a disappointment.

Big D, indeed.

I hadn't forgotten what they looked like—how could I? Even here, the Agency promotions find their way into our lives.

Sian cocks are similar to human cocks in function... less so in form.

The hard length hides those thick tubes under skin that is ridged along the bottom, as though they had once had the physiological ability to lock themselves inside of their mates.

But the strange, textured softness... The stiffness of those three tubes beneath the skin.

No manufacturer could replicate it, no matter how hard they tried. And like everything else about Sian men, they're bigger.

My fingers don't touch as I wrap my hands around him, running them up and back down the mouthwatering shaft.

If I hadn't done this once or twice—*before*—I might have started to rethink my plan. But I don't have to get all of him in my mouth.

There are women at Margot's who could.

A sliver of jealousy stabs at me as I wonder if any of the women there knew this had been hidden behind the dark fabric of his pants.

I shove it away.

Thoughts like that have no place here.

Not with something so gorgeous waiting for me to have a taste.

Sliding my fingers over him, I feel the phantom sensations of the last time I'd…

The desire I'd long since kept locked away pressing at the door I've kept it behind.

Edan hadn't let me see him before he'd taken me the first time. If he hadn't been so frantic to claim me, I might have thought he'd done it to keep me from being afraid.

D isn't frantic. He watches me, arms spread wide over the back of the couch. But I can see the tension in the line of his jaw.

His hands are claws, gripping the cushions.

"Is this okay?" I ask, stroking him and keeping my eyes on his.

His answer is a growled "Fuck yes."

Thank the saints.

The skin is so soft, I don't know if I could have stopped myself from touching him if I'd tried.

He's a heavy weight in my hand, and I imagine what it would feel like to have him inside me. *That* is a desire I'm still unable to give into.

I stroke him and clench my legs together to keep from squirming.

And for two seconds, I consider running back to the bathroom to retrieve the toy hidden in the bottom of my bag.

But somehow, riding a fake version while I have him in

my mouth seems simultaneously unfair to him, and like it would be a disappointment.

Still, the idea of it makes me shift forward on my knees.

I'm wet and hot, and I kiss the tip of him to stop from asking for more before either of us are truly ready for it.

The kisses I trail along his cock are definitely a stalling tactic, and he knows it.

Fingers sliding into my hair, he says, "Just tell me what you want."

I lick the ridges from base to tip to buy myself more time.

"I want to suck your cock," I say, channeling all the confidence I've seen Hannah and the other women at Margot's wield.

His breath hitches as I say it. His cock twitches in my hand.

"And then..." That confidence falters, but I push through it. "I want you to fuck my face."

His tongue pokes out to sweep over his lips and when he reaches out to run his thumb over mine, he's smiling. "Better open wide."

Fuck.

Those words send a shock of pure need straight to my pussy, and I can't stop myself from squirming this time.

I lick him from base to tip.

That ridge on the underside of him drags across my tongue, reminding me exactly how those hard ribs would feel as he withdrew.

Scratching this itch was such a bad idea.

Swirling the flared edge of his cockhead with my tongue, I look up, meet his eyes.

Watching him watch me as I do what he said and open wide.

When my lips wrap around him, his eyes flutter closed.

It's just for a moment. It's the sort of pause that makes me think of disbelief.

I'm having a hard time believing it myself.

He's hot and warm, and taking him in is easier than I thought.

But only for that first inch.

When I pull back, I suck, and his eyes widen on a gasp.

His clenched hands hover an inch above the cushions. And he lets out a hiss from behind grit teeth.

His eyes move from mine to where we're joined, and as I dip down onto him again—able to go a little further this time—he reaches out.

His hand is a gentle weight against the back of my head. Not pushing me down, but reminding me he could —will, when I ask him to.

That pressure is a promise that has heat coiling in my belly. I sigh at the thought and then laugh when he twitches in my mouth, bobbing my head in a different direction.

"Kimba." My name is a harsh growl from his lips. "You have no idea how long I've wanted this."

He lapses into the Sian language, one I understand perfectly, but the switch sends a thrill through me.

I know women at Margot's who claimed to have made men forget English entirely. Until now, I'd never understood why they were so proud of the accomplishment.

Pulling back to catch my breath, I ask, "Do you like that?"

"I love it. Please don't stop."

I'd had no intentions of stopping… but teasing him is too tempting.

Pulling away, I watch his face while I keep my hands occupied with his cock.

"What do I get when I make you come?"

His lips curve in a wicked grin. "I have something in mind…" But he doesn't say what.

The threat and promise is too heavy to ignore. But I bite my lip to keep myself from rising to his bait. "Let's see if I deserve it."

Getting my mouth around his cock is still a challenge. I know it never gets easier, the strain was just more familiar when I was in practice.

He lets out a deep moan as I press further down onto him, and the sound cuts through me. Makes me want…

I thought I could get through this without needing to ease my own desire, but I have to take something off. I'm wearing *way* too many clothes.

Pulling back from him with a suction pop, I sweep my shirt and bra over my head.

He uses the moment I'm away from him to slip his pants the rest of the way down. And he yanks his shirt off too.

He's *finally* fully naked for me, and that pulse of desire pushes harder at my core.

The skin of his thighs brushes against the sides of my breast as I lean in and take him again.

When I meet his eyes, they're hooded. His jaw is tight.

"Fuck, you look so pretty with my cock in your mouth."

I try to smile, but I can't quite manage it.

I have to rise up on my knees to swallow him, and the cool air caresses my damp and needy pussy. My shorts and underwear are no barrier.

Since I only need one hand to hold his cock steady for me…

I trail the other down my stomach, slipping it into the

fabric and touching myself, like I have so many times to the thought of him.

I imagine slipping these shorts off, getting fully naked with him and crawling up to straddle him.

It's so easy to imagine lining his cock up with my pussy instead of my mouth.

Swirling my clit once, I stroke my fingers down, pressing my pussy open as if to invite the cock currently between my lips inside that part of me.

My eyes flutter closed and I can't stop the moan that escapes me.

As I lower my mouth onto him, I slowly move from stroking the wet line of my pussy to pressing both fingers inside of me.

I want him so badly.

He sits up, the movement forcing his cock further into my mouth, and I pull back to look at him, but he doesn't let me go far while he repositions himself.

His fingers lace in my hair, and I have to use my free hand to hold his thigh—to hold myself up. Because he grips my head a little tighter and then he's the one who's controlling the motion. He's the one who's fucking my mouth.

Just like I asked.

He's gentler than he needs to be... but much more of this, and I'll come. I'm not sure how much more abuse my clit can take.

Every thrust is a promise of what I could have if I would just let myself take it.

I look up, relaxing my jaw as much as I can. But each time he presses me further down, I have to close my eyes.

There's just too much of him.

My body screams at me that I'm wrong. There's too much for my mouth, but I press my fingers into me,

78

knowing how easily he would enter me if I pulled away. If I just stood and straddled his gorgeous cock.

He would fit into me like our bodies had been made with each other in mind.

And then he would be *mine*.

The tightly coiled heat that thought brings to mind is dampened by that ever-present reminder of what could happen if I let it.

I shove the thought away.

Right now is about what we *can* do.

I knew it had been a while for him, but I hadn't expected...

His face contorts, and I feel the tug as he tries to pull me off, but I don't let him.

As much as this is about him, it's also about what I want.

And I want it all.

I never did this for Edan. He was always too frantic to breed me. Even when we realized he couldn't, he wasn't willing to risk the chance that I might swallow the load that would have impregnated me. And that's why...

D's cum is startling.

Like human men, it's hot. But it's not salty, like I remember from my days on Earth.

It's not sweet... but it has the potential to be intoxicating.

Addicting, even.

My head swims as I pull back, swallowing the first spurts so that I can take the rest.

They come so much more than human men. It's one of the many reasons it's so easy for human women—other human women—to get pregnant.

It's a literal deluge, and I have to close my eyes just to focus on drinking him down.

79

Ridiculous as it is, I don't want to spill a single drop. I want to wear that accomplishment as a private badge of honor.

His cock twitches once more, and I pull back, watching him as I flick my tongue over his tip one last time.

Leaning forward, he runs his thumb along my lower lip, still slick with him, and then gently presses it between them, silently telling me to suck the last little bit of him from his finger.

"How is it possible," he asks, still in Sianese, "that the saints granted me such a gift?"

"I was thinking the same thing."

His brows rise, just a fraction.

"Have I mentioned the brotherhood is going to hate that they can't whisper about you when you're around."

"And what would they have to whisper about?"

"Jealousy." He pulls me forward so I'm leaning over him, knees on his thighs, his cock resting against my stomach. "Because you're mine."

He's still hard.

Another difference between Sian and human men.

I slip my hand between our bodies, stroking him again.

"You don't have to—"

"I know. I want to." I press him against my stomach, sliding his cock between my hand and skin, stroking him.

There are women at Margot's who work in pairs. Someone else could do what I can't yet...

I don't think I could share him.

Wanting has been my constant companion. Admitting it, my constant fear. I slip from him, back to the floor and run my hands down his thighs.

I want to feel his skin everywhere.

That's why I lick him clean, making sure I've swiped

80

up every last drop, and then, I stand and shimmy my shorts down, swaying my hips in an abbreviated dance.

His gaze is hungry.

He's seen me naked before... thousands of people have, but this is the closest I've gotten to a man with my clothes off in years. And he knows it.

"This is dangerous, Kimba."

"You'll keep me safe." This time, I don't sink to the floor.

Slinging my legs over his, I straddle him, pressing myself to his chest. "You'll never hurt me."

He wraps his arms around me, holding me up so there's no chance I'll sink down onto the cock I know is pointed directly where we both want to put it—directly where it can't go.

I take one of his hands, sliding it down and guiding his fingers into me. "Feel how wet sucking your cock made me."

His hips shift and it nudges the tip of his cock against my clit.

I don't think it was a conscious movement. His body wants mine as much as mine wants his.

Another growl rumbles from deep inside his chest and he shifts, one hand smoothing down my spine until he presses it between my legs, curling up and into me... Blocking his cock from doing the same, but leaving my clit perfectly placed...

I rock my hips and the movement draws my clit along those ridges.

The curse I whisper into his mouth makes him chuckle and he moves his hand, fucking me with his fingers while I grind my clit against his cock.

Arms around his neck, I kiss him, pouring all of the frustration I feel into it.

But mine isn't the only frustration steering this moment.

D pulls back from me, his teeth grit. "I want you so badly…"

He picks me up, slides me back to the ground and fists himself. "I don't want to risk giving into the temptation."

All it would have taken was moving his fingers and he could have been inside me, completely…

"Thank you." I kiss him and sink back onto my heels as he strokes himself.

I watch as his face contorts in pain, as he moves in a rougher grip than I would have attempted.

I run my nails along his ridges and they flare more than I expected.

They *always* come twice.

The thick lines of his cum stripe my breasts and stomach. Warm and sticky, this spray is less forceful than the first… less voluminous.

Swiping my fingers over my breast, I suck his cum from them. "See how much nicer it is when you give me what I want?"

We could have been doing this for months.

Maybe that's a lie.

Before now, something like this would have probably sent me running.

But the rules have changed—everything has changed—and I'm not going anywhere.

DRIFT

Kimba looks up at me with a coy smile, and my head spins as she licks my cum from her fingers.

But I'm not so far out of it that I've forgotten about the hand she had snaked down between her legs.

She's kept me from leaning forward until now, but it's my turn.

I catch her other hand and draw her fingers to my lips, sucking the taste of her from them.

It's nearly my undoing.

The wetness that coats my tongue sends a fire through my veins that is almost primal.

I push her back, just enough so I can scoop her into my arms and turn her, so she's the one on the sofa.

She's short enough that she's lying nearly all the way down. Only her head is propped up. It's the perfect angle to look at me. And I want her to watch.

"I've wanted to taste you since the moment I saw you step onto that stage."

"Then you'd better make up for lost time."

I drag my pants back on. Sealing myself up so that neither of us can get too carried away this time.

I can't bury my cock in her pussy, but getting the taste of her on my tongue doesn't feel like I'm "settling."

She's wet from both of our fingers, and I stroke her, imagining how easily I could slide into her right now.

I'm already hard again, and there's a haze of lust in her eyes that makes me think she might be reckless enough to let me do something neither of us is ready for yet.

I'd never forgive myself.

"I just want to taste you." I say it low enough, I'm not sure Kimba hears me.

But it's a reminder for me, more than it is a reassurance to her.

"I want that too." She nods. It's a jerking movement. Her eyes are hooded.

And I wonder... just how long it's been.

But asking would just be my ego, searching for an empty prize.

Kissing the inside of her thigh, I don't let myself devour her. Don't let myself take from her the way I desperately want.

Devouring her would be for me. This is for her.

I sigh against her skin, letting my breath warm her already heated core, and she moves beneath me.

Wanting.

But I can't give it to her just yet. I *need* to pace myself.

Pressing my lips to her other thigh, I shift, moving so I have better access, so I know I'm not accidentally going to wind up crushing her legs.

Her chest rises and falls as she watches me, as she waits. When she bites her lip, I smile against her skin, knowing how easy it would be to give her an orgasm and be done. But I'm not *just* trying to get her off.

I'm trying to convince her to give me all of her, to trust me… and this is just a part of that.

I cover her with my mouth.

She tastes *perfect*.

Flicking her clit with my tongue, I hold her hips tighter as they buck beneath me.

The movement reminds me of how she might look on top of me, riding my cock.

Dragging a finger along her slit, I swallow as she shivers. I press into her, trying not to imagine it's another part of me.

I pull Kimba closer to the edge of the sofa and cover her again, using my tongue to tease. Using my fingers to rub and swirl at her clit.

I've waited for this—for her—for so long… I'm honestly surprised I haven't devoured her whole.

But I know no one else has had her since her bondmate's death.

No matter how much I want to hear Kimba cry out as I

fill her, making sure she's ready to take what I want to give is more important.

My cock twitches against my pants again, already struggling with the biological imperative to be inside her in the most binding way.

I fight that compulsion by paying more attention to the way she moves beneath my tongue.

Pulling away, just to catch my breath, I slip one finger in again, testing her. She's tight, but not so tight I need to stop there. On my next stroke, she rocks into me. Exactly as I'd hoped.

She's so responsive.

Whether that's because it's been so long, or—and my pulse quickens at the idea—whether it's *me* she's been waiting to do this for, I don't know.

Honestly, I don't really care.

I crave her.

Her skin is warm on my cheeks, her pussy warmer on my tongue.

Finger buried inside her, I stroke, wanting to pull that sugared bliss from her lips.

Grazing my teeth over her clit, I—

Kimba's gasp is sharp, and her pelvis flinches away from me. I drag in a breath as I look up her naked body to meet her gaze.

She got herself so close while her mouth was on my cock.

Still…

"If you want me to stop—"

"I don't."

"—at any point. Just say."

She nods and it shakes her whole body, moving her on the finger still inside of her. The finger that slides freely now.

Dipping down to press a kiss to her, I pull my hand away, just enough to realign myself. And this time, I press in two. Her moan makes my cock twitch.

She moves on me, pulling away to press back down on my fingers, pushing me deeper inside of her.

Watching her face, my gaze traveling up the length of her body, I see the bliss as it begins to haze her eyes.

Her hands grip the cushions, and each breath pressing her breasts a little higher.

Releasing her hips, I reach up her, needing to touch them. Needing to feel the softness of her.

Wanting to take them in my mouth as I take her with my cock.

"Fuck, D." She spreads her legs wider, wiggling as though she might get closer to me than she already is. "I want so many things I can't have."

"I'll give you anything."

But I'll start with an orgasm.

She bucks as I pressed my thumb to her clit, rubbing her harder, drawing a roughly traced circle.

I slip my hand under her hip and lift her closer to my lips. I want her to come, and I'm not going to stop until…

Arching off the couch, she cries out with a soft sob as she comes apart. The name that floats on the broken sound isn't the one the Maker gave me, it's what she's called me from the start.

"D!"

My cock stiffens back to full attention. She'll be the death of me, if I let her.

I pull my fingers free slowly. The pulsing vise of her diminishing orgasm makes it difficult.

Kimba's still shaking as she comes down and I keep fucking her with my tongue, lapping her up. I'm not done yet.

"That was…"

I lick her again in one long stroke and she flinches—still sensitive from before.

"If I get two, you get two."

This time, I press three fingers into her, stretching as I work her open.

Eyes closed, she bites her lip, but her moans escape as I curl my fingers, stroking.

Her sigh is a harsh curse that turns into a sharp mewl.

The sound drives through me like a spike of pure lust.

I can't take the pressure anymore. Shifting her so that my shoulders support her legs, I spare one hand. Reaching down to free my aching cock, stroking myself as though my hand was her mouth all over again.

I flick her clit with the tips of my tongue, working them back and forth. As she tightens around my fingers, I tighten my hand around my cock.

Her pussy would be a vice on me, and I want to line myself up… I want her to beg me to take her.

Fuck.

I need to come. *Quick.*

But Kimba comes first.

Her shattering cry echoes off the glass and I stroke myself, watching the beautiful bliss wash over her face again.

I want to see it every day.

Every morning when we wake, and before we go to sleep.

I want this—her—always.

When her face softens, the last of those waves crash over her. The tide of her passion ebbing, I kiss her one last time, and sit back on my heels… trying to decide if I should finish here, or leave her.

I don't have a chance before she presses up onto her elbows.

She sees me and shoots me a half-hearted glare. "Naughty."

"Don't worry, I'll take care of it."

"No," the words are a breath, and she shoves me onto my back, sliding to the floor to once again take me in her mouth.

She pulls back, her soft laughter caressing me. "I could get drunk off this... and you're not even in my head yet."

Yet.

I don't even think she realizes she said it.

Working my cock with her lips and tongue, watching me from where she sucks, her mouth is pure molten pleasure.

A sigh, painted in disappointment, brushes against my wet skin. "I want to fuck you so badly."

I doubt I was meant to hear it, but it's the tipping point.

She takes me into her mouth and I come—harder than I ever remember doing before—and she drinks me in. Pulling back, only when I'm finally done. She licks the tip of me, and hums... like a content, purring zurgle.

I reach for her, and drag her up my body.

We've lain like this so many times before, but not here... not with her naked and me all but. It's wholly familiar and foreign. And I want to stay like this until all the light fades from the sky. Feeling her beside me as our bodies cool.

"Someday, I'll have you. Someday, you'll come apart on my cock. Someday, your pussy will be full of me. But *not* until you're ready to give every part of yourself to me."

She said *yet.*

And I'll wait an eternity for her if I have to.

CHAPTER
SIX

KIMBA

AN HOUR LATER, I've got real clothes on and am sitting crisscross applesauce on a stool upstairs, staring at men's profiles scrolling across the tablet in my hand and trying *not* to look down at the map that reminds me of a giant playset for dolls.

But only points of light dance across the shimmering surface that projects the entirety of the Shadow Zone—the glacial valley that spans between the two caldera rims like a very wobbly donut.

I force myself to study each man's face as if this isn't worse than actually looking for a guy on a dating app.

"Recognize anyone yet?" D asks, stretching in my periphery.

I shake my head without looking up and then I stop, because I do recognize the man I've just flicked onto the screen.

Luthiel.

He wasn't one of the men waiting for me at my building. But he does make me think...

There's always a possibility this *is* about me.

Not D.

I don't even know how many times I've turned Luthiel down. I don't know how many men have been turned away without my even hearing about it.

But I'm just being silly and self centered.

Men here aren't like men on Earth... not like *that*. They can be possessive and jealous, but I've never heard of a single one *hurting* a woman just because he couldn't have her.

But maybe I'm wrong. Maybe Sian men aren't that different from human men after all.

I skim Luthiel's information. He works with the CSS, so he could have found a way to dig into my past and find out who I am and what I've done, but does he have the connections to get those men, or men like them, to come after me?

I shove that thought away. It's ridiculous.

Even if Luthiel, or someone like him, wanted D dead because he had me when they didn't, they wouldn't want to incriminate me in his death. They'd want to be the one waiting to be a shoulder to cry on.

His eyes are piercing in the photo as it stares up at me and I can't help but feel unsettled.

"What if it's me?" I ask, turning away from Luthiel's unseeing gaze.

D looks up at me, waiting.

"What if the reason someone wants you dead is because of me?"

D's brow crumples for half a heartbeat before it smooths again, and he nods.

"I thought you were going to tell me it was ridiculous."

Shrugging, he scowls at the keys in front of him. "If he was stupid enough to think killing me was a good option,

I can think of a few reasons he'd want you to be the one who did it. Or at least the one they could blame."

I couldn't. "Like what?"

"If you were on the run, I would do everything to keep you safe. Like I am now... He could have planned to do the same. To sweep in, whisk you away somewhere where you wouldn't be caught and use your fugitive status as a way to keep you in line." He pitches his voice oddly. "You have to stay here, or they'll lock you away. You have to do exactly what I say, or I'll turn you in."

"That's a little far-fetched."

"Is it?" D lets out a long and low breath. "He might want to punish you for being taken, just as much as he would want to punish me for taking you."

"I was never his." Whoever this anonymous *"he"* is.

"I know. But human men aren't the only ones who can become... incorrectly possessive of women." He stretches his neck and the tense muscles of his shoulders shift. He comes to me and when he sees Luthiel's file, his posture changes. "I think... we should take a drive. Ask some questions."

"Do you think that's safe?" I don't like being afraid... I like being afraid for him even less.

"Luthiel won't try anything in his office."

"You know him?"

"Yes and no." He doesn't offer me any more clarity as he pulls up an address.

I nod. "Okay. We'll go."

He doesn't ask me to stay behind.

I don't want to let him out of my sight either.

I'm not used to being cooped up. Getting out of here for a few hours will be nice.

He sets an auto search function and then slips downstairs to get dressed. The bags from my car are next to the door, so I rummage through them until I find my heaviest coat and pull it on.

I almost argue with him when his car pops open as soon as we step out of the garage. Mine's nicer, but there was a heavy snowfall last night and I'd rather he's in something he is comfortable with.

D doesn't say a word when we get in the car, but it's an easy silence, and I don't have anything to say either. More snow falls in flurries and clusters as we drive the dark ribbon of road into the city, but we both curse when we get close enough.

Usually a bright beacon in the skyline, Margot's is dark.

I don't have to ask him to make a detour.

He turns off the route and his navigation chirps at him, trying to redirect. We both ignore it.

The parking lot at Margot's is empty. Not a single light washes the building's walls.

"What the hell?"

D holds my hand, locking me in place. "Margot's inside."

He doesn't let me go.

Not yet.

He scans the parking lot again, and his brows dip in confusion. "There's no one else here..."

And there should be.

Three o'clock in the afternoon, any day of the week, Margot's should be packed.

"We need to go in and see what happened." I pop the roof of the car and get out before he can ask me to stay behind.

An empty parking lot isn't eerie by itself, it's the lack of lights.

Those are on all day, every day.

Without them…

It feels *dead*.

We go to the main entrance and D puts his hand to the lock, but it flashes red, so I try mine, and when it slides open, I don't hesitate to jump inside. The ride to the top is dark, none of the rooms are lit, and Margot waits for us at the top, arms crossed over her chest.

She looks so strange without her usual rainbow-bright makeup. And with her hair pulled up like it is, it almost looks completely black.

"Welcome back." She says, irritation—not meant for us —seeping through.

"What's going on? Where is everyone?" All the lights are on inside and I wince, wondering how bad it is for D.

"I'll tell you, if you promise not to apologize for something that was in no way your fault."

I cringe and she chuckles.

"Just tell us, Margot. Please."

"Fine. But if you say sorry, you're buying me a drink."

She looks up at D, eyes narrowed as if she might tell him to fuck off, and then she shrugs and leads the way.

"Guy came in yesterday, late night, one of the ones who's gotten attached to you through no fault of your own. Anyway, he wanted to see you dance, said something about an anniversary. He even brought you flowers. And when I told him you weren't working, he looked like he might cry." She nods her head toward the bar. "He had a drink to nurse his heartache and then he got into a bit of a disagreement with another patron. Words were said, a barstool was thrown and now… we're closed and he's never going to get to see you again."

"I'm sorry—" it slips out before I can stop it.

"Don't be, now you owe me a drink."

She points to a patched wall with neon green words

spray-pointed over it that say "Don't damage this, Assholes," and then goes around behind the bar. "He couldn't have picked a better spot if he was *trying* to fuck me over. Killed our power for six hours. I decided to stay closed for the rest of the day. Partially as a collective punishment. Remind the boys who come in here that if they play shit games, *everybody* wins shit prizes. And, it's nice to have a break... I haven't been closed for... it feels like eons, but it's only been about a decade."

She looks sharply at D. "Since I have you here. You can help me with a little heavy lifting."

Margot points at a new PA near us. "Take that to the front of the stage, please."

D shoots her a long suffering glance, but does as he's asked while Margot pours me a drink.

"How's living in sin treating you?"

I don't ask her how she knows that we aren't bonded and that I'm not pregnant. The idea of an unbonded pair spending a night together and *not* winding up bonded wouldn't even occur to anyone else.

Margot has bio scanners embedded in the elevator that read the bonding chemical, how much stopper is in a man's blood, if a woman is pregnant... all the fun things.

"We both know things are complicated."

"Yes we do. I'm not judging."

No, Margot never judges. She *nudges* and she hints.

"You wanted him to get away from us for a reason... what was it?"

She tips back a shot of water—I know her secrets too, and that bottle is one of them.

"I watch men profess their love for the women who work here on a daily basis. I know when they're lying. I know when they think they're telling the truth, but aren't. And I know when a man has fallen for a woman and will do anything it takes to stay by her side... even if he doesn't think he's ever going to get between her legs." Margot looks past me and something soft passes across her face. "You two are fated, girl. Do you think I would have let just anyone alone in a room with you?"

"Of course not. Do you think I would have let just anyone put me alone in a room with someone?"

Margot smiles at me and purses her lips like she has something she shouldn't say.

And maybe she says it anyway.

"That man is in love with you. And you better figure out real fast whether or not you love him too. Because he'll take you either way. But I don't want to see you again until you know."

"Are you firing me?" Prickles of anxiety flutter over my skin.

Being here, working with the women who love their job just as much as I love mine... that *saved* me after Edan.

She knows it.

"It's for your own good." She squares her shoulders. "Figure out what's going on with the people who want him dead and then figure out if you're going to keep him. You can have your job back once you know. Either way."

D comes back and he looks between us, but he doesn't ask what we were talking about. "We stopped in to see if you were okay, but we really need to be going." He looks at me. "Luthiel's office closes in about twenty minutes."

"Luthiel?" Margot looks at me, disgusted. "Why do you need him?"

"Just checking off boxes," he says, and Margot casts a questioning glance at him.

"He wanted Kimba in an unhealthy way. So I have no doubt he would do something stupid if he thought it would get her. But from what she told me about the men

95

who want you dead... Luthiel doesn't have the intelligence or the resources to make that happen."

"I'll keep your opinion in mind." Glancing at me, D turns for the exit.

I let him go, let him ensure that it's safe, because I know arguing isn't going to get me anywhere. But when I turn to follow after him, Margot catches me with a glare.

"Promise me one thing."

I raise a brow, not willing to commit to anything until I know what I'd be signing up for.

"Promise me you'll seriously consider giving that man what he wants. Because I think it's what you want too. It's a risk, I know. But you can't let fear keep you from something that could make you happy."

She's right.

I've been afraid for a very long time. But I'm not afraid anymore.

"I'll see you soon."

I lean over the counter and kiss her cheek before hurrying through the oddly empty club, back to D.

He holds out his hand, and I take it.

DRIFT

I don't *dislike* Margot, but I don't enjoy the way she always looks like she can see straight through me.

I don't *like* when people seem to know more about me than they should, and Margot knows more about anyone than a person should.

So I take a deep breath when we get back outside, and exhale all the anxiety that itches at my skin from her scrutiny.

We get to the car as another one pulls in, but it's just a trio of guys who pull right up to the front and each try their hand at the access pad. Red lights all around followed by grumbles as they slink back to their car. I wait until Kimba belts herself in and then turn the car back for the direct route to Luthiel's office. Except, Kimba gets a call and even though Margot's quiet on the other end, I can hear the conversation well enough to punch in the number.

Luthiel has already gone home for the day and Margot has his home address... something I wouldn't have been able to get.

Kimba thanks her and hangs up, pressing her lips together. I wish I knew what she was feeling. I wish I knew if it was simple worry or some deeper dread that made the corners of her mouth turn down like that.

"Since we're not on a time crunch anymore, can we make a small detour?" She looks up at the skyscrapers and takes a deep breath, "I'd prefer to do it in daylight."

"Sure, where are we going?"

She puts the address into the navigation as an initial stop and then drops back to the chair. "I want to see if they've trashed my place."

I know where she lives... I couldn't rest easily without knowing she was somewhere secure—though not secure enough, it would seem—but I've never been to the building. I've gone out of my way to *stay* away.

But I follow her directions and I park in her assigned spot in the garage. The light in front of the car flashes red until she hops out and slides her hand over the panel. And I feel a little more at ease when she slips her hand in mine before we head for the entrance to the building.

The garage is deserted... thank the saints. And she gives me a confused glance when I hit the button for the ground floor.

"I want to look at the security cameras first."

"Oh. We need to go to five."

She hits a few buttons, canceling my request and sending us straight to the fifth floor. "I didn't know they could do that."

"You're not supposed to know you can do that." She offers me a smile and when the door opens, she leads the way around to the far side and steps into a room that is floor to ceiling, wall to wall, security monitors.

"Hey Kimba," the guy behind the desk barely looks at her, his attention solely on me. "Get yourself a bodyguard?"

"Yep." She says it as if it's not a lie… and maybe it isn't. "He wants to see some of the feeds."

She looks up at me and waits.

"Can you cue up the camera that shows her door and go back to the last time she left?"

"Sure." He hesitates, looking me over again, not hiding his suspicion.

That's good. He should be suspicious if he's sitting in that chair.

"It was about eight o'clock," Kimba tells him.

He pulls up the right camera and the right time and I see Kimba walk out her door, loaded up with the bags she had in her car.

"Can you bring it down to one of these screens?"

Again, he looks suspicious and then moves out of the way as I take over the controls. My eyes sting as I take off my opaque glasses and when I focus them on the screen, I flip the speed to the fastest it will go, watching random residents pass by, the day change to night change to day again.

"How can he…?"

I ignore the man's unfinished question and don't look at him. I don't need to. I already know he's seen my eyes and that his have flown wide. I keep my focus fixed on the screen in front of me and a few moments of silence later, I nod and put my glasses back on. "No interruptions in the feed, no one messed with your door."

"Good."

The security guard watches me, still. But it's with a little bit of awe mixed into his suspicion.

"Fancy new SecSys tech?"

"Sorry kid," I slip my glasses back on. "You can't buy these eyes. You have to suffer for them."

"How badly?" He wants them... he doesn't know how wrong he is.

I ignore him and let Kimba take my hand again, leading the way to the lifts. She doesn't need to hear how many times the Maker made me want to die before he finished piecing me back together.

Kimba is silent until the elevator doors open on the seventy-third floor. And I let her lead the way down the hall, but I keep close behind her.

No one's waiting for us.

When she palms open the door, I wince, even with my glasses on.

"Sorry, I didn't think about it." She slips her neural link over her ear as I close the door behind us, and a moment later dark shades slide down over the windows.

Her home is easier to see without the daylight trying to destroy my lab-grown retinas, but I don't love what I find when that awful brightness disappears.

All of the base elements of this place are white and sterile. All of the things she's brought into it are deep blue and soft.

She's found a way to live in this space, but it doesn't seem worthy of her.

"Make yourself comfortable, I just want to grab something I forgot." She hurries up the stairs and I follow her with my eyes as she goes. The lower part of the apartment has a kitchen behind me and a large living space between me and the now shaded windows. But the thing that draws my attention, immediately, is the flat shelf set in the center of the wall to my left.

There are flower petals there and stubs of incense and signs of things that once lived there, but were hastily removed.

I know what hung from the peg above it.

This was her shrine to Edan's memory.

I put my hands in my pockets so I don't touch anything. She's lived here with his ghost for years. It feels like a tomb to me, and even though that isn't what it is to her, I won't desecrate this space.

But the hollowness I feel, as if I can find the grief in the space deep in my chest I've set aside for her, that aches deeply enough I can't be down here alone.

I climb the stairs to the loft-like space above the living area. There are no walls, only glass barriers of varying heights.

The view at night is, no doubt, amazing.

The disarray of her departure is more evident here. There are clothes hanging halfway out of drawers, the table beside her bed is a tangle of knocked over trinkets… but her bed is perfectly made, and beyond it…

"Hannah refers to it as a trophy shelf," she says when she comes out of the bathroom and finds me staring at the collection of brightly colored facsimile cocks.

"It's a conversation starter, at the very least," I say.

"No one comes up here… only a few of the girls from the club have even come over, and it's not like they'd be offended." She shrugs and stands next to me.

"You didn't want to take any of them with you?"

"One's missing," She catches her lip between her teeth, and then a little laugh escapes her. "I don't really use the others anymore…"

"Why not?"

"I found a favorite." Her gaze drops to my chest and, for the first time in all the time I've known her, she blushes with embarrassment. "One that reminds me of you."

My cock twitches painfully against my pants and my imagination tries to kill me with the idea of her, lying in that bed, fucking herself while she imagined me over her… riding it while thinking of me underneath her.

"You're not supposed to take your work home with you."

"And you've never been work." She pulls me down to her as she presses up onto her toes.

When she kisses me, it's like it's the first time all over again. Her mouth is tentative, her lips soft, and her fingers hook in my coat, drawing me closer and holding me at a distance all the same.

I don't move closer, even though I want to. There are so many reasons to set her away from me and walk back downstairs to wait for her, but I'm not as strong of a man as others think. I'm not even sure I'm as strong of one as *I* think.

The temptation of her will always drag me close to the edge.

And I think she knows it.

Muscles tensed, I let her control every part of this.

When she curses, it's only an echo of the words floating in my head.

We're tiptoeing on a very precarious ledge.

"I want to, but…"

I hush her. "I know. But I don't want to leave you needy."

101

Eyes wide, she watches as I step back from her and go to the shelf. I pull one of them from the line at random. It breaks free with a suction *pop*.

And when I look back at her, she licks her lips, but her gaze is locked on me... not the toy.

Because she wants *me*. Not the toy.

My cock strains against my pants, reminding me that I can give her what she wants.

It can wait.

She finally looks down at the cock in my hand. "If I didn't know you grabbed the first one you touched, I'd say it was a good choice."

When I'm close enough to her that she has to take a step back to look up at me, she says, "I'm not sure there would be a bad choice while you're the one wielding it."

I lean close, and instead of begging her to want me badly enough to tell me to put it away... "Do you want to come for me right now, Kimba?" I ask, breathing a kiss across her skin. "Do you want to show me how you want my cock to spread you wide?"

Her neural link flutters blue and the lights downstairs flick off, the ones up here dim even more than they already were, and soft music flutters through the speakers hidden in her ceiling. Then she slips it from her ear, looking up at me with eyes blown wide with desire.

Tucking it in her pocket, her eyes never leave mine as she shimmies her coat off her shoulders and slips her hand around mine... guiding my hand up until she's placed it over her heart.

I don't tell her I can see her heartbeat in the pulse at her neck.

"Sometimes, it scares me how much I want you," she says.

"Me too."

She nods, letting free a long breath and then she releases my hand. "I trust you."

With a nudge, she slips free of me and she walks slowly back toward her bathroom, stopping when she's halfway between it and her bed.

It's not until she turns back to me, one strap of her tank top sliding down her shoulder, that I realize she's not walking away, she's giving herself room.

I've never asked her to dance for me, but I've always hoped I was the one she was thinking of when she took to the stage at Margot's.

This isn't about anyone else.

There's no one between her and me, drooling at the sight of her.

It's just us.

I slip off my coat and sling it over the chair, but that's all I'm taking off here. And when I sit on her bed, she doesn't look the least bit surprised.

This isn't like the dances she does for other men to watch. It's softer… smaller. She moves her hands over her body and I *know* she's imagining they're mine.

When she slips her top over her head, she throws it to the same chair that holds my coat. She sways to the music, and my hands itch to reach for her, but I stay put.

Kimba doesn't. She toes off her boots and slinks toward me, "I've thought about what I'd do if you ever let me dance for you, downstairs at Margot's."

"And what did you come up with?"

She shakes her head, hair softly brushing against her jaw. "Nothing was ever right." She steps between my legs and turns before dipping down. "Because I don't want to dance *for* you. I want to dance *with* you."

She leans back against me, raising my hands to her breasts and tipping her head back so she can kiss me.

"Is this okay?" She asks, and I know why. Because it can't go where my straining cock wants it to.

"Yes." I squeezed her nipple before letting that hand coast lower. "I want to hear you come one more time before we go back to our problems."

Her stomach flickers when my palm coasts over it, and I'm the one who slides the zipper of her pants free.

She rocks against my hand, working it down her body with that rhythm and spreading her legs wider when my fingers reach the wet heat of her pussy.

Saints, she's the embodiment of perfection.

When she'll let me, I'll bring her back here and I'll sling her over my legs like this when we're both naked. It will be some dark night when we can leave all the lights off and raise all of the shades—to give the unwitting world a show—and I'll whisper in her ear that she's mine and remind her that thousands of men want to be where I am…

Thousands of men want to be where I am *right now*.

It would be so easy to shift her, just enough to slip her pants off, just enough to free my cock and slide her down onto me.

Too easy.

I lift her off me as I stand, turning and laying her on the bed. She's so gorgeous it hurts.

She smiles up at me like she could love me one day.

That thought punches me in the chest.

Some day.

She shimmies her pants down and catches her lower lip between her teeth as I pull them the rest of the way off.

This trust she's given me is something I'll never break. I'd rather walk out into the Zone and let the monsters or the cold take me first.

The toy has rolled to rest against her hip, and she picks

it up, inspecting it for a moment before her eyes lock with mine again and she sucks at the tip.

I feel mine weep in response.

Dropping to my knees, I pull her to the edge of the bed and cover her wet pussy with my mouth.

The taste of her makes my eyes flutter closed.

The whimper my tongue draws from her makes my cock strain against my pants, and I grip her thighs more tightly.

Each lick and suck draws a new and beautiful sound from her lips, and then... it draws a strangled one.

I look up in time to see her pull the silicone cock from her mouth and draw a deep breath, and I know what I want to do.

Standing, I pull her flush to the edge of the bed. "Come here."

She props herself up on her elbows, watching me with heavy-lidded eyes.

Slipping it from her fingers, I ask, "Can I fuck you with this?"

Her throat moves as she swallows, and she nods, eyes following the movement of my hand.

But I don't draw it along her wet and waiting pussy. I open the fly of my pants and fit the flared base inside.

Her eyes widen and she wiggles her hips, inching closer. The "fuck yes," she whispers under her breath nudges my cock against it, making it bob.

She watches me ease her open, and when the tip of the toy presses into her, she exhales in a single, heavy whoosh.

I still have to hold it, but entering her this way, even when it's not *my* cock, sends the best kind of shiver up my spine.

Rocking into her, I watch her consume the silicone

cock, and when I'm halfway inside of her, I finally raise my eyes from where I've entered her.

She is beautiful with her face crumpled in need.

One last gentle thrust of my hips, and it's buried inside her.

Her gasp makes my chest ache and when I trail my gaze down her body, it *looks* like she's mine.

But she's not. Which means I don't know how she feels about any of this. And I can't guess.

Swallowing back the selfish need that tangles in my throat, I ask, "Do you want me to keep going?"

She takes a deep breath, meeting my eyes. "Yes."

"Are you sure?" Saints, I wish I could feel her answer before she had to give it.

"Yes." She smooths her hands up my arms and says, "I've wanted to come with you over top of me for too long, D. I've dreamed about you in this bed... It can't be what I want, but we can get close."

There's something in the tilt of her eyebrows and the way she chews on her lower lip. A question... a fear.

I kiss her and pray that's enough to drive whatever that look is away, and then I move back. I reposition myself so that I can get a better grip on the base, and so that I can hold her in place and use my thumb to tease her clit.

"Saints." The word is a whisper and I wish I could feel the way I've just seen her tighten on the cock.

Knees bent, back arched, fingers twisting in her sheets... Kimba looks like a goddess pulled from my deepest fantasy.

I just want to hear her cry out in ecstasy.

I want her to come apart with bliss and to forget—even if it's just for a moment—anything that doesn't make her deliriously happy.

Dipping down, I flick my tongue over the peaked buds of her nipples and smile against the soft flesh as she lifts closer to me, pressing her breast to my mouth.

I want to hear her make these sounds every day for the rest of my life.

When I rise back up, she wraps her arms around my neck, coming with me. And when she's half upright, she rides the dildo, rocking it against my cock until she comes and I... don't. Thank the saints.

I'm painfully hard and she's eerily still.

Both of us breathing in the silence of her home.

"Fuck." She whispers the word against my skin. "I wish condoms worked with you."

There's a tremor of fear in her voice and I pull back from her and take her face in my hands, making her look me in the eye. "I'm never going to do anything to hurt you. No matter how much we both want something."

She licks her lips, biting the lower one before she nods.

Easing back, I pull the wet dildo from her body first and then work it free of my pants next. It and my hand are both soaked and the scent of it... the scent of her makes my nostrils flare.

I lick the thing like a lollipop and she makes a strangled sound.

"Fuck that's hot."

She shimmies down, going to her knees on the floor and all but tears my pants open, stroking me just long enough to guide me into her mouth.

It's on the tip of my tongue to tell her she doesn't have to do this—again—and then she looks up at me with the most amazing smile I've ever seen, and I don't have the chance to warn her.

Her eyes widen, and she laughs a moment before I come, and that laugh turns into a gurgle. When her eyes close, she drinks me down like I'm the most delicious thing she's ever tasted.

I watch her in awe as my abdomen convulses and I pour into her mouth.

She doesn't pull off me until I'm done and when she looks up at me, her eyes sparkling, my cum dripping down her chin and onto her breasts and tightly clenched thighs...

I could never have asked the saints for this. I could never have imagined such a gift.

KIMBA

It was probably a mistake to come here, but I can't bring myself to regret it as I stand in my shower with warm water cascading down my back and D standing in front of me. His hands massage circles along my spine.

"Careful. I'm going to fall asleep if you keep that up," I say.

"You can sleep when we're home."

I nod, agreeing with him before my mind catches up... before I realize that I am well and truly screwed.

I shouldn't think of his outpost as home. I shouldn't already feel like I'm his.

But continuing to fight against those feelings is foolish.

I've kept the lights off, but D sets me away from him and when he steps out, drying himself and slipping out to put his clothes back on, he flips the hand switch.

The light, somehow, makes me colder. It feels wrong, now. Like dimness is a default and anything brighter is wrong.

I don't linger in the shower. I finish cleaning off, and when I step out of the bathroom again, D is waiting, staring at the windows as if he can see through the shades.

Maybe he can.

"You okay?" I ask.

"Just letting my imagination run wild." He holds my shirt out to me and I pull it on, watching him, but not asking any of the hundreds of questions in my head. Because I can imagine him... at night, with the stars and the city behind him... loving me.

I swallow back those thoughts and hurry to put my shoes on.

We've already spent too much time distracted.

We spend the elevator ride in silence and I drop my head to his shoulder as he drives us through the garage and out into the darkness of dusk.

It's not a long drive to Luthiel's home.

The upscale neighborhood he lives in reminds me of the place Edan and I used to live in Gongii province.

Luthiel always made a point of boasting about his money—or so the other women at Margot's told me—and his house is exactly what I would expect from someone who wants everyone to know he's rich.

The second I had put through the visitation request at the front gate, the metal had swung wide. And now, as we pull up to the front of his house and D kills the engine, a flutter of anxiety starts in my stomach.

I don't know what Luthiel expects, but I doubt the man stalking up the steps behind me is on the list.

I feel the slightest depression as I place my foot on the third step and know that it's triggered a bell somewhere deep in the house. He should have been expecting me, so I'm not surprised when he opens the door before I've made it to the top.

The massive wooden door swings the rest of the way open as his smile fades and his gaze slides to D at my back.

"I had thought this was a surprise house call." He grimaces, and I ignore it as I stop in front of him. "But I don't think you'd bring that kind of muscle if it was."

"A house call for what?"

He mutters something under his breath and then steps aside, "Well, since you're here, you might as well come in."

I glance back at D. This could probably all be done on the stoop, but he nods and so, I step inside.

The house is even bigger than it looks on the outside. And we're not even inside when Luthiel closes the door. The courtyard is open to the night air overhead, and I tip my head back to look up at the stars.

"To what do I owe this pleasure?" He says the last word with the appropriate amount of disbelief and stuffs his hands in his pockets.

Luthiel looks like he hasn't slept in days. His usually impeccable shirt is rumpled, his hair is a mess, and his eyes are bleary.

"You look rough, issues at work?" D asks, and Luthiel's lips purse in a sharp line.

"I could answer that question if she wasn't here. But she doesn't have your clearances, even if she is your mate."

We smell like each other. Luthiel's nostrils flare, and I let him believe it.

"You know who I am?" D asks.

"Of course. What I don't know is why you're here."

He walks past me, leaving us to follow him and I do, after a quick glance at D to make sure we're still good.

The stone path from one front door to the next curves around an enormous and tasteless fountain, and the interior of his home isn't much better.

Luthiel may have money, but I wouldn't be surprised if it was *all* tied up in the furnishings in his home.

Honestly, nothing about Luthiel screams murderer. He's the kind of guy who's too absorbed in himself and his image.

He might be our first option, but it's a long shot. One I don't know how to account for.

If he was any weaker of a suspect, he'd be a plastic bag.

I stop in the middle of his living room—one designed with no attempt to accommodate a future human mate—and I don't bother going to the sofa.

"Drink?" Luthiel asks, holding up a bottle from a set up that reminds me of a sliver of Margot's bar and looking at D.

"No thanks."

He shrugs, pours himself a full glass and tips it back like a shot.

"I'm glad you're alright, Kimba." He pounds the cap back onto the bottle. "After what happened at Margot's... she wouldn't tell me anything about how you were, or *where* you were."

"That's policy."

"I know." He sounds bitter when he says it, but he takes a deep breath, turning to us, leaning back on the counter and crossing his arms over his chest. "Showing up at my house randomly isn't policy."

His mouth twists in a frown, and his eyes dart between us once again. "What *do* you want?"

I'm trying to decide how much I want to give away, and how soon.

D takes my pause as an opening. "Are you trying to kill me?"

Okay... all of it. And now.

I look back at D, not really certain how to let him know

111

I hadn't meant to give Luthiel that easy of an out, that quickly.

Better to let him stew.

But D isn't looking at me. He's staring at Luthiel in that way that feels like he can see straight into someone's soul. Someone's mind.

It's something I don't ever want turned on me.

Even being this close to it is unnerving. I want to step away, move myself so I'm behind D, instead of beside him. But that's not the image I'm trying to project.

Luthiel snorts and grabs that bottle again. "Don't flatter yourself." He then looks at me, "I knew you had a bond-mate and yeah, I wanted to fuck you, but I'm not delusional enough to think that killing your bondmate would be my in."

D lets out a little huff of a breath and I wonder if Luthiel knows he's laughing. But D says, "He's not lying."

"Why would I lie about something like that?"

Taking a deep breath, I look up at D for a moment before I turn all my attention to him. "We have a problem."

"What kind of problem?" Luthiel's attention is now firmly fixed on D.

D might be the looming danger, but I'm the one who's going to get the answers we need from him.

"Someone threatened me and tried to kill him."

Eyes wide, his focus snaps back to me. "Who?"

I shrug. "If I knew that, we wouldn't be here."

"You think—" His face transforms from shock to anger to something that stabs at my gut. "I would *never* hurt you or any one of the women who work at Margot's."

"Would you hurt me?" D asks. "I'm standing in your way. In the way of more than just *her*."

Luthiel starts to argue and then his shoulders drop. His eyes narrow. "We can't talk about that with her here."

"Read your rule book again. Anything we know, our bondmates know."

I clench my teeth because I can't argue with him and still get what we want.

"Fine," Luthiel does sit this time. He looks like he's eaten something disgusting as he goes to the sofa and then drops his elbows to his knees. "I vote the way I do on that asinine measure, because I know it isn't going to make it past the five of you."

"But your name is still on the pro column."

"And if I thought for even one moment that Roiban would win his extermination bid, it wouldn't be. But I need him on my side for other issues. The CSS's problems are vast. What happens in the caldera is something you freaks should be left to deal with on your own."

Luthiel looks from me to D again. "I may have more reasons to dislike you now, but I have never hated you, and I certainly don't plan on being the vote that actually results in a bomb being dropped."

My whole body chills. I have no idea what they're talking about, but it isn't good.

"I guess I'll find out if you really mean that at the next vote, won't I?"

"You should look into Roiban. If you die, the brotherhood falls into the hands of an unknown. It would make his position stronger."

"I'll keep that in mind." D's hand tightens on my hip. "And we'll leave you to the rest of your evening."

D leads the way out and Luthiel doesn't stand to follow us.

But I don't ask my question until we're in the car.

"What has he voted for?"

D grits his teeth and pulls away before he tells me. "There are certain members of the CSS that want to remove the brotherhood from the caldera. They want to drop a bomb on the cavrinskh population and be done with it."

I stare at the opening gates, confused. "Dropping a bomb into a dormant volcano sounds like a bad idea… even if you ignore all of the other problems."

"There are precautions in place to keep it from erupting. But I don't know how they would hold up against a bomb."

"What kind of precautions?" I grew up close to a dormant volcano on Earth… there were no "precautions" taught in my science classes.

"Timed pressure valves to cycle magma through chambers and let it off-gas to the surface. Trench would be able to explain it better. His mother designed and implemented the system decades before she died." He shrugs. "Most people have forgotten that the Zone sits over a volcano at all. They don't read the information we give them. They just want an immediate answer to a problem that's too complicated for a simple fix."

"And that's why you think they want you dead? Because you're stopping them from doing it?"

"It's a possibility." He turns the car for the mountains and says, "I think we can safely cross him off the list. He didn't know you were unbonded."

"True. But it's possible that he hired someone to kill you and *they* figured me out and approached me without giving him the details."

"He doesn't like hiring people to do things for him. If he did, he'd have a maid."

I look at him askance, and he holds up his hand. "He

114

was cleaning when we got there. He still had a soap patch on his left hand."

"I didn't even notice."

"Few would have."

"I spend too much time looking at you to notice things like that."

He smiles. It's different from the ones I've seen before, and a little piece of my heart melts.

It's the kind that comes from soft memories... We don't have many of those yet. But we might.

And we might not.

A cold slice of dread solidifies the part of me that had softened. He puts himself in very real danger, danger he might not ever come back from.

If not for someone trying to contract me to kill him, I might never have known. One day, he might simply have disappeared.

Swallowing, I have to look away. I didn't realize the thought would sting.

CHAPTER
SEVEN

KIMBA

THERE'S a teal blue car in the drive when we get back and I look at it hesitantly before I turn back to D.

"It's Richter," he says, sliding the car onto its charging plate.

When he gets out, looking at their car, he seems to relax. Though I can't guess why, even when he continues, "And he brought his little spy with him."

I don't know what he means until we get inside and a gorgeous blonde woman turns to look up at us.

Richter is a pretty orang-ish red colored Sian who doesn't have any of the scars the rest of them do. The unbroken patterns of his skin look wrong with the snowy backdrop out the windows.

His mate slides from his lap, but he doesn't let her get more than a step ahead of him as they come to us.

"Kimba, this is Richter and Laurel." D says, in Sianese —Laurel must already be fluent.

"Hi, we were recovering, or else we would have been

here sooner." She smiles, but it's weak and I remember the words 'attempted murder'. Maybe we have more in common than the average woman who crossed galaxies to be here.

"It's lovely to meet you."

"You too, I've seen you dance. You're amazing." She shakes my hand and then steps back into Richter's arms.

"Thank you."

She's pregnant. I can tell by the way Richter's hand rests protectively at her waist, how they move around each other.

"Have you met the others yet?" Laurel asks, her smile somehow even brighter.

"Which others?"

"The other bondmates." She gestures between us, including me in the group she's just mentioned.

"No." I say, my mind trying to find a way to tell her that's not what I am without stabbing D through the heart. But I can't think of anything that isn't at least partially a lie.

Suddenly, his hand on my shoulder feels more posses-sive. Suddenly, I understand how this looks.

"Well, we'll have to figure out a time to get together. Compare notes," she says, conspiratorially.

"Yes, of course." I say it in a rush that her light words didn't warrant.

D squeezes me gently before he says, "I doubt this was a 'getting to know you' visit."

Richter mutters something about business and holds out a dark triangle—their version of a microchip. "We scrubbed the data from Laurel's handler back on Earth. I couldn't find much, but I figured now that we've done the groundwork, you can dig into it and see what they want with us."

D glances at me for the briefest second before he takes it. "I'll look into it."

"I also have some cavrinskh information that wouldn't make sense without a face to face." I catch the smallest glance he sends toward Laurel. He doesn't want to let her out of his sight, but he also doesn't want her to be a part of the conversation.

"Why don't we go sit down and talk while they deal with the gory details." I hold my hand out for Laurel and she takes it, more than happy to not hear about the monsters, I assume.

"How long since you got here?" I ask, knowing it can't have been long.

"It feels like days and years all at the same time." She laughs as she sits and then her spine straightens as she looks over at Richter.

"It's a little unnerving sometimes," she says, shimmying her scarf over her head. "The way they watch us."

It's easier for me. I *know* D watches me, but I don't feel the heat of the emotions behind that gaze. None of his feelings tangle up with mine.

I almost wish they did.

I almost wish I didn't have any other choice but to give in to what I know we both want… what I'm still too scared to take.

Luckily, Laurel can't sense my melancholic thoughts either.

"So, you speak the language… I don't know why I'm surprised, you've been here a lot longer than I have."

I nod. "Edan needed me to be able to talk with the others. Needed to be sure I gave a good impression. He was one of the people who pushed hardest for getting the Agency set up and bringing over those of us who fit the parameters."

She smiles in that way people smile when they feel like they should know something and they don't. "I'm so sorry. Who's Edan?"

"No, I apologize. He was my bondmate."

"Oh." Her smile is no longer strained, it's non-existent. "I'm so sorry."

Mortality isn't something that comes up in the brochures. Even with Richter out in the Zone hunting monsters, I doubt she's given much thought to the possibility that one day he might be gone.

This is a routine I should be used to by now. How many times have I had to break the news to a woman at Margot's that their bondmates are fragile creatures... no matter how thick their textured skin might be.

I force a familiar smile of my own. It's false, but I've practiced it so well... "It's been years since he passed. I've endured the worst of it."

She glances at D, and then something seems to click and her face clears before she turns to me. "Wait... how long have you been here?"

"Almost fifteen years."

Laurel blinks at me, stunned to silence.

"I was the fourth human woman to set foot on the planet." *Hand in hand with Margot.*

She whispers "*holy shit*" under her breath and then her eyes narrow as she studies me. "So, you're like... the reason we're here."

"I guess, kind of? They needed us more than they realized... everyone but Edan. He's the reason we're all here."

"You talk about him like he was a saint."

Sometimes I think he was. "He was a perfect partner. And there's not a day that goes by that I don't miss him."

"Still. I'd be willing to bet I never would have had a chance without you working your magic."

119

"I didn't dance back then, if that's what you're thinking. I mean, I've always danced, but not as an enticement. Margot has always had that side of things covered." I don't really know how to explain, "I was more of an ambassador. But in a way that men who had no idea what to expect from human women would accept."

She gives me a skeptical look.

"I know you haven't spent much time with Sian men outside of the brotherhood. But I can assure you, many of them are not like I assume Richter was with you—especially back then. Most of them think of women as if they are spun glass. We're too fragile to be left on our own. We're rare and therefore precious. We need to be protected at all times. Like some resource they could lose at any moment."

"You're right. I haven't experienced that." She pauses, looking at the white out the window, and there's something sour in the response. "Is that what you experienced at Margot's as well?"

"Not personally, but I hear enough stories." When her brows quirk quizzically, I say, "Margot and I have a deal. I dance. I don't fraternize." I refuse to think in past tense. She didn't *actually* fire me. "I'm not bonded, I can't sleep with anyone until I've decided if I want to bond again."

"But, Drift…" Laurel shoots a confused glance at the men's backs.

"He is the only exception, and only to some of the rules." I let her decide which she thinks I've let him break. "Margot trusts him. So I trust him."

She looks back and forth between us, eyes narrowed and if I had to guess, I'd think she was doing math. "I didn't know you could be here, unbonded."

"There are a few widows, like me. But it's rare." At least, that's what I've been told.

If it isn't, the Agency certainly wouldn't advertise it.

A faint blush covers Laurel's cheeks and she shoots a glance at Richter.

I've seen that look a dozen times before, and I'm not surprised when he comes to collect her.

"It's time to go home," Richter says, holding out his hand to help her up.

"And feed me." Laurel laughs as she gets to her feet. "I didn't realize I'd be so hungry."

"That's normal."

Again, I get a look.

"I've been here for a very long time, and I've spent years around women who come and go when there's a weeun on the way."

Thankfully, they take that explanation without further question.

It's the first time I've said the "w" word out loud in a long time and it's a sour taste on my tongue.

Goodbyes exchanged, they disappear into the garage, and D hesitates a moment before handing me my coat.

He takes my hand. "Come on, we can watch them go."

There's a set of stairs I hadn't noticed before, tucked behind a column that leads up instead of down, and the door he steers me through at the top of them opens on a frigid blast of wind.

We step out onto the roof, and I draw in a sharply cold breath. All around me, nothing but icy mountains and the deep valley between the calderas, lit by near and distant moons.

From here, even in the half dark, it feels like I could see forever.

The way D looks out over the caldera… maybe he can.

I watch the bright car drive around the bend and off toward Richter's outpost, taking the sharp fractals of light with it. Kimba does not.

She stares at the mountains that block our view of the city.

"I don't know the last time I was outside and *couldn't* see the city. It's so... isolated here."

"It can feel that way."

"Does it bother you?" She turns and looks up at me. "Being alone all the time."

I shake my head. "It might feel that way to you, but that's because the brothers are staying away. There are people here semi-constantly."

"If I'm in the way—"

"You're not."

"I haven't forgotten what it was like to be bound to a man with an important job, D. I know how to stay out of the way if I need to."

I don't want her out of the way. I want her in my way and in the thick of things.

"I'll tell them to stop treating us like we're newly bonded. They're going to have questions for you."

"And if I don't want to answer them, I'll go downstairs and they'll have to deal with it."

"Because you can't get away with pretending that you don't understand what they're saying."

We haven't spoken English since Laurel and Richter left.

"No, I don't suppose I can." She shivers, but she doesn't even look at the door back to the inside.

She looks out at the expanse of the caldera and I wrap my arms around her hoping it will help keep her warm.

"Did you know our language before you came over?" I ask, needing to hear her voice again.

"No. Edan taught me. He slowly transitioned to the point where we spoke it exclusively in the house. So I had years of immersion before he was gone, and then... the women at Margot's liked to practice with me. They thought it was fun to bring home their new skills to their bondmates, and several of the clients were more comfortable, or hadn't learned a human language yet."

The mention of *years* tugs at my mind.

I knew she'd been bonded before, but there was one element I hadn't considered before now. "You never had weeuns."

I don't mean to say it out loud, but it slips free.

She's quiet for a moment and then exhales, long and slow.

"I know, it sounds impossible, but Edan... couldn't." She shrugs and snuggles further into my arms. "By the time we found out, we were okay with it just being the two of us."

She's distant, her gaze on the inner caldera. Her words are a whisper. "But now that he's gone... I'll admit, I wish I still had a part of him."

"He'll always be with you." I kiss the top of her head.

"Kids were always a part of the promise for coming here, even before the Agency was in place. And even though I passed all the tests, I spent years thinking maybe it wasn't him. Maybe it was me..."

"Is that why you've never thought about rebonding?"

She swallows and I wait a moment longer for an answer that doesn't come.

She looks up at me and the sorrow in her eyes is so deep, I worry we'll both drown.

"I'll go get tested if you want." I brush my lips against her hair. "You have to know I'd do anything for you."

"I do." She blinks a little too fast.

And even though it's probably too soon, I say, "I'm asking you to take me for your own. It doesn't have to be today or tomorrow. I'm offering you everything that I am, and I would wait for the rest of my life if that was how long you needed to be sure."

Her lips part, and then she closes her mouth in a tight purse.

I spoke too soon. Again.

I can see for miles if I need to, but I'm not always clear on what's right in front of me. And I've never been more unsure of anything in my life. Ever.

"If you don't want that—if you don't want me—I'll take no for an answer." I'll hate it, but I will let her go if she asks me to. "And even then, I'll still do everything in my power to protect you."

"I know." She shivers, but I don't think it's from the cold.

"Let's go back in. We don't have to talk about this anymore if you don't want. Not right now."

She nods, and I let her go when she pulls away, following her back inside, sliding the bolts behind us.

I am hyper aware of her, as ever.

When we reach the bottom of the roof stairs, she takes off her jacket. When we get downstairs, she slips off her shoes. And when she sits, she looks up at me with a caution I wish didn't exist.

I want her to be sure of me... even if she isn't sure of anything else.

"You've sacrificed a lot to protect people you don't even know." Her voice is quiet, and I wonder if this is a conversation she knows she isn't going to enjoy.

124

"A lot was sacrificed for me." I sit, giving her enough room that she won't feel crowded, but close enough that if she wants to...

She moves to my lap, pulling her knees up to curl into a human sized ball. Her face buried in my chest, I let the rise and fall of her breathing calm me.

"None of us chose this job. It was given to us. They say it's because we're the only ones who can do it... I think they want to keep us away from the normal population as much as they can."

"You couldn't have refused?"

"We weren't given the opportunity." I tell her. "Loathe as I am to say it... without this job, no one would have tried to kill me and you would still be in your ivory tower, always out of reach."

"If you were someone else, I'd probably be worried you set up your attempted assassination just to get me here with you. But you wouldn't."

Her gaze goes to my lips and she licks hers.

Flashing sparks in my periphery, and I glance to the side at the virtual screen projected there. I've kept it out of the way all this time. I'd rather see her.

But perimeter breach warnings can't be ignored.

"I have to go." Four words I hate the moment they leave my lips.

With a stoic nod, she slips from my lap and stands, waiting for me to join her.

"What can I do while you're gone?"

"You don't have to do anything."

"I know, but I want to help."

"You can access anything upstairs. Check the classified files for familiar faces. Maybe you'll be able to find the man who tried to hire you to kill me."

"Why do I have access to classified files?"

125

I consider telling her they're accessible to anyone inside the outpost, but I don't want to lie to her, ever. "I've coded you into the system as my mate."

"Oh." She looks like she wants to say more, but she presses her lips together instead and hurries upstairs.

By the time I have my suit on and make it upstairs, she's rearranged three of the monitors to create a little pod and is scanning through so much data, it should make her head spin.

CHAPTER
EIGHT

DRIFT

I KNOW I'm not needed before I get there, but I join Trench anyway. The thing had come into the Zone in my territory and had crossed into his right before it would have passed the old proximity markers.

Like it knew where they were.

The creatures are intelligent. If we could just reason with them, my life would be so much easier.

"An easy one?" I ask, boots crunching in the snow as I go to where Trench stands above the carcass taking measurements and samples. The others call him a ghoul. It's another one of those sacrifices he gets to make.

"You'll have to ask Arc." He looks up at me with an irritated pinched scowl. "I asked what he was doing patrolling my sector and he told me the correct words were 'thank you, brother, what would I do without you?'"

"And did you thank him?"

"Of course. And he promptly told me to shove that thank you up my ass."

That certainly sounds like him. "What was he doing

over here?" I'd put three sectors between the two of them for a reason. They were actual brothers and for reasons unknown to me, Arc couldn't stand Trench.

"Was he intact?"

"You know Arc. Luckiest bastard of the lot of us. He says he caught it off guard. He was riding the base of the inner caldera, and came at it from behind."

I move around the carcass, trying to get a good look at it, but there's nothing to see. It turns my stomach, and if Trench wasn't willing to deal with the carnage, none of us would be studying the things—no one would be trying to find an alternative to killing them one by one.

"You didn't have to come out for this," he says.

"I did."

He laughs, mirthlessly and pulls a tarp from his bike. "We knew the brotherhood would change when mate-bonds started clicking into place. Just because you don't have a real one yet doesn't mean you can pretend you're the same as you were a few days ago."

I help him wrap it up. He's not taking this one home, but we can't leave it here.

Cavrinskh are drawn by the scent of their dead.

Grabbing a shovel, I bury all of the blood I can see while Trench preps it for the ride to one of the flow chambers where we can incinerate it.

Even if we could bury it, normal scavengers will trip the proximity sensors just as easily as the cavrinskh. Best to not give them a reason to venture into the Zone.

"There's twenty minutes until the next flow. Think we can make it?" He asks.

"We'll find out."

I follow him across the frozen Zone until we get to a patch of ground that is all rock, no snow.

The perfectly square hole cut into that rock has already started to release its heat mirage.

"You're cutting it close."

Trench doesn't say anything to me as he hefts the creature off the back of his bike. When he drops it—holding onto the tarp only—the body rolls out and over the edge of the lip, hitting the bottom with a hard crack before I hear the hard sizzle of the magma consuming it.

This system Trench and Arc's mother made has been the biggest single help in dealing with the cavrinskh that want out of the inner caldera. If we didn't have a way to get rid of them, more and more would come.

I watch the pit, not daring to get any closer to the slick shimmer emanating from it. The invisible smoke already hurts my eyes.

"Why are you still here?" Trench asks, glancing from me and then toward my outpost.

He can't see it, of course.

But when I turn and look that way, I can. I can see Kimba's silhouette in the windows upstairs. I can tell that I need to show her where the thermal vents are if she needs it to be warmer...

"You love her, right?" Trench watches me like he expects me to confess some deeper secret.

"I do."

"Then you need to find a way to keep her after the immediate threat is over. The powers that be might let her live on her own as an unbonded widow, but I don't think they're going to let one of their biggest sellers stay away from the stage for long if she's not bound to you."

"Even if she does take me, I won't make her quit dancing."

"Not sure I could do that." Trench laughs again and tosses an enzyme packet onto the tarp. "Guess it's a good thing I'm not signing up for a mate again. I'm too greedy to be kind."

"That's not greed. And if you ever change your mind, I'll sign the documents the minute you send them over."

"My life is death and gore. I'm not going to bring a woman into that again." He picks up a handful of snow and scrubs at the blood covering his hands as the packet dissolves the remains of the cavrinskh from the tarp, leaving ugly white streaks behind.

He's the only man I know who has gotten a bondmate and had her refuse him. He's the only man I know who has given his bondmate a *chance* to reject him.

Death and gore had been the two words that had featured most heavily in the paperwork that came through after he took her back to the Agency—a drive he did not return from as the same man.

Trench has been looking for answers inside the cavrinskh for years, and he has barely scratched the surface. He needs help, but there's no one we can ask.

He needs a partner.

The magma consumes the dead creature faster than any normal fire would, and it flows through its cycle a few minutes of silence later.

"You should go home and get out of the cold."

"It's always cold here." He shakes the chemical remains from the tarp and starts to fold it.

"It's warmer if you want it to be."

"Don't pull that nonsense on me. Exercise your own advice, first." Trench rolls his eyes at me. "Besides, who in their right mind would want to warm a ghoul? The rest of you can play at being lovers. I'll stay where I belong."

He straps the folded tarp to his bike and hops on, waiting for me to do the same.

"Ask her to stay," he says. "It's easier to live in that

limbo, but you're not like me. You'll be happier if she says yes."

"And if she says no?"

"I guess you'll have to learn how to live without her."

The bike rumbles to life, Trench throws a small salute, and then I'm alone in the vast icy expanse again, as I have been so often before.

I only get halfway home before a buzzing in my ear makes me slow, almost to a stop.

"Riann." I say when the call connects. "What can I do for you?"

He's on a full screen and with my helmet on, I can see him in my display, but he can't see me.

"I know it's late, but I figured you'd be awake. I need a consultation." Grimacing, he glances behind him. It's a crime scene and I see blood, but not a body. "It's better if I don't say too much over comms."

"I understand. Send me the address and I'll be there as soon as physically possible."

KIMBA

D is tense.

His jaw is set tight and when we get to where we're going, I don't blame him.

CSS officers swarm the lawn of a suburban home.

They look at us askance when we get out of the car and one comes up to D, telling him we can't be here—he doesn't look at me. He barely gets the full sentence out before someone shouts and all eyes turn to the man in the doorway, waving us forward.

I know him.

He's been at the club before—I'm sure most of them have—but something about that man in particular is memorable. Maybe it's the dark purple of his skin, or the way he holds himself.

Broken glass crunches in the grass as we cross to him.

"Riann," D says, taking his offered hand.

Riann, that's right. He was Jillian's favorite before she decided to retire. She said he was special, but never went into detail as to how.

"Kimba, this is Riann, one of the junior officials of the CSS. He is a friend when he wants to be."

Riann smiles as if that is a long-standing joke. "It is a pleasure to meet you. You are a bit of a celebrity, so I hope you won't mind that I try to get you out of sight before people start asking too many questions."

"Not at all." I follow them inside and listen to the other officers trying to sort through the scene.

Nothing in particular catches my eye until…

I stop, boots scraping on more glass.

There is a dead man on the floor, staring up at me like he was waiting, just for me.

Again.

"I'm sorry. I should have warned you." Riann says softly and I see both of them shift, uncomfortably, in my periphery.

Don't they close their eyes here? "I recognize him."

"From the club?" D asks.

I shake my head, unable to look away from those dead eyes.

He hadn't looked like he wanted to be anywhere near me that day. But he'd been alive. I remember the way he shifted his shoulders. *He'd been alive.*

D steps between us. The loss of the sight of him kicks my brain back into gear and I shiver. "I recognize him from… the *incident* in my parking garage."

"You're sure?"

I tap my cheek. "I've gotten in the habit of noticing scars. Even when I don't want to. Even when I'm scared shitless, apparently."

"That's a good thing. It gives us someplace to look *and* it's one less of them that can come after either of us."

I take a deep breath, meet his eerie eyes, and nod. "You're right. And you're right."

"I feel like I missed something." Riann looks back and forth between us, the sharp ridges of his brow quirked.

"You did." D squeezes my hand, still looking at the other man. "But this is not the place to fill you in."

"As you say." Lips pursed, Riann dips his head in a nod and glances at the other officers. They're all decently far away. "We know *who* he is and you know why I needed you here. The coroner is the only other person who's going to walk through that door and possibly know what they're looking at."

I was so shocked by the familiar face, I barely registered that the man's body had been ravaged.

When D turns, I look at the man again. He's a bloody mess and I'm certain what killed him wasn't Sian, human, or even a zurgle. And with D called in...

"Another one got out?" I ask, as quietly as I can manage.

"It would appear that way." Riann is the one who answers me.

D is too busy looking around us. His eyes don't change color... not really, but they are different.

He points toward the floor beneath the sofa in the distant room.

"Floor safe." He takes a deep breath. "Have your guys move the couch and I'll see if I can get it open."

"As long as you don't have to do that creepy eye thing again."

"All my 'eye things' are creepy. You've just gotten used to some of them."

Riann actually laughs and calls two of the officers to help him move it.

"You've known him for a long time?" I ask, watching Riann supervise.

"Not too long. But he's never given me a reason not to trust him, and he's trusted me with certain secrets that could kill more than his career."

"He didn't seem surprised that I'm with you."

D looks down at me, the places where his pupils should be look like brightly lit crystal balls—clear and haunting. "He is, in some ways, our unofficial CSS liaison. He knows you're with me. He doesn't know why yet."

I glance toward him, "But unlike others, he's not going to assume we're bonded."

"Unlike others, he *knows* we're not."

Right, because he'd have access to Agency information.

But if D trusts him... I'll trust him.

We wait for the other officers to leave and I ignore the way they stare at me once they've realized who I am. It doesn't bother me, I just don't want to engage with it right now, so I step to the side and use D as a shield as we make our way away from the dead man.

With the sofa gone and the rug pulled back, the dark disk of the floor safe's lid is obvious. It's a dark spot in the otherwise brightly enamel-coated floor.

D stands over it and Riann gives me an oddly sympathetic smile before we both turn to watch him.

He stares at it for a long moment, mouth screwed into a scowl. "It's an old-style keyed lock. Did he have keys on him?"

Riann pulls out a brick from his pocket and tosses it to

D. He doesn't even look up, catching it while still scowling at the floor.

Almost everything can be programmed to a neural link. If they have something fully offline, they didn't want to have to register it.

D cracks the brick in half and the keys—circular and spikey—splay out for him. He doesn't have to try a few before he finds the right one... he just looks at them and knows.

The safe opens with a soft and solid *thunk* and D lifts the lid away, setting it aside and looking down into the darkness of the little hidey-hole.

The first thing he pulls out is a familiar metal stick. He hands the datafilm to Riann, who opens it and immediately starts reading.

Why lock the film when you've locked the safe?

"The rest is just physical credit blocks."

I look around the house. It's ultra modern. "He didn't collect antiques. So he was getting paid for something he didn't want anyone to look into." *Like playing muscle to whoever wants D dead.*

Look where it got him.

Riann mutters something under his breath as he looks through the data scrolling across the film.

While Riann reads, D goes to the far wall and lifts a sculptural wobble off the wall, setting it aside and revealing another safe. He grimaces.

"We need a human CSS officer as soon as possible. Are there any on site?"

Riann looks at him askance and then steps to the doorway, shouting at someone outside.

"Carrie will be here in a second," he says as he comes back. "What's going on?"

"He wasn't alone in the house." D stares at the safe

door, key already in hand, and an uneasy coil starts to tighten in my stomach.

Carrie arrives and offers me a quick smile before she asks, "What's up?"

But D has already opened the safe door. There's space, the depth of the wall, and then another. When he opens that, light spills out and a woman inside lets out a little chirp of alarm.

"Oh." Carrie says. "Oh!"

She hurries forward and tells the woman everything is going to be alright.

D draws me away, and Riann comes with us, giving Carrie and the woman space to sort things out.

"How did you know she was there?" I ask.

There's a faint glow when he turns to me that has nothing to do with his neural link. "The walls aren't that thick. I can see through most things—sort of—if I want to."

He grimaces and turns to Riann, so I don't ask any more questions.

D glances toward the two women. "It wasn't a Lasap-lined room like last time, but it's a little too familiar."

"I agree. At least we know this woman is alive. Beyond that..."

"There's nothing else here your team hasn't already found." D looks around the house again, even though he sounds certain.

I watch Carrie help her out of the hole in the wall and she sits her down in a place where the woman can't see her dead captor. And then, she comes over to deliver her report.

"Her name is Sharon," Carrie says, focusing on her, even as she talks to us. "She got here on an Agency ship yesterday. She thought everything was kosher, but when they got here, his demeanor changed and she doesn't remember how she got in the room. They weren't bonded, so she didn't feel him die. She doesn't have any clue what's going on, or why he did it. She's just confused and feels betrayed. Reasonably, she's freaked out."

"Of course." Riann nods and glances at the woman too. "Get in touch with the Agency. She needs someplace safe to stay. Get the rest of her statement while you wait for them to come. And whatever you do, don't let her see the body."

"If it was me, I'd prefer to *know* he was dead," I say.

Riann studies me for a moment, and then says, "If she wants proof, she can see him at the morgue, tomorrow."

After he's cleaned up.

Nodding, Carrie pulls up a comm unit and walks away from us as she calls the Agency.

"She's going to be alright," Riann says and I'm not sure if it's for my benefit, or D's.

"But this is *definitely* related to the Company," D says.

"I can't see how it wouldn't be." Riann turns toward the door. "Coroner's here. I'll go through the data from the floor safe and get answers."

"Keep me updated."

I'm not going to be cut out of this. "Keep *us* updated."

CHAPTER
NINE

DRIFT

KIMBA TELLS me she isn't going to be cut out of this and I agree.

I tell her everything that happened with Laurel and Richter... and try not to take her concentration as a guarantee that she'll still be here when we get all of this sorted out.

"But I don't see how my death, or yours, would further the Company's goals." I say.

Kimba takes a deep breath, nodding, without looking at me. "Still, you can't deny the connection. And I don't believe in coincidences."

"Riann is sending the dead man's information to us. We'll know more when we get home."

She seems a million miles away in thought when I pull into the garage and close the harsh chill of the evening behind us.

I follow her inside and don't even pretend to be surprised when she goes straight to one of the consoles and starts pulling up information.

While I'm not going to stop her, I do make her pause long enough to take her coat off.

By the time I've put both of our outerwear away, Riann's information has come through and I send it straight to her. We could work at different screens, but it's an excuse to be close to her. So I take it.

She doesn't protest when I pick her up and sit her on my lap so that we can both go over the file.

"He wasn't anybody," she says after a moment.

She's not wrong. Tefir was a normal Sian man who checked all the boxes and garnered no fanfare.

He just existed. Didn't step on any toes. Didn't have any great achievements.

"Do you think this is real?" She looks up at me, brows knit. "I mean... he was working with a guy who hired me to kill you and threatened me... and he had a woman in a secret room and a floor safe full of untraceable credits. That doesn't just happen overnight."

"It might." I pull up the housing records. "He just moved. He *won* the house a few weeks ago."

"From who?"

The group name is unfamiliar, but I pull up the name on the nexus and a glaringly bright information site pops up.

She winces at it too. "They raffle off houses for unbonded men to move out of their bachelor pads?"

That's what the site says, but... I throw the information into the CSS databases. "They don't exist."

"Are you saying it's a front? How is that possible?"

"I don't know what that means. But I'll make sure Riann is looking into what's going on with it. He'll be able to find out more than we can."

She nods. Looking down at the file, I wonder what she reads in it that I can't.

She knows things I've never even thought to try to learn.

"Do you care if I ask Margot for her file on him?"

"Of course not. I have a feeling her records are more thorough than mine."

I stay there as she sends the request over and then, before she can dive back into this problem, I stand, swooping her up.

"Hey!"

"Sleep first. Answers later, when we can attack them with a clear head."

She looks at the timepiece on her wrist and agrees. "I lost track of the time."

"I know."

Deflating a little in my arms, she lets me carry her all the way downstairs and to my bed.

KIMBA

The results of the database search on the description of the man who'd tried to contract me had gotten us nowhere— not that I expected a miracle.

Margot's information on Tefir is non-existent. "She's getting in touch with the woman who runs the club in Gongii."

Saying the name of the province I once lived in used to make my skin crawl.

It still makes me sad, but the rush of memories is just a dull ache.

"The other Company man had a similar story. He did his time at a club outside our city and then moved here right before his match came through."

"We have to find something to call them other than Company men. It makes them sound like the CIA."

He looks confused, but in the "I'm going to look that up later" way, not the "I'm going to derail this conversation" way.

"Cavrinskh are getting out and finding their way to town to kill these specific men. That is a huge change in behavior."

"I know."

"Do you think your opponents on that council are going to try to use this to push for that bomb?"

"No. Two men dying isn't enough to sway the others. They may not even believe it's true if presented to them by one of the opposition."

"But you'd tell them it was true, if they asked."

"Of course."

I pinch the bridge of my nose. There's something else that's bothering me.

They changed their behavior completely.

"If they can be trained..." I let the thought die in my throat, because who could possibly be training them?

D looks toward the console at the far end of the room a moment before a tone sounds.

"You have to go out again?"

"Maybe." He stands, walking away from me. "Let me figure out what's going on and where and I'll let you know."

He goes to his work and I go back to mine.

No. This isn't my work. It's not my job.

Too bad I can't teach myself to not care.

I let the description search continue in the background on one of the screens, hoping something might pop, and move on.

Sifting through the enormous amount of data D has access to, I open the file labeled "archives".

A direct translation would be irrelevant. But nothing feels irrelevant anymore.

"What are you?" I pull enlarge a cluster of data, glaring at the names.

There is a file labeled "Threats" or maybe "Concerns", depending on the translation.

I'm fluent, right up until things get technical.

But maybe Luthiel isn't the only one we both know who would qualify for either of those translations.

I open the file and take a deep breath. That's not the kind of threat cataloged here.

These are the monsters that children are told to fear. The monsters that D and his brotherhood protect us from.

And they are so much worse than I thought.

We've only ever been given vague descriptions of these ugly creatures.

But now, I have photographs in front of me. Tables with weights and measurements.

A long line of images fans out over the top of the screen. None of them are a complete cavrinskh—a name we've only ever translated as "monster".

Not even the sketched out versions here look... complete.

They've never had a good look at a whole one.

I skim through the reports. They're too fast, their movement patterns too erratic and killing them usually left behind fragments. They decompose too quickly, too. Trench only has a day to study them.

I shiver as the ick of what I see sends icy fingers down my spine.

Closing the file with dissection notes, I rub at the skin on my arms. "No, thank you."

There are clinical assessments of trips out into the Zone. The oldest reports are entirely data with no conjecture. The new ones are stamped with analysis from someone named Andrea.

It takes a bare moment to find her information—Strike's bondmate, a woman with a data analysis degree from Earth.

Data is easy to stomach. Photos of medical procedures... not so much.

And now I know how D got some of his scars. I can guess about the rest, easily enough.

I used to sit in rooms like this, reading reports like these. I used to analyze them front, back and sideways. *How do we do better? How do we make it out with fewer casualties next time?*

Those were games. This is real life.

When the next file has photos of Arc, I close it out immediately. I'm fine with other people seeing me naked. Bloody naked photos of the men who work for D? Not on my wish list.

Seeing D flayed open by those monsters... I'd *needed* to see it, but it made my blood run cold.

It would be so easy to lose him... without ever having him at all.

My lungs seize at the idea, and I shove away from the information.

I walk all the way across the room without letting a single thought enter my mind.

Looking out the long wall of glass, I wish my mind... my emotions, all of it... I wish it was as blank as that icy landscape outside.

That's where I am when D gets back.

He moves through the house in what I assume is his normal routine, shedding equipment and his suit in a methodical manner as he moves to the computers.

When I turn away from the reflection to see him, the

suit hangs around his hips and he glares down at an input terminal as he logs information.

Gaze coasting over his skin, I finally release some of the tension that had held me rigid.

No new marks mar his flesh.

"You're still in one piece."

He looks up and that scowl fades. "Fault and Arc beat me to it. They had it handled before I even got there."

"What was Arc doing there? Isn't the trio's territory miles west of here?"

His brow twists in momentary confusion and then, he glances at the data on my screens. "You're a quick study."

He pulls a shirt from a hidden place inside the equipment and tugs it on, I almost stop him.

"Arc has a habit of doing laps around the inner caldera. He's restless and it wouldn't surprise me if the other two kick him out rather than suffer through his harassment. Honestly, I think one or both of the other two are going to ask to be reassigned to one of the empty outposts."

"Is there room for that?"

"There are four outposts that are technically abandoned." He pulls up a map and four points glow dark blue. "The trio don't need heating, so they're the only ones who could take them, anyway. They're abandoned because they don't have access to thermal springs, or that one," he points at one of the dark dots, "need serious repairs."

"As long as I don't have to have a roommate."

"I'd be even less tolerant of him than those two." He laughs and closes up his report, turning to me.

But the smile that came with the comment slides from his face as he looks at me. "What's wrong?"

Nothing.

And everything.

Because I want him.

144

Somehow I want him more than I've ever wanted anything in my life. More than I realized I could ever want anything.

I *need* him.

And he's here.

Offering to be mine.

All I have to do is reach out and take him.

Shoving my fears aside, I step into him, running my hands down his chest, slipping them under his shirt then pressing up again, traveling over that warm marred skin I've memorized.

"I want you. All of you."

"Every part of me was already yours." He looks down at me, eyes searching mine with something like fear.

"And if I want more?"

"That's already yours too." He presses a kiss to my forehead and slips his fingers between mine, squeezing my hand gently. "I'm going to go downstairs and clean up. Give me a few minutes and we'll talk?"

Nodding, I watch him disappear downstairs and then, I go to the computers, letting them continue on in the background.

I don't plan on coming back for a while.

I hear the running water when I follow him downstairs and slip into "my room". It's silly to care what I wear for this.

Ridiculous to think it matters…

But the gossamer-soft slip is a whisper of fabric as I slide it over my head.

It's the only piece of clothing he's ever given me and I want him to know I have it. I want him to know how often I've imagined the silken fabric was his hands ghosting over my skin.

I've spent years preparing my body for men to see. This time it's different.

It was always going to be different.

Slipping into the darkness of his bedroom, I move slowly, sweeping my hands in front of me, sliding my feet along the smooth stone. I get to the bed a moment before the water turns off.

I climb to the center as the faint sound of the towel sliding from its hook reaches me.

My heart flutters so fast as I watch the darkness, trying to see any sign of movement, but I can only hear him.

I hear him stop.

"I knew that color would be perfect on you."

I wonder what it looks like in the dark. I wonder what he sees.

There's a sharp fluttering in my stomach, but I ignore it.

The problem with fear is that it only protects you so far.

At some point, you have to give it up, get past it, or it will hold you down. It will suffocate you like someone who says they have your best interest at heart, when really, they just want to keep you from changing. From being who you are.

Who you need to be.

D was always a risk.

He's always held me at arms length, even when he's gathered me close.

"What's wrong?"

He hasn't moved. Still so far away...

This would be easier if I could just do it without talking about it. But we *have* to talk about it.

Nothing is *wrong*.

"I told you upstairs. I want all of you."

146

The room is so silent, I'd almost question if he was still there, except a small blue light flares and then dies. His lens...

"Are you sure?"

I nod. I'm so sure... If he was Edan, I'd already be on my back and he'd already be inside me.

But he's not Edan. And I'm not Nadine anymore.

Edan wasn't the man Kimba needed. But D... he is.

Hands wrapping around my arm, then under my ribs, he pulls me forward. The sheets, once again, put up no drag.

Despite the fact I know he's been in a hot shower, he's ridiculously warm. And I melt against him, even though I know I need to talk, not sleep.

"I want you."

He nuzzles my neck, kissing from my jaw down to my collar bone, and I slip the strap of the negligee down. The smallest pressure on his head directs him to my breast, and he feasts as though I've given him the sweetest fruit.

"Kimba. Are you sure? I need you to say the words."

"I want you to be yours as you would be mine. I want you to be my bondmate."

He lets out one long exhale, and then, he's on top of me, devouring my mouth as his hips press mine into the bed.

I'd almost forgotten how ravenous Sian men could be about bonding. Almost forgotten how intoxicating it was to be needed so wholly.

Skimming the fabric up my sides, he stops leaving the gown bunched around my waist.

I can't see him, but I feel everything.

The roughness of his hands as they trace back down me, the too-soft pants he needs to take off before I go crazy and tear them off... even his ragged breath brushing

147

over my stomach before he kisses me. It all drives me wild.

He drags away the covers, throwing them fully off the bed, and pulls me closer.

"Do you really want to be mine?"

"I'm selfish. I want *you* to be mine."

Thankfully he laughs.

"These," I snap the band at his waist. "Need to come off. Now."

"Anything you want Kimba. From now until eternity, it's yours. I'm yours."

He lifts away, just enough to slide the pants off to tangle by my feet.

I don't wait for him to take control again. I stroke him. He's so hard, it makes my mouth water.

But I will not get distracted by drinking his cum. Not this time.

"I've dreamed about fucking you so many times," he says as he runs his fingers up the inside of my thigh.

On a gasp, I confess what he already knows. "Me too."

Hands on me, his fingers slip inside, I'm slick and wet, but we're both old enough to be cautious this first time.

"Please tell me you have lube."

His voice is strained and he leans away. "I was hopeful."

A drawer opens and closes.

A bottle cap snaps.

His hands return to me, cool liquid joining the warm wetness my body managed on its own.

He slips his fingers into me, one, two, three at a time.

"Fuck. I don't think I can wait anymore." Pressing my legs wide with his thighs, he cages himself around me. The tip of him rests heavy and hard against me. "Are you sure?"

"Yes. And if you ask me again, I may scream." I take hold of his head with both of my hands and try to meet his eyes even though I can't see them. "I've been yours for so long... I've just been too afraid to admit it."

When he enters me, I can't stop the sound that escapes my mouth.

It's been so long and he's so big.

It's that beautiful fullness I'd almost forgotten.

He's larger than Edan was, and gentler. He rocks into me, and I gasp with each slow thrust.

"Tell me if you need anything. I know it's been..."

"Five years." I say the words without meaning to. Neither of us *need* the reminder.

"Saints." The word is a growled whisper against my neck.

"We're not there yet," he says, pulling out of me, so that only the tip of him rests against me. "We can stop. I don't want to push you into this."

"You said it was my choice, right?"

"Of course."

Dragging my nails down his back, I reach his ass, and pull him forward. It's the hardest thrust yet, and I cry out, despite the fact that I was the one in control. He's buried inside of me to the hilt and this time I do need a pause.

I hadn't realized he'd taken me so shallowly before.

With him fully inside me, I'm not sure where he starts and I end. Maybe it's the shock of that that's making it hard to breathe.

Lifting himself over me, his thumb brushes my cheek. "Still sure?"

"More than."

He smiles, a feral flash in the darkness, and then he starts to move.

Somehow, I'd forgotten how much I love actual sex. Being with a man, the skin and scent and heat…

D kisses me so deeply, I have to pull away to draw in breath when he lets me go.

The delicious warmth of his body wrapped around me, inside me.

"Kimba…"

My name flutters against my skin, punctuating every caress and kiss of his mouth.

I'm full of him. Each thrust driving that stake a little further into my heart.

His hips rock into me and sensation builds like a shimmering spark. I want to come and I want to claim him and I want to be claimed as well.

He's heavy on top of me, but I can still play a part.

Dancing for so long has given me a mobility I didn't have with Edan and I rock against him, taking him as much as he's taking me.

He whispers my name against my skin, cursing and praising the saints in a single breath.

"I've longed for you Kimba. I didn't realize—"

His next thrust drives the bond home and his emotions flood into me. I feel everything he's admitted and everything he hasn't yet said.

The bond connects us through every nerve and sinew.

I'd forgotten this particular *fullness*.

I'd forgotten how two people could be separate and yet one at the same time.

The sheer force of his desire spikes my pleasure and the moan he's tried to hold back slips free from my lips.

He jerks and I rock, and movement bleeds to instinct as our lust and yearning bounces off of and through each other.

It's too much.

My desire coils into a tight little ball of ecstasy, and my eyes fly wide. The room is brighter than it was before and my nails dig into his back as he spills into me. I don't know which of us cries out. All I know is that the sound is exactly what I feel.

The world is a pinpoint of bright swirling sparks and I know I'll never get enough of him.

At some point, reality starts to blur back into the pleasure that held us so high.

D's breath is a stutter of silent laughter against my neck as he lifts himself onto his forearms. "I've never come that hard."

I'd heard stories of men blowing both of their loads at once during bonding, but I hadn't expected to experience it. "And you probably won't again."

He chuckles as he eases back and his cum spills from me in a rush.

"We are a mess." I say, some eerie light letting me see the shimmer of his cum.

"We're perfect."

Yes, we are.

Amusement filters across the bond to me. "You're happy," he says.

"I am." The room has already started to dim and I wonder if that's a side effect of the bond... or if it's just my imagination.

"I need to go clean up." He lifts me, and we both drip as he walks me to the doorway. "I'll change the sheets while you take care of that.

I nod and I'm so glad he's turned away when I take my first step.

Of course I'm walking funny.

Cleaning up isn't a problem. Margot had slipped some wipes into my bag a few months ago and I simply never got rid of them. When I go back to his doorway, D's waiting for me.

I wonder what he sees when he looks at me now.

"You're mine now." I whisper against him.

"I always was."

At some point as we come down, satiation takes over, and I don't realize we've fallen asleep until something rouses me. D, muttering in his sleep.

Hours have passed.

He's slumped against me, head pillowed on my shoulder, one hand lax on my chest, cupping my breast and I'm open to him. Cool air coaxes my pussy as my leg is slung over him.

Muscles I'd forgotten I have are sore, and the room around us smells like the glorious aftermath of sex so passionate…

D stirs beside me, rolling on his back, dragging me along with him. His cock is hard, and I consider…

He's mine now, and I'm his.

CHAPTER
TEN

DRIFT

THE SOFT BRUSH of Kimba's fingers wakes me immediately, but I don't move.

I watch her play with me in the darkness, unable to see. She hums sleepily to herself as she rises, wrapping her fingers around me and finding the tip of my cock with her lips. They brush over me just as softly and I moan, despite trying to stay still and silent.

I feel the breath of a laugh against my skin and she looks up at me without being able to meet my eyes. "I want a midnight snack."

I don't correct her that it's past midnight. The dark clock on the far wall tells me it must be nearly dawn.

"You can have anything you like."

"Good. Because I like you."

She moves with the same grace she always does, slipping her leg over me and using that grip to slide my cock against her and I twist my hands in the sheets. She hums as she rocks against me. "How many times have I dreamed about waking up as you slid into me?"

153

She slips me inside her and eases down my length. Head tipped back, she shivers and sighs as her body eases to fit me.

A small part of my sleepy mind had worried I'd dreamed our bonding.

The warmth of that relief is replaced by the overwhelming flood of lust. "Do you think it was more times than I have?"

"Definitely." Her hands slide up my chest, up my neck until they find my face and she holds me still as she leans forward to kiss me, the move drawing her off of me until the tip of my cock is all that is left inside of her. "I think I sleep more than you do."

It's my turn to chuckle, and hers to moan, when I take hold of her hips and move her back, sliding her onto my cock, exactly where she belongs.

But she doesn't stay there for long.

I keep ahold of her, but gently. She's doing all the work. I'm just here to support her.

There's no possible way to describe what I feel through the bond.

It's one thing to know. It's another to *know*.

No explanation could have prepared me for this.

Kimba's everything I have ever wanted… and she's finally mine.

As she rocks and rises over me, I try to fathom how I possibly got this lucky. How an attempt on my life gave me something so precious as this connection… someone worth living and dying for.

"I'm going to have to teach you how to focus." Leaning down, squirming on top of me, she presses her beautiful full lips to mine, kissing me so deeply I forget what was distracting me. When she pulls away, her lips still brush mine. "The only thing you should be thinking about is filling my pussy with cum."

I twitch inside her, and the burble of joy and ecstasy that filters through her into me makes me twitch again.

Nails scraping my chest, she rides me.

In the dark, no one else could see her like this. She is mine and I'll do everything I can to keep that look of bliss on her face.

"Keep thinking those thoughts, and I might blush."

She can't hear them, but she can feel them. Just like I can feel the building desire in her.

She's *mine*.

"You're mine now." I repeat the words that echo in an ever-growing chorus in my head.

"Yes." The word is a breath in the cool air around us.

"No one else can have you."

She laughs, but it's a sharp agreement that courses through me.

"They can look, but they can't touch."

"There's no one else I even wanted to touch. I've wanted you from the first night I met you." She rocks forward, eyes closed, and I wish she could see me. "I wanted to take you into my mouth, drink you in."

"And now, you have me, you can do everything you want… anything."

"Good. Because I plan on taking you every way, every-where, I can think of."

I want that too.

"I have no idea how we're ever going to make it to one of those other places."

I've imagined her on every horizontal surface in this room, and every vertical one, too. Imagined her in the middle of the war room floor upstairs, flirting with the danger of interruption.

I've dreamed of taking her in the most inappropriate places...

My fingers tighten on her to keep from bucking her off of me so I could drag her to the dresser on the far side of the room. It would place her pussy at the perfect height for my cock...

"I like when you think about fucking me." She lets out another breathy sound that is partially a laugh. "My tips doubled when I knew you were watching me perform... I wonder how much I'll make the first time I dance when I can *feel* you watching me."

"That will be an interesting experiment." I kiss her and wonder if I could make her come while she dances. Wonder how many men that would bankrupt.

Our lust is on a feedback loop and even though it's a slow and steady ride, each rock of her hips—each thrust of mine—builds, and when I adjust my grip so my thumb can snake down...

The moment I press her clit, the sensation hits me, and I come before I even realize I was that close.

That feedback loop pushes her over the edge too.

Fuck.

I don't know if one of us said it or if I thought it... but the sentiment rings in my veins.

She doesn't say anything as she kisses her way down my chest. Her lips leave a warm trail and I struggle to breathe as she slips off of me, cum pooling as it pours out of her.

My eyes fly wide and I push up onto my elbows to look down at her as she draws her tongue up the ridges beneath my cock.

"You taste good." She says, as if she can hear the question through our bond, "I'm not going to start sucking on the sheets or anything like that."

156

She snorts a little laugh and then, I notice her eyes have a faint blue shimmer.

"You can see me."

She hums in agreement. "A little. I think it's a mixture of the bond and your cum inside me... It went away quickly last night. I don't expect it to stick this time."

She takes me into the heat of her mouth and I almost drop back onto the bed, but I force myself to stay upright, to watch her clean my cock with her tongue and take me into her deeply enough that her eyes flutter close.

It feels too good and I was already too near that edge.

"Kimba," I thread my fingers into her hair. "I'm so close, susre."

She pulls off of me just long enough to say "good" and takes me into her mouth again. Her tongue flat against the ridges of my cock, she sucks at the tip of me. The pressure, her pleasure, it coils tight in me until I burst.

"*Saints.* You want to push me over that edge, don't you?" I tighten my grip on her on accident and it sends a jolt of pure lust through the bond to me. I groan, gritting my teeth as I flinch against that feeling.

Hand twisted tight in her hair, I hold her still as I rock my hips into her and shudder through the last of my release, shocks of pleasure pulsing through the bond each time I reach the back of her throat.

And when I'm done, I hold her there still, selfishly wanting to see her draw back from me, wanting to see my cum pour from her mouth.

When I let her go, it spills down the front of her, making her skin glimmer. She draws in deep breaths, looking at me with a smile so wicked it makes my cock twitch again.

"Did you know that most people don't leave their

homes for a month after they've bonded?" She asks. "Did you know that?"

"I know that there are usually considerations made with employers." And perhaps I should have given the bonded men in the brotherhood longer. "And I can understand why." I drag her up me, ignoring the cooling cum that has made us both a mess.

"If given the choice, I would lock this outpost down tight and live inside of you."

KIMBA

"You liked when I pulled your hair." D's words are soft, but it's so quiet in the room, he barely needs to speak them at all.

"I did." A flutter of anxiety passes over my skin, I can still see him in the dark. It would probably be easier to admit this if I couldn't. "Edan didn't really know the concept of gentle sex. I didn't realize how much I missed being... used like that."

"If that's what you need from me, I can learn."

"Gentle is good too." I slip my arms around his neck and press myself against him. "We're not replacing him, right? I'm not trying to make you into a new version of him. I want *you*. And I want you to love me the way you do."

He tips my chin up. The effects of the sex are already starting to fade, but I see the smile on his lips before he kisses me.

"I will love you every way possible. And if you want, I'll find impossible ways to do it too."

I don't care if he's being serious, that's too ridiculous not to laugh. But he catches that laughter in a kiss and then rolls over top of me, scooping me up and taking me with him when he rolls again, standing this time.

But he doesn't leave me at the hallway, he carries me across into the room that is "mine" and I don't protest when he sets me down in front of the partition to the commode, because he goes to my shower and while I take care of that necessity, he turns it on and tests the temperature.

The lights are still off, but the windows let in enough for me to see as I join him and he goes to his knees, washing the remnants of cum and sweat from my skin.

"Careful," I say, drawing my finger over his brow ridge. "Look at me like that for long and you're going to get fired for not being able to do your job."

He grins so widely, I should probably be scared, but then he draws my leg over his shoulder and drags his tongue across me. One tip on either side, toying with me.

In the dark of his room, I'm forced to focus on what I feel. Here, I get to watch.

He presses his tongue inside of me and then his eyes flutter shut.

The only thing that breaks the silence of the next few minutes is the splatter of the shower, and the sharp breaths as I try to keep myself upright.

When I come, the soft sounds that echo off the shower walls send satisfied tremors through our bond.

And I look down at him, still on his knees, licking his lips.

"I wish I knew what you see when you look at me," I say.

"I wish you could see it too. You are so beautiful it hurts, Kimba."

We manage to finish cleaning up and get out of the shower. Towels wrapped tightly around us before I realize

Edan's picture was on the counter, watching us this entire time.

"Do you think he would be mad?" D asks, my sudden apprehension making its way through the bond.

"I don't know."

"He loved you. And I will honor his memory the only way I am able. By loving you the way he would have, if he had been given the opportunity."

I swallow back the lump in my throat and remember the downside of the bond's emotional tether.

"I don't think he would have *liked* watching you love me. He was jealous and possessive at times... even when he didn't need to be. But I *hope* he wouldn't begrudge us this."

The two people I spoke to on Earth—before I cut them and the planet out of my life entirely—hadn't understood the shrine... the funeral rites... any of it. And there were so few women on the planet who had been in my position...

I didn't imagine D would be the one who made this easier to bear.

CHAPTER
ELEVEN

DRIFT

I KNEW, of course, that the bond would be a distraction. I knew that feeling her, always with me, would make me want her even more than I already did.

But I hadn't realized how hard it, *and I,* would be.

Kimba and I lost two days. We moved from bed to bed, and I had to reprogram the cleaning robots to deal with the cum that covered the floor when I'd fucked her against the hallway wall, the kitchen, the window, over the back of the sofa and every other place the "mood"—as she calls it —struck. I was dizzy with a constant need for her, and she was no less affected.

Even now, fully dressed and surrounded by the faintly beeping machines of my war room, I placed equipment between us or nothing would get done.

If I could reach her, I would drag her over it and we'd wind up back where we started.

She looks up at me with an amused smile before going back to the map she's been studying while I've *tried* to pay attention to the data Andrea sent over yesterday.

"There's something here." She snatches a light pen from the top of the console and circles the place on the screen, leaving a glowing border around it. "I'd bet everything I have that *this* is why so many have managed to slip past the sensors closest to the inner caldera."

I move around beside her and can't stop from touching her, even though it's probably a mistake. She leans into me. *Not a mistake.*

"I think this is your problem." She taps it again.

"I want you to tell me why," I say, but I hold up a hand so she doesn't start now. "But wait until the others get here. You shouldn't have to explain this twice."

"The others?"

I've already sent the summons.

"Shouldn't you be the one to tell them?"

I dip down to kiss her and then immediately pull back. We're about to have guests. We can't get distracted.

"I did not fall in love with you because of what you currently do for a living—"

"Assuming Margot does let me have my job back."

"—and I didn't fall in love with you because of what you did when you got here, or even before that. But I am very happy that you can fit into all aspects of my life and they're going to learn that's the case soon enough. This is a partnership. Completely."

Something simmers, low in the bond. "I don't want to do your job."

"I'm not asking you to take over. But I also didn't ask you to sit in that chair and find what you did." I kiss her again, hating her ill ease. "If you don't want to be the one to tell them, you don't have to, but if you don't want to be a part of this, you're going to have to stay downstairs… I don't think you know how to turn off that part of your brain when there's a puzzle on offer."

Tension pulls taut and then snaps. The release vibrates across my skin.

"I'll tell them," she says, not perfectly at ease, but she knows herself well enough, and I'm right.

"Thank you."

She presses up onto her toes and kisses my cheek, just beside the corner of my mouth. "You may come to regret it."

Closing my hands tightly, I shoot her a look, because she knows how badly I want to slip her pants down, bend her over the console and fuck her before the others get here. She blows out a breath and steps back, pursing her lips.

"It gets easier," she says, clasping her hands behind her back. "It doesn't diminish… it's just easier to resist after you've been fighting it for years."

And that's why it doesn't seem to be affecting her as much as it is me. Because she's done this before. "Promise?"

She bites her lip. "No. Sorry." But she doesn't look particularly apologetic.

I glare at the location she's circled and pull up the newest of the maps Core and Richter made and then send a drone out to see if it can't capture better imagery.

"They'll be here shortly."

"They don't know who I was… before I became *me*. What makes you think they'll take me seriously?"

"If they don't, I'll throw them out the window?"

She laughs, "I'm being serious."

"They are going to listen to you because you are the one speaking, and they will take you seriously, because they are going to hear you. Anyone who hears you is going to know you know what you're talking about."

She nods, but she's fidgety as she goes to the couch, so I give her space as we wait.

I haven't found anything else useful when I see the indicator that someone has pulled into the garage.

Kimba's focus is out the window on the swirling snow, and I'm glad she's all the way over there when Arc hops off his bike and pulls his helmet off.

He's been out patrolling, but he isn't wearing a suit. I'll have to talk to him about that. Again.

"Sorry if I'm interrupting," he says loudly as he opens the door.

I ignore the speculation on his face when he finds us yards apart. "The others are right behind you."

"Goody." He goes to sit on the couch and I catch the odd glance between us. He knows. And maybe that's why he doesn't say more than a "hello" to her before pulling out the game he and the other cold boys play instead of actually talking to each other anymore.

Trench and Richter arrive next and I'm surprised that I don't see Laurel in tow, but I imagine she is at home with a promise not to go near any doors or windows.

Arc shoves the game away as soon as they arrive, like he's hiding it, and turns a bored glare on his brother.

"Find anything interesting digging through your latest dead body?"

Trench doesn't give him the satisfaction of being offended, so he adds, "Or do you just like playing with corpses."

"I'd offer to dissect you, but your skull is empty and the rest of you is just piss and wind."

"Are you two always this mean to each other?"

Arc blinks at Kimba like he'd completely forgotten she was there. "You'll have to excuse us. My brother and I are

164

like… what is the Earth saying Jen likes? Oil and water, I think."

"They like to stab at each other verbally, because I won't let them do it with knives." I say, sitting beside her.

"They're among the very few of us who are biological brothers," Ric says, earning a glare from Arc, as if he hadn't just admitted the same moments ago.

She looks between them, "I suppose I can see that. There's something similar about your chins."

Both men suddenly look very concerned about the mentioned anatomy, and it shuts them up.

A moment later, Hazard comes in and goes directly to the fridge, as always.

He pops a bottle top into the trash and joins us with a small bow to Kimba.

"So glad to see you're here to stay."

Trench and Richter both look at us and ask the same question.

"Yes, Kimba and I are now bonded," I say. "But no, that's not why you're here."

They congratulate us all the same and I'm a little unsettled by the sincerity in Arc's delivery.

Richter yawns and Hazard offers him a drink from his coffee—Hannah got him hooked on the stuff while none of the rest of us can stand it.

"What are we in for?" Ric asks, pushing the bottle away.

I don't need to set anything up for Kimba. She's spent years performing to others, years before that charming and selling her entire race. So I signal to her and let her take a completely different stage.

"We haven't been able to figure out who tried to hire me yet. We're still working on that. But I was looking at the Zone maps and noticed something odd in the location markers of where the monsters are popping up." She takes the remote from me and changes the window behind her to the map. Its lights flicker as a pre-programmed simulation cycles through. And I sit back to watch.

KIMBA

The only time in my previous life that Edan had made me feel uncomfortable was when he'd first pushed for me to be the one who *sold* the CSS officials in the southern hemisphere on maintaining a permanent Agency port. I had a passable grip on their language… and he wanted to show me off.

But it is the reason I no longer feel uneasy about men watching me. It's why I don't feel awkward explaining to the four men on the couch opposite how they may have been failing at their jobs.

I use the equivalent of a laser pointer to make sure they're looking where I want them to.

"This crescent shape, here, shows the normal areas the cavrinskh trigger your sensors on this side of the caldera. You've got three known exit points from the underground cave systems you've managed to block off, but the rest seem to come over the edge of the interior caldera, right?"

I don't wait for a confirmation.

"Outside of this crescent, you have these." I circle the points that made me ask questions. "Abnormalities that could be indicative of a serious problem."

When I look back, Arc has leaned forward, elbows on his knees, a scowl twisting his face. "I'm confused. Are you, or are you not, one of Margot's dancers."

"I am." I don't explain my CV to him. In the end, he'll respect what I have to say, or he won't.

"They're clustered here. But these outliers," I circle the

pinpoints that are well outside of the normal range. "They're testing you. I think they've been looking for a way to get around you. Looking for ways to get further into the Zone before they trigger any of your sensors."

"I wouldn't be surprised. They're incredibly intelligent." Trench scowls at the board before he looks at me. "Why didn't we put this together?"

"Maybe because you've been looking at it with each individual occurrence? Maybe because you haven't considered the possibility there's more to this than just wild animals?"

And I have found that Sians as a whole are far less suspicious than humans.

Maybe not these ones, though.

"We still should have noticed." Arc looks pissed. Not at me. He glares at the map like he, personally, is responsible for the places they've gotten through, even though they're not in the trio's territory.

"Each time one of these outliers pops up, it's during or right after severe weather. If you were writing them off as being confused by zero visibility in a snow storm, I wouldn't be surprised." I look back and three of the four of them glare at the map like they're trying to memorize it. "If they are intelligent and they do want to get out of the caldera to kill the rest of the women and children on this planet…"

"Not going to happen." Arc practically barks the words at me and D says his name with a quiet harshness that makes the air cool a few degrees. "Apologies, dajzha. We take this task we were given very seriously."

"I'm glad." I take a deep breath and brace myself for their next reaction. "Especially since it looks like they've found a way out. At least twice."

I was prepared for confusion or anger... The stillness makes my skin crawl.

"What?" Richter is the one who breaks the silence. "What do you mean, *twice*?"

"I was going to bring it up at the meeting." D says, pulling their attention away from me. "My CSS contact called me in because he recognized the wound on a dead man. He'd been killed by another cavrinskh."

"Another *man*." Richter's jaw tenses.

D nods. "Another Company man, it seems. No other casualties."

They descend into a harried conversation. Questioning the changes I too would like answered, but that's not the right focus right now.

"We need to stop them from getting out before we worry about why they aren't going after women and children like they normally would."

The four of them go silent the moment I speak and I ignore the amusement D feels at that.

"We need the brotherhood to find the exit point. We need you to figure out how they're bypassing the sensors. And we need to make sure that stops."

D turns sharply to Arc. "Don't even think about going out to hunt them down until you've gone home and changed."

The pale green man settles down into the sofa, a scowl on his face. "Wouldn't dream of it."

Trench watches me and I know he has a question. "Ask it."

"How does someone go from a spec ops cadet on Earth to a statesman's wife in Gongii to a dancer... and then wind up here, second in command of the brotherhood?"

A hard lump coils in my throat and then drops to my belly. "How do you know what I did on Earth?"

"A name change doesn't erase your files. And he was in love with you." Trench turns a sharp glance toward D. "I had to make sure you weren't the one behind the assassination attempt."

"Be very careful, friend." D says, muscles coiled like he plans to lunge across the room and strangle Trench.

I squeeze his hand and push some of my own calm through the bond.

Trench cared enough to check. I won't be mad at him for that.

He looks at D and shrugs. "It was a possibility. If it was someone else, you'd have checked it out the same as I did."

"Or," Richter says. "Maybe you'd call a meeting to expose her with half the information."

Something like shame passes across the bond, "I take your point."

"Will you show me how you dug that information up?" I ask, pulling their attention back to me. "If you found it, someone else could have done it the same way. Knowing how might narrow our suspect pool."

Trench dips his head in agreement. "Once you two register your pairing, it becomes public record and more people are going to look at your past."

"I'll talk to a friend with the CSS, see if he can't bury that past deeper."

"Is he bonded?" Hazard asks.

"No."

"You may have to convince him more than you would others." He looks at me with a half shrug of his shoulder. "Only one in fourteen hundred of the Sian men who are of-age and have marked an attraction to women have bondmates."

Richter scoots forward. "And until you have that bond, you don't really know what it's like."

Or, I think, glancing at Hazard, until you've fallen in love with a woman you'll never really be able to have.

"He'll help."

"Fucking—" Arc literally jumps out of his seat, turning to Kilo who had been standing behind him. "Where did you come from?"

"I've been here the whole time." Kilo smiles and takes the coffee from Hazard. "It's not my fault you guys like to forget I exist."

He turns that smile on me and I wonder, "Is that your thing?"

Dipping his head, he looks rueful. "That's me. Utterly forgettable."

"I hate when you do that." Arc goes back to his seat, glaring at the other brother.

"I promise, I only use my superpower for good... or to fuck with you, specifically."

I don't think I like that particular super power.

"But," Kilo says, turning back to D, "Your guy will help, even if he doesn't want a bondmate of his own."

Arc scowls and turns back to me. "So we pay attention to those outliers. We look for more patterns with snow-storms, and... then what?"

"I don't know." I shrug, ignoring the warmth down my spine—I'd forgotten what someone else's pride felt like. "Obviously we can't ignore the caldera, simply because someone's trying to kill D."

The look Arc gives me bordered on suspicion. "Okay, what do you want us to do then?"

I glance at D. This is his territory, and I'm about to trample all over it, but he doesn't look like he has a care in the world.

170

"D sent a drone to check these locations." I point to the map over my shoulder. "We'll see if there's anything there, anything they have in common. Once those come back, we should assess and someone—a team, probably—should go to inspect them physically."

Trench and Richter bounce ideas off each other, Arc asks me a few more questions about my previous employment. Kilo watches quietly while Hazard glares at the coffee in the other man's hand.

None of them look to D.

He lets me talk, lets me answer their questions. He only speaks when I look to him for an answer I don't have. And when he gives it, they immediately turn their attention back to me.

CHAPTER
TWELVE

DRIFT

THE BROTHERS LISTEN to her the way I had hoped... her past professions' authority seeping into her words.

In another life, she'd been trained to brief soldiers with the tone she uses on them now. Even between languages, that translates.

By the time they leave, even Arc has stopped his usual irritating nonsense.

They respect her in this position. Which is good. I would hate to have to replace windows.

They left us alone with a mountain of data. And while Andrea is working on it as well, Kimba has taken a stab at some of the overflow and I'm trying to help too.

But I can't stop staring at her.

If her help wasn't invaluable, I might be jealous she's paying more attention to the curious problem of the cavrinskh she is than to me.

But that certainty that I couldn't do this without her— previously just a theory—has settled into my bones.

She looks up from her work, meeting my eyes and smiles with an amused twist of her lips. "You are distracting."

"Sorry." I say.

"No you're not." She stands wrapping her arms around my neck.

Her smile is one of my favorite things in the world.

"I didn't realize it was so late."

We both look out the window and I don't point out that we watched the suns set while we ate dinner *hours* ago.

She raises her face for a kiss and I happily give it to her.

"You don't have to help with this if you don't want to," I say. I never want her to feel pressured. "You left that life behind, and I wasn't trying to drag you back into it."

"This is different. You still get to rally the troops. I'm just looking for problems. It's wildlife control, not combatants."

"You might feel differently if you were out there when one attacks." As soon as I say it, a flare of absolute conviction passes across my veins. She'll never be out there.

"No thank you." She pinches my chin. "Don't even think about me out there. I don't like the way it feels."

"Sorry."

"You can make it up to me." She interlaces her fingers with mine and drags me downstairs. She turns to me when we get to the bottom, spinning me around and then pushing me back onto the couch.

I land on the cushions as she lets me go.

She doesn't turn on the lights, but the moons are bright enough, their light bouncing off the snow, I know can see.

Kimba's grace has nothing to do with her ability to dance… it was always the other way around. She pulls off her shirt, doing a little spin as she goes and drapes it over

173

a chair. When she walks back to me, she moves as though she's floating an inch above the floor and I watch her, still a little dazed by the idea that she's truly mine.

"I like the way that feels," she says, drawing her hands up her sides to cup her breasts as she straddles my lap. "But you don't need to be surprised."

She moves my hands to her waist and I feel the shivering sensation of need across the bond.

"The women at Margot's would have fought me to have a go with you if they thought it would work." She kisses me, rocking forward, teasing my cock through both of our pants. "You are a catch… and now, you're mine."

Her mouth is hungry and her hands greedy as they trail over me.

But I need to know one more thing before we get any further. "Kimba?"

She stops, sitting back and looking at me with heavy-lidded eyes as she licks her lips, hips still rocking. "What's wrong?"

"Do you still want kids?"

Her spine straightens and her brows twist. "Of course I want to have your weeuns." She chuckles and pokes me in the stomach. "What makes you think I wouldn't?"

"I wanted to be sure." I trace her lip with my thumb. "I'll get off the stopper whenever you're ready."

She kisses me again, teasing me with the grinding motion of her pussy. "How long have you wanted to breed me, D?"

My nostrils flare as I inhale the scent of her, and my cock strains at the idea. "From the moment I first saw you. I knew you were the only woman I wanted to be mine."

I grip her hips more tightly, holding her still. "If I could have done exactly what my body wanted when I first saw you, I would have gotten up on that stage, torn the rest of your clothes off and claimed you right there, for everyone to see. I would have fucked you until you didn't remember a single word other than my name, and I would have filled you until there was no chance you weren't carrying my weeun."

"That would have been a very bad idea for all involved," she chuckles, but I feel the way her lust notches up. "I've never considered giving a show in the public room… but when you paint a picture like that…"

Her fingers go to my waist and she slips my cock free, playing with the tip of me like I'm a toy, made just for her.

"We could sell tickets. Margot would market the hell out of it and I bet she'd hit capacity."

"Neither of us need the money."

"I know."

I pull my shirt off over my head, throwing it… saints know where, and lift my hips. She giggles as she holds on. Getting my pants off is a challenge until she stands over me, giving me that little space I need.

"You think other men want to see someone else fuck you?"

"I think they'd sit back and pretend your cock was theirs. They'd stroke themselves like their hand was my pussy and I bet the floor would be three inches deep in cum before we were done.

"They'd see the way you spread me and they'd imagine being able to do the same."

She doesn't come back to me when I've finally gotten them off, rather she hops down, turning her back to me and then… she dances.

There are no flashing lights to distract, no other men ogling her.

And I force myself not to touch myself as she works

her pants off for me. I ignore my bobbing cock as she bends, and I grit my teeth as she twirls.

I've long since memorized every line of her body. From the full curve of her breasts to the softness of her belly... I know the shape of her hips and the roundness of her ass...

I grip the back of the couch and hold tight to it so that I don't reach for her.

No matter how much I want to grab her and take her to the floor, I know that patience will reap its reward.

And I know she can feel the impatience that zings through my body.

Margot had never been shy about telling me how much money men threw at Kimba. They tried to buy a moment's notice from her. It would be so easy to willingly bankrupt myself.

Kimba is the kind of perfect someone would die for a taste of.

And she's mine.

Now, I'll die to keep her happy.

Margot had never been shy about the men who tried to overstep bounds when it came to Kimba, either.

"Hey," she snaps her finger in front of my face. "Whatever that is, no thinking about it when your cock's out."

She catches my hand, sliding it between her legs, moving her hips so that she fucks herself with my fingertips for a moment.

When she releases me, turning back to finish her dance, I lick my fingers clean and she shivers, as though I'm licking hers.

This dance isn't one I've seen before—not a surprise, she doesn't have a pole here—and I like to think she's making it up, on the spot, for me.

When she turns back, the look she gives me makes my

176

mouth go dry. She slides to her knees in front of me, her hands trailing up my legs.

"Why didn't you ever let me dance for you at Margot's?"

"I wasn't there to make you work."

"I wanted to." She raises up on her knees, smoothing her hands up my thighs, leaning close so the sides of her breasts brush against my skin.

"You can dance for me anytime you want, Kimba." I draw my finger along the line of her jaw.

"Every time I've danced, for the last two years, it was always for you."

She pulls back, just enough to bite my finger. And when she looks at me, teeth to skin... that feeling that filters through the bond feels like it could be love.

Standing, she spins and dips down once more, skin brushing against skin, teasing.

She takes hold of my hand again, sliding it up her body this time. "Do you like when I tease you?" She asks, looking from my eyes, then pointedly down at my cock.

"What do you feel?"

Her smile twitches the same way my aching cock does, and she dips down to kiss it, licking the tip of it with a swirling swipe of her tongue.

But the taunting isn't over. She stands fully, cupping her breasts and then, she turns, kneeling over me, back to chest... positioning herself so that her pussy slides against my cock, but not onto it.

She leans back into me and it's my turn to take over where her hands have left off. I cup her breasts, pinching her taut nipples and she laughs. The sound too breathy to be true amusement. The fizzling sensation that pulses through the bond tells me it's simply a different kind of desire, and my abdomen clenches with want once again.

"I want you, Kimba."

She hums in agreement. "How badly?" She turns her head so her lips brush against my jaw when she says, "Bad enough to take me?"

"Yes."

"Good." She rocks her hips, sliding her lips along the top of my cock. "Fuck me the way you would have if there were no rules. If you'd walked into Margot's and dragged me off that stage and right onto your cock."

I lift her and my cock finds its place immediately. No need to guide it in. It knows where it belongs.

I thrust my hips up as I pull her down onto me and the sensation through the bond is like a microexplosion. A sharp breath pierces the air and I have to stop. I hold her there, overloaded by the shock of pleasure bouncing back and forth between us.

"It never stops being this good," she says, as her eyes flutter open and she looks back at me. "If you were worried."

"I wasn't." How could I be?

"Good."

She works herself over me and I know she knows that first load is so close. I wonder if it feels like her skin has drawn tight too.

Arm wrapped around her hips, I hold her down, sealing her to me so my cum floods her, as I pour into her, body and soul. I lose all touch with the world around us.

Head dropped back to the cushions, I stare at the ceiling, counting and trying to find my way back to reality…

But reality is Kimba… on my lap, full of my cum, kissing my throat as she waits for me to fuck and fill her again.

"You look so sexy when you come." The words are a

low whisper, but she's close enough to me there's no way I wouldn't have heard them.

Now that my own first orgasm is out of the way, I can feel how close she is, but it's fading fast as we sit here, waiting for me to get myself back in order.

I snake my hand up to hold her throat and pull her back against me with the arm that crosses her body.

The question in the bond isn't one she asks. She trusts me.

And delight flutters between us as I tip her forward, going to my knees.

"This is how I would have taken you on that stage." I trail my hand from her ass all the way up her spine to hold her shoulders down as I move within her, my cum squelching with each thrust.

"I would have laid you out like this, bonded you and bred you."

Her whispered "yes" is faint, but the corresponding sizzle through the bond isn't.

She is everything I want, and as she squirms beneath me, I grip her hips tighter. She isn't trying to get away, but I need the control.

I fuck her like our lives depend on it, rough and dirty. The need to push her over that edge, to return the favor before I come again, it's consuming.

It's almost like an addiction—needing to be inside her. Needing to possess her. Needing to *be* possessed by her.

I want every inch of her. And she wants every inch of me.

Her breath hitches as I pass my thumb over her asshole. "You said you wanted me to fill you up."

"Yes."

"How full do you want to be?"

"Bursting."

I press my thumb against her, slowly adding pressure.

Her pleasure crackles across our bond. Her little moans and mewls fill my chest with a fullness I can only equate with a type of pride.

"Lube," she says, questing her hand toward the bottle misplaced sometime before.

When I pop the top, I have to take a moment to catch my breath. Her pussy clenches down so tightly, but the pure need that flushes through the bond, *that* makes me dizzy.

She moans when I drizzle the clear liquid over her ass and my thumb.

"Have you fucked your ass with your toys, Kimba?"

She says "yes" even though I don't actually need her to anymore.

I maneuver my thumb until the tip has slipped inside. "Will you show me, later?"

She lets out a shivering breath. "Only if you promise to do exactly what I've shown yo—*fuck*."

Pure desire flutters across the bond, stiffening my cock as I ease my thumb deeper into her.

She moves on me, rocking and writhing and I watch her sloppy pussy slide on my cock. There's no room for it in her ass. Not yet. But my thumb—strangled by her, each time her pussy pulses on me—relays the possibilities to my brain.

She's slick with my cum and I'm not worried about hurting her, so I take what I want, paying attention to the feelings that make their way across the bond.

I'll take everything she'll give me.

Every panting breath drives me to find her completion. And when I tip my hips one way, it's like lightning through the bond.

She says, "Yes" on a harsh inhale and repeats it again and again with each thrust.

"I'm going fill you with my weeun." I say, not sure whether the words are in my mind, or against her skin. "You don't get to drink any more of my cum until it's growing inside you."

It's the flash of heat from her that lets me know she heard every word, lets me know how much she wants that weeun too. That drive and desire. That need pushes me over the edge.

When she tightens around me, the sounds she makes fracture, not words anymore, and this time, her orgasm doesn't creep up on me, it punches me in the gut.

We come apart together.

My whole being seizes. The world stops...

And when it starts again, I have to haul in a huge breath.

She smiles up at me over her shoulder. "Hi."

Chuckling, I squeeze her hips as I remove my thumb. "Hi."

I pull back from her, legs shaking as I release them from the tension that had kept me upright.

Cum rushes from her, pouring down my legs and hers.

"It's a good thing you don't have rugs." She wiggles forward and rolls onto her back on the floor. When she holds her hands out to me with a lazy smile on her face, I force myself to stand.

Helping her to her feet, I let her pull my face down to hers to kiss me, but when she draws back, she doesn't release me.

"I love that you want me to be the mother of your children. But if I want to drink every last drop of your cum, I will and you will thank me for it."

"Understood."

"Good. Now, let's go get cleaned up so we can get messy again."

I scoop her up and throw her over my shoulder. Shrieking, she slaps my ass so I squeeze hers.

Cleaning up turns into a soapy hand job that turns into sex against the shower wall, and by the time we collapse in our bed, I should fall asleep immediately.

But my mind buzzes. She's mine, but she's not safe yet, and until she is, I'm never going to rest *easy*.

"What thoughts are bouncing around in your mind right now?" She watches me, eyes faintly glowing in the darkness.

"You're everything to me now. The first thought on my mind when I wake, the last before I fall asleep. You are my every dream." I draw her close. "You're the one I want to tell all my secrets and the only one I'll share my troubles with. If there was no one else in this universe but you and I, I would be content, simply because you are mine."

She kisses me and the feathery warmth through the bond soothes me.

But when she draws back, she says, "That's not what those thoughts felt like."

"I need to figure out who tried to turn you into my murderer."

"I think you mean *we* need to find out who's trying to kill you." She pokes me in the chest and then stretches, pressing as much of her body against mine as she can. "You're everything to me now too. I'm not going to let anyone take you away from me."

KIMBA

Sex with D provides a sort of clarity I've never experienced before.

And it's not just the fanciful notion that I can somehow see better afterward. It's like I can breathe again. And when that air finally reaches my brain, I can dig through the scattered and jumbled thoughts that wouldn't organize themselves before.

He gives me every opportunity to clear away the mental cobwebs.

The honeymoon phase had startled me the first time around. With D it's... mellower. And not in a bad way.

We've still managed to fuck each other on every available surface upstairs and down, but we make progress in between.

Tangled together on the stairs—we didn't make it all the way down this time—I run my hand over D's skin, staring out at the vast expanse between the two ridges of the calderas.

The Shadow Zone has no shadows at this time of day. Everything's a little too bright.

I've sorted through so much data, at this point, I might know more about the caldera than D does, but there's one thing I don't know.

"You said there's a system that recycles the magma and stops the caldera from erupting."

D doesn't say anything. Breath heaving, he turns his face toward the window, and a schematic projects from his eye onto the glass.

The information is from the lenses he wears. The projection...

Any time I learn some new trick of his eyes, I have to remind myself it's not magic.

But the process I see on the reflective surface might be.

"How did they manage that?" The system allows magma to flow out of a dozen ports in the sides of the main chamber walls. They travel out to open pits inside the Shadow Zone and then through a different slope that takes it back into a chamber below. The pressure eventually works them back into the main chamber and it starts again.

Even looking at it, I don't actually understand how it works.

Blinking the image away, D turns back to me, nipping at my lower lip. "That was built a long time ago by people far smarter than me. It's been in place since before I was born."

"I don't think that system is enough to ensure a bomb *wouldn't* cause an eruption."

The fizzing sensation of confusion prickles in my mind and D asks, "You're afraid it would crack the surface and draw magma up?"

"Maybe? My geology and volcanology background is pretty rudimentary. That may be something from a really old movie, not real life. Field trips do not an expert make."

"I don't know half of those words." He laughs and draws me further up him so that he can kiss me properly. "I'll ask Trench if he knows, or knows someone who can answer that."

"If I'm right, it's another bullet in your proverbial gun."

"They're going to think I took you for your tactical skills if they ever find out."

I snort at the word *took*. "That's alright, we'll both know it was for my pussy."

D hefts me even higher and I squeak in a little protest as his tongue circles my nipple and his lips latch onto me.

"We're never going to get anything done if we—" My thought ends on a shuddered breath and I wriggle against him, sliding myself across the slickness of his precum.

"We'll get plenty done in between."

In between.

I had almost forgotten that that was what the rest of the world would become: the in between moments.

"Life" was every second spent with him. Everything else existed outside of this—of us.

All it takes is pressing myself up and levering back, and he's inside me again.

He mutters curses that feel like kisses across my skin.

The robots have already cleaned away the previous mess where his cum had dripped to the floor below… but the stairs beneath my knees are still slick and I don't have any leverage.

I'm still sloppy enough that I slip and slide on him.

It's not enough, and he knows it.

Hand firm on my hips, he holds me down on him and stands, but we don't stay upright for long.

My back presses against the warm tile floor and D drops over me, holding me down with his weight as he fucks me like I might try to get away from him.

As if there was any danger of that.

"I could live on your cock," I say, lips pressed against the hard line of his jaw.

He chuckles, but he doesn't loosen his grip on me. "That would get awkward when we have company."

Fingers gripping the back of his head, I hold him closer —as if that was even possible—and bite my tongue to keep from asking him to promise me he'll never leave me.

A familiar sound echoes through the outpost… like the saints heard me and decided to say "fuck you, *personally*, Kimba."

Groaning, I feel the frustration and need coil in the bond as he finishes the best possible way, rough and ragged.

"I will be *right* back." He kisses me and I laugh at him

through the bond as he leaves me there in a pool of our cum.

There are so many worse places I could be.

But he doesn't leave me there for long. D comes back, lifting me up and managing to wrap me in an enormous warm towel before carrying me into "my" bathroom.

"This one does need me," he says, waiting for me to be on stable footing before he lets go of me with a lingering kiss. "I won't be out there any longer than I have to."

I sway a little when he goes back into the dark cavern of our room.

I'm in the shower when I feel the chill as a prickle on my nape. The cold outside doesn't actually touch me. But discomfort when the cold tightens the fabric of the suit he wears... I feel that.

It takes a few minutes to clean myself up, but I take them, sorting through the possible issues I might have overlooked and as I'm toweling myself dry, I start to think they might not exist. Not even this sexual clarity can reveal things that never were.

Pulling on my shirt, I glance toward the corner of the vanity and freeze.

Edan's picture is gone.

All of the pieces of his shrine, gone.

No one else could have stolen them, and D wouldn't have...

I button my pants as I walk out into the living area and my eyes go to exactly where Edan should be if this had been his home as well.

And he's there.

I stare at it for a long moment.

His picture is hung straight, the mementos of his life are placed exactly the way I was told they needed to be. There are new incense cones and fresh petals.

D did this.

I can see his fingerprints on the glass orb that holds Edan's carbon remnants.

D made this place for Edan in his life, because without his memory, I'm not whole.

Breathing deeply, I manage to keep myself from dropping to the floor and sobbing. But I could easily imagine turning into a puddle the bots would slurp up on their next pass.

I climb the stairs with an odd static in my limbs. It feels like relief, but not a kind I've ever experienced before.

D has known for so long that he would change his life to fit me into it… it's only fair that I do what I can to fit into his.

He hasn't asked me to do what I used to do, in either of my previous lives—he's just let me do what I want—but I can do some of that without feeling like I've betrayed the version of myself that is here, now.

But making that decision means I need to know all of the information.

There's one part of the outpost that I haven't seen. And only one way to get there.

I take the elevator down to the lowest level, glad my feet are cozy in warm socks when the doors open to a cavernous garage. There is one snow bike left inside it… but it looks like it could hold two dozen if the need arose.

There's a person-sized door beside the one for their bikes and I go to it, looking out at the icy wastes beyond. I scan the swirling blue.

I *can* see better.

Wind howls on the other side of that door and I shiver, despite the balmy air.

There's a secondary medfac down here—good—and an ugly mechanical room, but otherwise, the space is empty.

Unused utilitarian shelves line the walls.

This space is waiting to fulfill a purpose.

I hate that it reminds me of myself...

I don't like it down here. I doubt I'm supposed to.

A flashing in the corner draws my attention... except, there's nothing there. It was just a light wraith... but another draws my attention upward.

Someone's here.

I know it, even though there's no reason I should.

And sure enough, when I step out of the elevator into the top floor of our outpost, Core is there with a petite blonde woman. *Cindy.* My memory supplies her name.

The enormous pink Sian man smiles lovingly down at his mate and Cindy... is *literally* glowing. It hurts my eyes.

"Hello." I say, trying not to wince or squint.

"Hi!" Cindy's excited peal bounces off the walls as she hurries over to me.

She hugs me before she speaks.

"I'm Cindy. You're Kimba, this is amazing!"

And I can't help but chuckle. "Yes, it is."

It's not even an uneasy chuckle.

She's as warm as she is bright, and I relax into her without really thinking about it until it's already done.

Squeezing me tight once more, she laughs and this time, *hers* is uneasy, but she turns back to Core and shoots him a half-hearted glare. "I am not being overbearing."

"I didn't say anything." Core very definitely thought it though.

"Congratulations," I say, and she blushes.

She, like Laurel, is very definitely already pregnant. It's hard *not* to get pregnant on Isia.

"Thank you," Cindy turns, sweeping her coat to the side and looking down at her stomach, "I'm not going to lie to you. I'm a little mad I haven't started showing. I am determined to beat Andrea to it—just for fun, of course, she doesn't care one way or the other. She'll be at the meeting tomorrow? The day after next? I can't keep track of things."

She looks back at Core and he says, "The day after next."

"Right. You'll get to meet her then and we'll find out if I still have time to win."

"It's not a competition." Core says, but it's clear that he's hoping she does.

"What is the use in being small if you don't get to 'pop' first?" She asks, turning big puppy dog eyes on me.

"I mean, being short's never been a negative in my mind," I assure her.

Cindy's only an inch or two shorter than I am, but she makes a show of looking up at me. "Tell me that after you've moved the stool for the tenth time because you need things from *EVERY* high cupboard to make your cookies."

"Lucky for me, I don't bake."

"Well, I do." She beams up at me. "I brought you an assortment of cookies and a loaf of banana bread. Don't worry, no nuts were involved in *any* of them. I made sure everything was safe before I started work on your batch."

"Thank you?"

"Don't look too worried. The second Drift registered your bond with the Agency, I got a packet with first aid info. I have not gone snooping through your files and won't unless an emergency comes up or you ask me to."

That makes sense. "Thank you, again."

She nods. "That is part of the reason we're here. I haven't gotten a ping in my files that says D is off the stopper yet, but I wanted to come by and make sure you know how to check the medfac when the time comes. I mean, and to introduce myself, of course."

"I came to threaten you."

I look up at Core and for a moment, I can't tell the intention behind his jagged tooth smile.

"Be good to my boss," he says.

I don't like the low prickling those words wash over my skin. "Or what?"

"Or I'll send your weeun a harpsitar for their first birthday."

Cindy hasn't been here long enough. She likely doesn't know how serious of a threat the percussive string instrument is.

"I think that would be more of a punishment for your friend than it would for me."

His smile falters and I see him think it through. "Point taken."

"Don't worry," Cindy says before looking back at him affectionately. "I wouldn't let him finalize the order."

They smile at each other, their gazes lingering and I'm glad I feel D come back into the warmth of the outpost. I don't want to have to tell Cindy she can't go downstairs.

"So!" She claps her hands together. "Your medfac has everything you'll need when the time comes, but the lingo can be a little odd, even if you speak the language fluently."

"I think I'm going to be okay, actually, but thank you."

Her eyes go wide as the door pings softly behind me and I turn to D, grateful that he's in one piece and alone.

"Something wrong?" He asks, glancing from Core to Cindy, clearly expecting her to be the one who answers.

"Nothing's wrong. Just wanted to swing by and make sure the medfac was ready to go for your bondmate."

She beams at him, but something unpleasant coils in the bond, like she's slapped him.

"Thank you for your concern. It is fully functional and I have already set all of the parameters to English."

Her smile tightens. "That's great. But I should still probably check it out."

"The downstairs is off limits." D says, once more. "Even to medical professionals—outside of an emergency."

Cindy tips her head to the side, eyes narrowed. "Fine. But the second you need something, just know, I'll be here."

"I'm sure we'll be fine."

"If you say so. We just don't want anyone else being run off the road or falling into the caldera."

I don't know what one has to do with the other, but at this point, I'm also on team 'Get them out the door.'

Looking at Cindy has started to give me a headache.

So when D manages to efficiently herd them out and we're alone again, I relax a little more than I anticipated.

"What's wrong?" D's hand grips the back of my neck, squeezing at the tension. "You've been in pain since they got here."

"I think there's more to bonding with the brotherhood than there is to other Sian men."

His eyes narrow and I can sense his confusion.

"Cindy was glowing. Literally. Not the 'she's pregnant and beaming' thing that Earth people say." I rub at my eyes. "She was actually glowing. And I think I saw her from downstairs. Not like fully. But there were these light wraiths… I'm not sure how to describe them."

D tips my head back and looks down into my eyes.

"There is something different… when did you notice it?"

"It started the first time we had sex, it's been kind of on and off since then. I can definitely see further."

"We should go down and see what the medfac has to say."

I remember that Cindy has access. "Not right now."

He wants to argue. "You're sure?"

"Yeah."

"Let me know if it changes."

If it changes. "Do you think I'll get to see shrimp colors?"

His brows quirk. "I don't know what that means."

Shaking my head, I laugh as I press my cheek into his palm. "I'll see if I can find the comic. Earth science may have debunked it, but I'm hoping you've got at leas one more miracle up your sleeve."

He nods, leaning down to kiss me.

"You registered our bond." I say when we break apart —instead of jumping up into his arms.

"I did. I hope that's okay. Did you want to be the one who did it?"

"No, it's fine. It explains why the number in my mailbox has been climbing steadily." I haven't looked at my messages beyond scanning them since I arrived.

"You have physical mail too." He nods toward a little box beside the upstairs kitchen.

The drone network here delivers everything possible. Even mail to the middle of nowhere.

I pick up the stack and sort through. There are half a dozen cards among them and I pull those out, ignoring the solicitations from local businesses wanting to help me "set up" my new home.

D changes as I open the first one.

"Oh dear." I hold up the *very* expensive card. "Luthiel sends his well wishes. I can't be certain if they're genuine or not. He's very good about tiptoeing around calling you a liar."

D laughs. "It was a foregone conclusion... I think we all know that."

There are a handful of cards from women at Margot's and then one from the woman herself.

"Margot would like to say 'Told you so' to both of us." I read on and don't quite understand the "sisters" comment she makes at the bottom of the card in the PostScript.

I'll ask her when I get back to work.

Second to last is a very pretty envelope. It's utterly human and I've no doubt it was bought from one of the Earth stores. Probably Hannah, but it's not Hannah.

The name makes me freeze.

"What's wrong?" D is at my side a moment later, looking down at the same well wishes, not understanding why my blood has suddenly run cold.

"He had a brother." I can't manage more than a whisper.

"Who?"

"The man who killed Edan. The one *I* killed."

Has Kylan been keeping tabs on me?

There's a sliver of trepidation in the bond. I'm not sure I want to know what he's been thinking.

"The man who approached you knew who you used to be..." He trails off, but it's easy to guess what he's thinking.

"He knew what I'd done."

He nods. "Did Kylan know what happened?"

A prickling sensation tickles at the nape of my neck and I reach back, scrubbing at the skin, even though I know it isn't going to help.

"The records were sealed. As far as I know, only the

people on the scene and the judge who pardoned me know…" A face flashes in my memory, clear as day.

How could I have forgotten Kylan was *there?*

"What did you remember?" D asks. Of course he knows why my skin just went so cold I'm shivering.

He pulls me tight to his chest and rubs my back. "What happened?"

"He was there afterward. He saw—" *everything.*

"Do you think he could have been behind this?"

"No." I shake my head, but I'm not sure. "Maybe?"

It was years ago. Kylan… Kylan had looked at me like I was a murderer. And he was right. He'd seen me on the floor, covered in two Sian's blood… and he knew I was the reason his brother was gone.

"I didn't really know Kylan. I don't know what he did or who he was." I take a deep breath, trying to only remember the relevant parts of that horrible night. "I doubt he processed the fact that his brother had killed Edan first. Neither of us were in a state for rational thought."

"It's been years, if he's behind it, we need to figure out why. And why now?"

"Do you think it was me all along? That you're simply convenient because you're the only man I was ever close to."

"I don't know what to think, but he's a possibility we have to rule out."

He hadn't come to my trial. He hadn't tried to contact me since. But I didn't know him.

I don't know what he is capable of… or if he held grudges.

Then again, knowing someone means less than nothing.

I knew his brother, and knowing him hadn't warned me of what was to come.

I check the return directions. "He still lives in Gongii."

It's almost a full day's drive away—but it's only a two-hour flight. If Kylan had slipped in and out of Ilidi City for legitimate reasons, it wouldn't raise any red flags. He could probably have organized the men in my garage without even leaving his home.

"Then maybe we need to take a trip to Gongii."

CHAPTER
THIRTEEN

DRIFT

LOOKING OUT THE WINDOW, I can see the heat trails of two bikes headed our way. Trench and Arc will get here at the same time.

"Why those two?" Kimba asks.

She's wrapped herself in a thick sweater and snuggles it close as she looks out over the Zone, scanning the blue snow.

"Because, sibling turmoil aside, they're the two I don't feel any guilt asking favors from."

She raises her brows and I feel her need for a better answer through the bond.

"Arc never seems to want to go home, and Trench jumps at any distraction I give him. Arc might joke that they'd like to see each other dead, but they manage to work together better than most. So they're who I call."

She nods and looks up at the ceiling, as if she could see through the stone and into the garage. "What is their problem with each other?"

"Arc hates everyone. He just hates Trench a little more."

She doesn't like that. "Why?"

"I have spent years trying to figure that out." And failing miserably. "They're here."

The sliding light of the lift that goes from the lowest level of my outpost to the top (and nowhere in between) passes up the wall behind the stairs.

She watches it for a moment and then nods, going to the kitchen, instead of up to greet them.

I leave her downstairs packing, but I know she can feel how unsettled I am when they arrive.

Silence is more startling than their usual jabs, and I wonder—but don't ask—about what might have been said in the elevator.

"We've found tunnels," Arc says. "They've been reburied. Like they didn't want us to find them."

"Okay." I don't like the sound of that.

Trench nods. "It's not good, but it's something."

"Kimba and I have to go to the Gongii province. We'll leave at first light tomorrow and be back before dark the next day."

Trench's eyes narrow and I wonder what he sees. "If you're leaving the Zone while we don't know how they're getting out, it has to be serious."

Maybe not as serious as he would like.

"You guys can handle it. Just don't burn the caldera down."

Arc posts up behind the counter, back to the refrigerator he's just closed, hands wrapped around a bottle of the black soda he prefers. "You could have given us more notice you were going on honeymoon."

"We need to check on a man who might want Kimba dead, or incarcerated."

Trench scowls at me. "Then one of us should go with you for back up."

He might be right, but I don't think so.

"Honestly, neither Kimba, nor I, are particularly concerned about this guy. It's a long shot, but one we have to check into."

I feel Kimba join us a moment before their attention shifts behind me.

Arc straightens and dips his head in a greeting, while Trench smiles brightly. She knows it's forced, but she doesn't bring it up.

"You two going to be okay while we're gone?"

They exchange a glance, and it's Arc who speaks. "We promise we won't throw a party and trash the house, mom."

If he'd said it a different way, one—or both—of us might have made him pay for it. But for once, he wasn't being a smart ass.

———

Trench is already upstairs when I take the bag up and set it beside the garage door.

He's made himself breakfast and slides a glass of marbaroo tea to me.

"Can't drink that anymore." I should probably have already thrown it all out.

"No?"

"She's allergic."

Trench nods, snatching it up and tossing it down the sink. "Would you like me to get rid of the rest of it while you're gone?"

"Sure."

Kimba yawns as she reaches the top of the stairs. I probably should have let her sleep longer.

"That smells delicious," she says, looking at his plate.

"It is." Trench smiles at her. "Bring him back in one piece and I'll make it for you sometime."

"Don't worry. Kylan isn't dangerous on his own." She says it, even though she's not certain.

"Then why is he on the list?"

She casts a sidelong glance at me. She doesn't really think he should be.

"Because any lead is a good lead," I speak for her.

She doesn't tell me I'm wrong. Not out loud anyway.

But Trench looks back and forth between us and I see him grimace. It's the smallest movement of his lips, but I know... he doesn't like being around bonded men. I imagine we're unwanted reminders.

"You two hold down the fort. The others have been informed of our absence. They know to look to you."

Nodding, Trench says, "Have fun."

He heads for the consoles, still cluttered with Kimba's notes. He doesn't look at us again.

When the garage door closes behind us, Kimba pauses before she gets into the car. "Do they all have access to the outpost?"

"Yeah, but they don't come unless called—or, like today, have something scheduled—and they never go downstairs."

Something low and suspicious coils inside her, but she shakes her head and gets in the car. I toss the bag into the back.

The drive out of the mountains is quiet. Neither of us say a word until we're through town and on the long, wide, road to Gongii.

Her eyes are closed, her head tipped back against the seat. "Next time we head out of town, it had better be to a secluded love nest. Not the home of a man who's brother I killed."

"Since there aren't any others, I think I can promise that."

She drops her head toward her shoulder and gives me a weak smile.

"I can promise that the next time I take you away, I will spend ninety percent of the trip inside you... one way or another."

"Can we just skip to that trip instead?" She twists in her seat, her skirt bunching. "I can take off my panties and we can start right now."

Saints, how I wish we could.

"We've got to figure out what's going on first, so we can both live to make it to a second trip." I keep my eyes on the road, but ask, "What did you think of back there? Why did them having access worry you?"

"I just wondered... the brotherhood seems pretty tightly knit, but what if one of them wanted to take over?"

"You think one of them might have tried to take me out to take over control of the Zone?"

She shrugs. "Core joked that he was there to threaten me yesterday. There were plenty of people back on Earth who would kill for better positions, higher pay, the like."

"None of us need money, the CSS basically has an unlimited account for us. And believe me when I tell you, no one wants this job." Not even me on the best of days.

We do it because we have to.

"Not even Arc?"

Maybe. He spends enough time out patrolling...

She waits. Patience tasting like butter.

No. "He's an asshole, but he doesn't want to be in charge."

"Kilo?" She asks. "I keep looking for him, convinced he's just going to be there like a ghost, whenever I turn around."

"I know when he's there. And if you're right about your vision... you should be able to see him too."

"Is there any rhyme or reason to the things you can do?"

"No." I keep my focus straight ahead. "A different kind of monster made us to hunt the ones in the caldera. When you live through what he did to us..."

"I'm sorry. I wasn't trying to make you talk about him." She shivers. "If you say they're good, I believe you."

Sliding her arm through mine, she snuggles against me, holding tight to my biceps as she drops her head to my shoulder.

The worry is still there, floating like a fog at the bottom of our bond, but contentment hangs above it, and what anxiety I'd started to feel at the possibility of talking about that time diminishes.

KIMBA

Gongii city is not *terribly* different from Ilidi—the city none of its residents call by name. It's the same type of buildings in a different order with a different pattern of lights and a different train schedule.

It feels like it should have changed more since the last time I saw it.

D holds my hand in a soft grip. "We got here quicker than I expected. We can do this tonight instead of tomorrow."

"And we won't have to worry about a work schedule."

I don't know what he does. That wasn't in the public record.

His house is set halfway up the plateau wall, over-looking the city lights. There's a modest wealth in the structure. Something Luthiel could learn from.

As I step out of the car, I look up at the three floors.

"I feel like we're repeating history," D says, smiling at me, and a fizzle of humor bubbles through the bond. The similarities aren't lost on him.

I don't mention that his outpost is bigger than both of their homes combined… he just doesn't use most of it.

Kylan used to work with some kind of advocacy group that put him in Edan's circles. He never really wound up in my path—he didn't need convincing. But he wasn't a politician. He was something else…

We stop at the door and D waits for me to ring the bell. We're not doing this until I'm ready… except, I'm never going to be ready. Not really.

With a deep breath, I push the panel beside the door.

And wait.

After the deep tones fade, I hear him coming. Whatever he yells back to the other person in the house, I don't know, but it's a happy sound.

And he's smiling when he drags the door open.

That smile vanishes in a flash, replaced by blank aston-ishment. "Nadine?"

D shifts, and I know what he's thinking. I feel his stress. But I don't need protection right now. Linking hands with him, I focus on keeping him still.

"Hi Kylan." I squeeze D's hand. It won't make a differ-ence. I won't move him unless he wants to be moved.

D looks down at me, and I raise both brows, hoping he'll understand that he needs to back off.

Kylan shakes his head and the smile returns. "I'm so sorry, Kimba. I just wasn't expecting to ever see you again."

D stiffens behind me, drawing Kylan's attention. But he's... excited. "And you brought your mate."

"It's been a long time." I look to D for half a second before I turn back. "Kylan, this is Drift, head of the Shadow Zone Brotherhood."

"I know you by reputation, I've worked with the council before, but not you directly. It was a long time ago." He pauses, seeming to remember something. "Actually, this is great. Come in, please."

He hurries into his house, picking up random clutter as he goes, looking even more flustered.

I've seen this sort of tidy mess before. Whatever happened in the five years since I'd last seen him, Kylan has children now. And those tiny tornadoes invariably leave their mark on a home, no matter how big.

I think, for a moment, that I can hear them upstairs, but that's just my imagination. I shove those thoughts aside, focusing on the here and now.

Something oddly soft rolls through the bond, and when I turn back, I see what's made D stop.

There's a picture of me and Edan on Kylan's wall. It's not placed specially. It's just in amongst his family photos, as if we belonged there.

It only takes a moment to scan the photos: a bondmate, children... others I don't know.

His brother isn't on his walls.

Ahead of us, Kylan quickly clears away space on a long couch. Toys and clothes and clutter are piled on a chair in the corner.

Motioning toward the couch, he asks, "Can I get you anything to drink?"

D sits first, and I shake my head. "No, we're fine."

Kylan glances between us, a sad smile on his lips, and I

realize how odd it must be. Knowing I've rebonded is not the same as seeing it for himself.

His smile returns as he sits across from us. "I am really glad to see you. I didn't think you'd come back here. It wasn't my intention when I sent the note. I am truly happy you've found someone worthy of you again."

I believe him.

We didn't need to make this trip.

D relaxes beside me. He's as sure as I am that Kylan had nothing to do with the men who asked me to kill him.

"So," Kylan says, "This can't be a social call... what brought you all the way to Gongii?"

The idea of telling him the truth makes me hesitate, but D shifts, lounging back, trying to look non-threatening. "Do you know why your brother killed Edan?"

Kylan straightens, lips pursing in discomfort, but he doesn't try to avoid the question. "Yes."

There's a moment of silence before he turns to me, his brow creasing. "Don't you?"

I shrug, because it doesn't matter anymore. Not really. "A political disagreement gone wrong is what I was told. I wasn't present for the argument, only the aftermath."

Wincing, Kylan shifts, glancing toward the stairs that lead up into his home, and I know he doesn't want to say what he's about to.

"Sian men have been fighting over you since you got here. I don't know if you knew that. I can't tell you how many people asked Edan if he'd be willing to let them 'sample' you."

I did. "It came up once or twice."

Not that Edan ever considered it. He might have, if I had wanted to and if we already had children... but until then it wasn't even a question.

"Jax wanted more than just a 'sample', but he knew he couldn't have you."

"He never said anything to me." I try to remember... "I don't think he said more than a few sentences to me in the entire time I knew him."

"I think he knew what your answer would be, even if he wasn't willing to admit it to himself." Kylan lets out a long breath and looks down at his clasped hand. "Instead of moving on and getting over it... He stayed and he let it fester. And then he found out Edan couldn't have kids."

I don't know why Kylan knowing makes me so uncomfortable.

Edan's gone. His frustration and embarrassment shouldn't still prickle across the empty cavern where our bond used to live.

D's hand goes to my shoulder, gently massaging the tension away.

Kylan has the decency to pretend he doesn't notice.

"He thought he'd found his way in. Margot's was already around, as you know. Bonded mates had already proved that a second man joining in on the fun was socially acceptable, so he thought... why not. The idiot thought he'd come up with a great plan. He'd offer to do what Edan couldn't."

The distaste on his face is echoed in D's feelings across the bond.

Kylan pinches the bridge of his nose. "Jax made his pitch about a month before..."

He swallows, but he doesn't say it and I'm grateful.

"When he told me about it then, I thought he was insane. Not for offering. Up to that point, I thought the two of them were better friends than they actually were. But for being upset that Edan told him no."

A month... *I thought Edan told me everything.*

"But he didn't give up." D keeps his hands on me, and that contact keeps me grounded.

I don't want to hear any more. But I have to.

"He left some rambling message for me that night. I didn't get it until after I'd come home, after the police had called me and I'd already been to your house." Swallowing, Kylan stands and drags a hand through his hair as he paces to the window. "He went to your home to talk Edan into it. He said you would be his, one way or another. He actually thought you'd leave Edan for him. He was convinced you wanted children more than you wanted Edan."

For a moment, my brain stops functioning. Every piece of me, everything that I am, freezes in disbelief. "I barely knew him."

"I know that now. Even when I didn't, I couldn't fathom how he'd come to that conclusion."

D slips his fingers into mine, eyes still on Kylan's back. "But you think he went to their home, intending to kill Edan that night."

"I think it was an option he'd considered and accepted as more than likely." He takes a deep breath. "That's what I told the CSS back then, and it's what I still believe now."

"Then you know what I did to him?"

"I do. I won't lie to you—I refuse to insult your intelligence like that—I was furious. My brother was gone and you were the reason."

D's anger prickles across the bond, "No."

Holding up his hands, Kylan says, "I came to understand that very quickly, don't worry. How could there be any other answer as to why *you*, someone I knew to be so gentle, could do something like… that?

"Human-Sian pairings were still so new. I'm certain he didn't know what it would do to you." He runs his hand

206

over his head. "I don't think anyone expected the consequences of bonding to be quite so dire."

Because they hadn't known, not at first.

"Edan had sold the idea of a bondmate, using you as the example of the perfect human woman. And Jax... he wanted to buy." He deflates, like he's wanted to say that out loud for so long. "The Agency changed some of their screening criteria after that. And the clubs as well."

"I remember. I didn't realize why." It had been in the year I'd spent drowning in grief.

"There was a lot of discussion as to whether or not you should be involved. But some others lobbied for leaving you alone. And I know that was the right thing."

He nods, as if he's still trying to convince himself.

"Academically, I'd tried to empathize with what you went through and I thought I'd done a good job of it." He looks at those steps again. "And then... Rose came into my life."

"You bonded fairly quickly after that." D says.

"Yes, Rose and I had already been matched. The events surrounding Jax and Edan delayed things, but she came and I suddenly understood what I'd known only theoretically before. If someone killed her, I could see myself doing what you did... or worse, before the bond killed me too."

"I sincerely hope you never have to feel that pain, or that rage." I hate the sharpness of those memories, and how I know they're translating across the bond to D.

I also know that if someone kills his mate, Kylan won't survive it. That is the only true disclaimer in the Agency paperwork Sian men have to sign.

Like me, their mate could survive *their* death, but they won't survive hers.

"We should go." I don't want any more of the

unpleasant tremors rumbling across the bond before I can stop them. "We need to head home first thing tomorrow morning."

"Please stay. Just a little longer. I would really like you to meet her." Kylan glances up again and I wonder if he's sent some urgency through the bond.

I don't know why, but I feel like I owe him that. "Okay."

He takes a deep breath and nods. "Let me go help her finish putting the kids down and I'll be right back."

He hurries upstairs, and D stands, watching him go.

"They have three weeuns." He says, looking upstairs… likely able to see through the walls the way he found the woman in the dead Sian's house. "The youngest is giving her mother trouble."

"That's not surprising, from what friends have told me."

He looks at me and I know he felt the spike of despair through me. "We can go, if you like."

"No. I want to meet her…" Something tells me I need to.

A minute later, I don't have a choice.

Rose looks like a European super model and when she speaks, it's the first time I've heard Sianese with a French accent…

"Hello! It's so wonderful to meet you." She takes my hand in both of hers, not shaking it, just holding it. "I hope it will be okay to speak in their language. My English is not what it once was."

"That's perfectly fine."

"Marvelous! You are a legend around here, I did not think I would ever have the pleasure of actually speaking to you."

I don't know why, but her scrutiny is sharper than the men who come to memorize the shape of my body.

"It's lovely to meet you too, Rose."

She smiles so brightly. I wait to hear her jaw pop… but it doesn't.

"Kylan and I both agreed we wouldn't bother you, but since you're here…"

Kylan says her name softly under his breath and she ignores him.

"I'd like to solicit your help."

I don't think MLMs have made their way to this planet yet, but I'm cautious when I ask. "What kind of help?"

"Ky left the advocacy firm after we had our first weeun, but I work with a different branch and we… Well, we're here to help women like you."

I feel my smile melt away from my face like a strange out-of-body experience. "Women like me?"

She smiles, sadly. "Women who've lost their bond-mates and, thankfully, survived it. We know that most of the time they don't feel like it was a blessing, not at first, but *we* do. And we want to do everything to make sure they thrive, no matter how long it takes for them to rebond… if they ever do. We never push them toward it. The choice is entirely theirs."

Would that have helped me? I honestly don't know.

"I'm not asking you to take a job, just to be open, if we have questions or to other possibilities."

She isn't pushing. If she works with widows, I have a feeling she's learned to be very delicate.

"Tonight's not the night to talk about that." Kylan says, squeezing her hand.

She nods. "It *is* getting late. Send me a note and we can talk later."

D looks sharply toward the console table a moment before the phone goes off.

She apologizes, going to her phone, but her smile disappears and she excuses herself to take a call.

The perfect opportunity to escape.

It's a short walk back to the front door, and D pauses at it, just long enough to tell Kylan it was nice to meet him and share a glance with me.

He's giving me time. I'm not sure I want it.

"Thank you for seeing us."

"Of all the people on this world or any other, you are one of the few I would never refuse to see." He looks over my head. "I'm glad you've found happiness again."

"I found it before him." I say, glancing to where Rose has started pacing on her phone call. "But it has definitely eased some of the pain that Edan's death left behind."

"He is known for solving problems."

I follow his gaze, to where D stands at the car, moving without seeming to think about it.

"You could do a lot worse."

I laugh and see D smile, even though I know he can't hear the conversation. "My chosen profession made that abundantly clear."

"Edan would have been proud of you, Kimba. And he would have wanted you to love and be loved, even though it couldn't be him anymore."

His smile shifts to curiosity.

"Why did you come? Clearly there was a reason... but you got your answer before you asked the question."

I could ask him to leave it alone and I'm sure he would, or I could lie, but he'd been honest with me.

"Someone asked me to kill him. We haven't found anyone with a motive to kill him, so we were exploring the possibility of people who might want me dead or incarcerated."

He looks shattered by the implied accusation. "I guess if you didn't know why Jax killed Edan, I'm a logical enough choice for that." The scowl twisting on his face isn't meant for me. "I should have reached out a long time ago, to let you know I didn't blame you."

Maybe he should have. "The past is in the past."

He dips his head in a little bow. "Goodbye, Kimba. And good luck. Though, I don't think you'll need it."

Until we figure out who wants D dead... I think we will.

D hasn't gotten in the car yet.

Leaning against the back quarter panel, he watches me as I walk down to him. He knows what I'm feeling.

"Where are we going?"

I booked the hotel without telling him where, and I don't tell him now either.

"You'll see."

CHAPTER
FOURTEEN

DRIFT

THE HOTEL KIMBA directs me to has no sign announcing what it is.

It doesn't seem to have a staff, either.

We pull up to the front door and as soon as we're out and the car is locked, the drive opens up and lowers it down into a storage facility with half a dozen others.

"I've never liked handing the car code over to someone else," I say, "But I'm not sure this is better."

She chuckles. "This place is meant for guests who don't want to deal with people who might get excited by them. It's quiet and private. And tonight, I just want it to be you and me. No other people, no monsters. Just us."

I like that.

A tiny drone appears at our side floating with a low buzzing sound that ripples the air around it. Kimba holds out her hand for it to scan.

As soon as the blue light passes over her skin, mapping her palm print, the drone sweeps down and collects our bags, flitting away.

"They always remind me of hummingbirds or dragon-flies," she says. "Have you ever seen those?"

"I have not."

"We're definitely going to take some time for nature documentaries later."

"Yes, we will."

I like the idea of that, snuggled up on the couch as she tells me all the little details that are important to her that a narrator would gloss over.

The doors open automatically, greeting her softly by name, and when I follow her to what should be a reception desk, there's no one there to sort out our room or direct us.

A dish rises up from the broken stone and the automation gives her a physical key... like the one at Tefir's home.

It also provides two glasses of bubbling and fizzy alcohol.

I hear low voices down hallways and when we pass, I see others in the dimly lit rooms beyond them. Bars and spas and lounge spaces... but Kimba ignores them, leading the way to the lift and letting it scan her hand once more.

The thing takes us up and up, rising at an angle, until the doors open once more, directly into the room.

The lights are low and she doesn't raise them.

"Can you still see better than you could?" I ask.

"It fades." She goes to our bags—waiting for us by the bed—and shimmies out of her jacket. And then, she chuckles. "I'm beginning to think the more cum I have inside me, the better I can see."

She comes back to me and I lift her up so I can kiss her.

"I wonder," she says, sighing against my lips. "If that's a 'you' thing, or a brotherhood thing."

"If Laurel gets hurt, I'll tell Richter to fuck her and see what happens."

She snorts and hits my chest with her open palm. "You will not."

"You're right. I won't." I have a feeling Laurel would do more than swat at me if I suggested it.

"Are the city lights too bright?"

I glance out the window to where they flicker and shine. "No."

"Good." Her tongue pokes out and she licks my lower lip. "We have a few hours to spare before we need to sleep, and I find myself craving you more than room service."

I like that too, but, "Food first," I say, turning her toward a table by the window. "I plan to exhaust you. Eat now, or regret it later."

She does as I ask, and I'm not surprised, again, when food just appears, rising out of the table. She ordered ahead of time, and as a particular torture, she watches me. I can *feel* her thinking about fucking me again.

It's more delicious than the food, which is spectacular.

But I don't finish mine.

The second she's done with hers, I drag her from her chair and press her back to the window. The city glitters like a halo behind her. "Do you know what teasing will get you?"

"Exactly what I want?"

She's right—as always.

I kiss her, trying to reign in this vicious need for her. I don't know if the window is strong enough to withstand it.

"I've been thinking," she murmurs, between kisses.

"Always a good sign."

Hands on my chin, she holds me away from her, breath rising heavily, gaze locked on mine. "I want you to come off the stopper."

My heart seizes and my cock twitches. She can feel them both in very different ways. "You're sure?"

She nods, drawing her nose up the side of my neck and nipping at my ear. "I am more than ready for you to breed me, D."

I clench my teeth, trying to hold in the growl. I don't manage it.

She chuckles. "But... since you're still on it, and we've got time... I want you to fuck my ass tonight."

Groaning, I ask, "You've only taken my thumb, Kimba. What makes you think you can manage my cock?"

"Delusion?" She purses her lips and I can feel her laughing even though she doesn't make a sound. "Delusion and a *lot* of lube."

She nods to the side, and I see a literal jug of it beside the nightstand.

"I asked them to have it in the room when we got here."

She kicks off her shoes and using her legs and feet, she manages to drag her pants down too. "Every inch of me is yours... it's about time you take it all."

Stepping back, I let her slide down. Her eyes don't leave mine and I pull off my shirt. She pulls off hers too.

"You are lucky my teeth are blunt." Her hands go to my waist. "Because I constantly want to bite you."

"Bite away." I would wear the marks with pride.

"Only if you promise to bite back." She licks her lips.

I don't make that promise. *I* would leave marks behind. And I am *never* going to hurt her.

I feel her laughing at me and her smile makes her cheeks rosy. "Alright, fine. You don't have to bite back."

She goes to her knees, taking my pants with her.

"I won't bite where it will actually hurt," she says,

215

before leaning forward and scraping her teeth across my thigh.

She doesn't bite when her mouth wraps around the tip of my cock. She doesn't bite when her tongue swirls around it, or when she licks and sucks.

I keep my hand at the back of her head waiting for the dangerous flare I feel in her to turn into something more daring. There's a curious burble in the bond that makes me think she might try to choke on me.

I close my grip a moment before she can do it, and pull her back off of me.

Her smile makes my spine tingle and when I release her, she drops back to sit on her heels.

"Why did I think," she asks, taking a deep breath, "that being older and wiser would mean not being perpetually horny?"

"I don't know."

She looks up at me with wide eyes from beneath my cock, angling her face so the ridges on its underside rest against her cheek.

"I'm glad." Her hand wraps around the base of me again and she strokes. "I want everything with you, D. And I'm not willing to settle for less."

Dragging her to her feet, I haul the covers off the bed and toss her onto it.

"I want you all the time, Kimba."

"Me too."

Good.

She lets out a little shriek as I bury my face in her sloppy pussy. I would forego water if I was only allowed to drink one thing for the rest of my life.

It doesn't matter what the question is, I'll choose her.

Her nails dig into my skull as she rocks her hips, helping me to tongue fuck her.

216

Every stroke of my tongue, every little chirp and moan from her lips... my cock is already drooling for her.

"Saints, D." She draws a sharp breath and her muscles tighten.

The flush of her skin warms mine and I don't let her finish the sentence she'd started.

She comes on a broken cry, her thighs squeezing tight against my head.

I shouldn't be thankful someone wants me dead. Their attempt gave me the woman I love.

But I haven't told her...

Her grip eases, and when I can, I crawl over her.

"I love you, Kimba." I kiss her and don't let her speak. I have more I need to say first. "I knew I wanted you the first time I saw you. I knew I loved you the first time you fell asleep in my arms. I will give you everything, because you are my everything."

She swallows, and for a moment, I think she's going to cry.

"I don't know when I fell in love with you, D. I certainly didn't mean to. But I do. And I can't imagine not falling for you. We would have gotten here, eventually, but I can't hate that we got here faster than we would have if someone hadn't hired me to kill you."

She kisses me, and I fuck her with slow and languid strokes.

Being with her like this, knowing with complete certainty that it *is* love I feel in our bond... this has to be what humans call heaven.

Eventually, she pulls back from me. "I think it's about time you stuff your cock in my ass."

I laugh. I can't help myself. "Just so you know, I didn't tell you I love you *because* of this."

"Oh, I know."

She bites her tongue as she smiles up at me, and I ease from her, sitting back on my heels so I can turn and grab the jug.

There is *so* much lube. I inspect the bottle and do the quick math of ounces in my head. "This could last us a week." Maybe a month.

"I only asked for a large bottle." She laughs as she turns over, going to her knees and wiggling her hips.

"Maybe they thought we planned to have a party." I press my slicked thumb against her ass and she draws in a slow breath.

"You're the only one I want at this kind of party." If she had anything more she wanted to say, it turns into a moan.

The lube is unbranded, but it's so slippery, my thumb presses inside of her as if her body has pulled me in.

She whimpers as I withdraw, squeezing around me, her pussy clenching.

"Still feeling delusional?" I ask.

"Yes." She points to her bag. "I brought help."

"Help" turns out to be three silicone cocks… two of them were *not* on her trophy shelf. They're smaller, different sizes… she planned to work her way up.

I feel both our surprise when the first one—drizzled with lube and oh, so slick—slides into her just as easily as my thumb.

"I am going to have to tell Margot about this," She pants as I work her open with the smallest dildo. "The lube, I mean. Not about how well you fuck me."

She grabs the second cock and hands it back to me. "I want yours. Don't tease me for too long."

When I swap them, this one doesn't slip in so easily and… my cock jumps when that resistance pulses a jolt of lust across our bond from her.

The pressure, the fullness... the way she loves it tightens a phantom fist around my cock.

She doesn't hand me the next dildo, so I skip it and press my cockhead against her lube-drowned ass.

Her fingers work her clit and she whispers "yes" over and over again as we ease together.

I can feel when her body relaxes and opens for me. I can feel when the pleasure starts to blossom.

Kimba's need shimmers through the bond before she's started to rock in that opposite rhythm.

"Not so delusional after all."

"If you could see the way you swallow my cock, Kimba." I shudder, and I feel it run through her in a tremor as well.

"Show me." The words are a whisper, but I feel them in the spike of desire.

Hands on her hips, I hold her in place as I move, dragging her back and then up against me so that I can turn us both.

Slinging her legs over mine, I sit, buried inside her as deep as I can go and letting gravity push her further down as she exhales on a whimper.

She looks at us in the reflection of the window and arches her back against me.

Her sweet, swollen pussy drips with the shimmering remnants of her cum and I stroke her, slipping my fingers inside. Slick with the evidence of both our desire, I fit three fingers in, so easily.

"I wish my hand was smaller," I say, the words soft against her ear. "I would shove my whole fist inside of you, just to hear you scream in pleasure."

"Try."

She's breathless and I'm tempted, but, "Not with my cock in your ass, Kimba. There's not enough room."

She lets out a breathless little whimper, but I'm not going to leave her unsatisfied.

I snatch the dildo we didn't use from the tangle of sheets, and she bites her lip as I squeeze lube onto it too.

KIMBA

I could look down, but the ghostly reflection of us captures my full attention as D pushes the dildo into my achingly empty pussy.

Holy fuck.

It's exactly what I asked for.

I'm so full I can barely think, and then his thumb flicks across my clit.

Crying out, I arch back and clench on him *so* tightly.

Women at Margot's had talked about this—though they'd meant two men.

It had been intriguing, but I'd never dreamed…

"Saints, D. I don't—" I can't imagine what I was going to say, how I planned to end that thought. D fucks me with the dildo and I pulse on his cock with every stroke.

I'm adrift in a sea of pleasure and all I can do is *feel.*

And I feel *full.*

D is close, but he's fighting it.

I don't want that.

Twisting and craning my neck, I draw his mouth to mine, kissing him and using my tongue to toy with his.

"I love the way you fit inside me D. I want you to cum in me." I want him to cum *on* me. I want to spend the rest of our lives locked together in one way or another and with the bond… we get that.

He curses under his breath and his fingers work harder at my clit. He comes a moment before I do. Head dropped back to his chest, I jerk and shudder and then I laugh.

He lets go of the dildo and it flops out of me onto the floor.

I expect him to lift me off of him. I expect the flood of cum… but he holds me tight, standing and staggering to the bathroom as cum leaks down the front of his legs.

"How many liters do you think your ass can hold?" he asks as he steps down into the empty tub and leans me over its edge.

"What to find out?"

We don't.

Neither of us is in a headspace to measure when he comes again.

We clean off and he draws a bath, holding me close.

Tomorrow we'll go back to a world that's trying to kill him.

Back to a world of monsters and murderers and responsibilities.

Tonight… tonight we're just two people from completely different worlds who found each other despite all the odds stacked against us.

I love him.

He loves me.

Everything else can wait.

CHAPTER
FIFTEEN

DRIFT

THE OUTPOST DIDN'T BURN down while we were gone. Trench and Arc are both still alive. The trip may not have uncovered my would-be murderer, but it did prove that I can leave them to their own devices for a few days.

Or, maybe not.

"What do you mean, there's been another cavrinskh attack?"

Riann grimaces, glancing away from his camera, and I wonder if the door to his office is open.

I hope not.

"There have been three more," he says.

"Why am I only hearing about them now?"

"Because they were all last night." Riann looks at me like he expects me to give away some secret. "While you were gone. It's like they knew."

"That's ridiculous," Kimba says as she comes to join me. "We know they're intelligent, but there's no way they're tracking individual movements."

Riann glances past me and dips his head, greeting her.

"Ridiculous or not, it's too big of a coincidence to ignore." He rubs his eyes and I can see the telltale signs... he hasn't slept in a few days. "No one sees them come in to the communities, no one sees them get back out. If we hadn't seen one in the incident involving Richter's mate mix up, I'd question if this wasn't just a weird cover up or attempt to blame the cavrinskh."

"Something has changed." Kimba says, slipping her hand into mine and squeezing. "We need to find out what."

"I think you need to get Trench digging a little harder. How do they say it on Earth?" He looks at Kimba. "Set him on fire?"

She tries to hold in her laughter, but it comes out as a snort. "I think you mean 'light a fire under him'?"

"Is that not the same thing?" Riann smiles, but I imagine he's embarrassed by the mix up.

"Not quite." She looks at me. "Maybe Trench needs some help? Fresh eyes... is there another brother who could help?"

"I have an idea." But I don't think anyone's going to like it. "I'll see if I can make it happen."

"You should know... all three of these men *also* have ties to the Company... One of them had two undocumented children. They've been run through every database we have. He wasn't their father and even though we have DNA matches, we can't find either parent."

A cold slither crawls through the bond and Kimba says, "That is a problem."

"Yes." A dull chirp echoes on his end and he mutters a curse under his breath. "I've got to go. But I know you wanted to be updated. If you can think of anything that might help me figure out where I should start looking for these guys *before* they get their throats torn out, that would be great."

"I'll see what we can come up with."

The screen goes black and my eyes adjust as I look down to Kimba.

She's still glaring at the darkness. "Why do they have children that aren't theirs?"

"I don't know." But I don't think I'm going to like the answer once we find it.

Kimba straightens her shirt and glances toward the door.

We're going to have company. Soon.

It's a meeting night.

"Here." I hand her the small case that was delivered a few hours ago. "If you have the same issues with Cindy... you're going to need those."

She pops it open and her brows quirk when she sees the two lenses, suspended in an inert solution.

"They're tinted, and they should help with the brightness, without making you act... oddly."

We'd agreed that we would take some more time to figure out the strange effect on her eyesight before we started asking questions of the other bonded women.

"Thank you." She goes to the bathroom on this level to put them in and when she returns, her eyes look black to me. I know they won't to anyone else.

"Just in time," she says, as a familiar teal car pulls into the garage.

Richter and Laurel are the first to arrive, but not by much of a distance. Core and Cindy are close behind. Hazard too.

They come in, greeting each other and congratulating Kimba. I watch for any sign they find her eyes odd, but they don't. And she doesn't wince when she sees Cindy.

226

As the rest of them arrive, I let them get settled. All of the brothers on this side of the caldera and their bond-mates—only three other women, right now—sit on that circular, sunken couch.

What few introductions are needed are made quickly and I tell them what we've learned.

Laurel's reaction to the cavrinskh and the dead Company men is as expected. Arc's... is not.

I watch him as he paces near the windows, but I don't tell him to sit down.

"I've done a little digging." Kilo says, and when Trench scowls at him, he says, "Discreetly."

"What kind of digging?"

"We all know there are people who don't want you here—in both of our home galaxies—I set myself up to be... approachable to that sort of person."

"And were you approached?" Kimba asks.

"Yeah." He points to the man on the screen whose skin is a deep caramel yellow. "By him."

There's a brief moment of pandemonium as the others start talking over him.

"Enough." Kimba pinches the bridge of her nose. "I don't need a headache. Let him talk."

Kilo smiles at her and dips his head. "Thank you, dajzha."

He scowls at the man in question. "He told me just enough to read between the lines, but not enough to actually incriminate himself if I was a CSS stooge." He turns and looks at Andrea and says, "What *is* a stooge?"

She looks at him like he's gone insane and then shakes it away. "I'll tell you later."

Nodding, he glances at Laurel. "Are you sure you want to hear this?"

"No, but tell me anyway."

227

"They're pulling women from the Agency roster by pairing them up with men who don't want them. 'Giving' them to men who don't qualify for bondmates and then putting the children into creches where they will have no human involvement whatsoever."

"They told you all of that?" Kimba asks, her disbelief echoes my own.

"Of course not. I followed them and let them talk to each other when they didn't know I was there." He glances at Kimba and the other three women with an apologetic wince. "I've left out the colorful commentary, so you didn't have to hear just how much these guys hate humans."

"Do you have names?" I ask.

He looks at me and unclenches his jaw. "Give me your CSS contact's information and I'll do what I can to help him find the others."

"You said they couldn't find the parents of the two children they found?" Cindy asks.

"That's right."

"Then they're either holding them somewhere... or they're dead." She says it with so much conviction, everyone turns to her.

She shrugs. "No woman who came here through the Agency's criteria would give her baby over and not be desperate to find it."

"She might be scared of reprisals," Hazard offers.

Kimba grimaces. I don't need to look at her to know it. "Did you meet this guy at Margot's?"

"Yeah, actually." Kilo says. "We don't really hang out in many other social settings, so I decided to start there. I got lucky."

"I'll give you the contact info," I say. "And I'm sure he'll have more questions."

"I don't see how any of this relates to you being on someone's 'hit list'." Hazard lounges in his seat, sipping on his coffee. "I mean, the escaped cavrinskh are a problem. The Company and these stolen kids are a problem... but do we think they're connected to Kimba being hired to kill you?"

"No." I say as she responds, "Yes."

She looks at me with pinched brows. "You cannot deny there's something here. All four of those men were in my garage with the guy we still can't find."

"If he hired men to go with him, it makes sense that he would have pulled from the Company's ranks. Bad men do bad things."

"I think she's right." Laurel says, staring me down.

I don't voice the question that leaps to mind. *Would you say that just to argue with me?*

"Me too." Cindy says. She doesn't look like she'd like to stab me just to see if the knife would sink through.

"Even if she isn't—and I'm not guessing one way or another—you should at least look into the possibility." Arc holds up his hands. "Stop thinking about this like you're invincible. Ric's the only one in this room that could take a bullet to the head and probably survive it. You are as soft and scraped up as the rest of us."

He runs his thumb over one of his own scars, as if he needs to prove his point. "But that is, of course, up to you."

KIMBA

The rest of the meeting is spent going over reports and observations since the last meeting.

Nothing said in this room truly required an in person

meeting. All of it could have been disseminated via comm, or relayed on a call.

But that's because it's not about the information.

I watch as Cindy and Andrea exchange notes. Laurel grills Kilo on the things he's learned… and Trench and Hazard talk about something I didn't catch to begin with and can't hear now.

These meetings are about making sure they come together. I look out at the Zone. The snow flurries are minimal tonight and from here, I can see the faint light of the closest outpost. They are so isolated, even from each other.

By the time they start to leave, I've heard Hazard demand a bakat rematch from Strike, Cindy has questioned me on my favorite baked goods and Andrea has let me know they're naming their weeun Kodi, after his mother, and that Margot managed to get mango imported for her.

D asks Trench to stay behind and I hang back with them, watching as the cold boys are the last to leave.

D's wrong about those three.

Shock and Risk aren't going to boot Arc out of their outpost. They're holding onto him for dear life.

They're so careful to constantly be in contact with him and he… something is broken, and I already know the three of them are going to have to figure it out on their own.

"I'm not saying 'no' to help. I just don't think you're going to find anyone willing." Trench offers me a smile as I join them. "As for the theory they chose to attack three men specifically because you were gone… how would they have known you were gone?"

"I thought it was ridiculous too," I say.

"Ridiculous or not," D glances at me. "We need to figure it out."

"I'll see if I can't figure out what's going on in their brains… with whatever pieces I'm able to collect."

He goes, and I take the lenses out. "They helped," I tell D. "But I don't like the way they feel."

"Me either."

He takes my hand and heads for the stairs. "Let's put those away and practice breeding you again."

CHAPTER
SIXTEEN

DRIFT

I LEAVE KIMBA SLEEPING, even though her exhaustion settles deep in my bones.

The sky is bright. No sign of a storm on the horizon… not even a cloud to obscure the moons that are still out in the pink haze of the morning.

I climb all the way upstairs before I turn on the news feed for the city. Even though I should pay attention to it regularly, I let it slip from my routine far too often.

Today, however, I want to know what the news is saying about the cavrinskh attacks… if they've started to figure that out at all.

It's loud enough I don't want it to wake Kimba. The man asleep on the couch behind me though…

Kilo has a strange aura around him. I've gotten used to it when other people are around—it's what tells me they can't see him—I didn't realize it happened when he slept.

The man slowly wakes up, and I ignore him as he finds his way back to consciousness.

The news is a constant drone, but it might give me time

to clear out my head and rattle free anything that might have gotten caught back there.

Automated reports scroll across the bottom of screens. Weather predictions for the next three days. Their reporting is a little different than the ones coming from the device in the far corner of the war room, but there's nothing on our readouts that will affect anyone but those of us up here.

Storms rolling in on the lower plains might give more water than anyone actually needs…

"You're up early," Kilo says as he opens the fridge. "I thought bonded men stayed in bed until mid day, if not longer."

"You have an outpost you could have waited at if you thought that was true."

"I could have, but I *didn't* know. And look at that, it's only been three hours since I got here. So, we both lucked out. You get to hear what I have to say. I get to go home and not have to come back."

"What did you find out?"

"Firstly, your contact is very rude. He would not see me, or even take a call. Secondly, the guys I've been able to pick out as working for the Company? They're spooked. I mean, I would be too if I found out monsters were hunting the people I associate with. Oh wait… monsters *do* hunt us."

He chuckles and scrubs a hand over his head.

"So you've hit a dead end?" I guess.

"No, I've found an opportunity."

I don't like the way he smiles.

"They're losing people left and right. It's time to start recruiting again."

"No," I say.

"You haven't even heard my pitch."

233

"I don't have to. I will not authorize you going in and attempting to infiltrate them."

He mutters under his breath. "I knew I shouldn't have told you."

"Kilo." I make him look at me. "Do not go looking for trouble."

He salutes me and leaves without actually promising me anything.

I'll deal with him later. He's not going to do anything today except go home and go back to sleep.

The news feed pulls up footage of Margot's. Lights blaze on the tall white walls, the parking lot is packed. There's nothing out of the ordinary.

Reading out a rote brief, the reporter provides her viewership with an update.

"The man who caused the damage last week that resulted in the outage at Margot's has been ordered to pay for the repairs required and attend mandatory therapy. According to the reports we've received, he has elected to pay the wages of every employee who was affected. But sources tell me that wasn't necessary, as Margot's employees were already compensated by the owner and many received tips from fans, even though they weren't able to visit."

She segues into a commentary on a new zurgle cafe that has opened downtown and I'm about to flip away when she grimaces.

"In less cuddly news, I'm afraid I must inform you of a death in Shiga Heights."

She says more, but I don't hear it.

My blood runs cold as I stare at the face of the dead man.

Kimba shakes my arm—

I didn't even realize she was holding it.

She blinks up at me, face pale. "What's wrong?"

KIMBA

He's stopped.

Frozen.

It's like someone hit the pause button.

Gaze locked on the wall screen.

When the dread that's on his face flushed through our bond, I moved without thinking. And now, when I turn to look at what's caught his attention, I'm glad I understand their language.

It's why I know that the man on the screen is dead, and that the fact he was murdered isn't the only reason he's being featured. He doesn't fit the pattern of the Company men who've died.

Mada Klen isn't a name I recognize, but it's clear D does.

"Who was he?"

D pulls in a long breath, shakes his head, and some of the warmth returns between us.

"He was a member of the council with Luthiel and I. One of the ones I know—I *knew*— who was never going to be okay with dropping that bomb."

The reporter offers her condolences and mentions the possible connection with other murders.

D stares at the picture. I know what he's waiting for.

They haven't said *how* he died.

I watch him a moment more before I leave him, still keeping an eye on him through the bond. I go to the closest console and tap through the string of commands required to shift the screen from the Zone databases to the nexus. I read as I close up the pants I'd barely gotten on before I'd raced upstairs.

"Mada was found in his office, with an antique Earth letter opener through his eye."

Nothing indicated there was a cavrinskh involved. But the article linked the other deaths the reporter referenced.

I open the larger article and two more faces enlarge on the screen next to Mada.

Three *new* deaths.

Nothing links them except for the length of time between their deaths—a few days—and the way that D looks at them now that he's joined me.

"More council members?"

He nods.

"Also on your side of the vote?"

"We were split five to four."

"One of them was killed the night I was supposed to try to kill you." I take a deep breath so I don't shiver. "This was always about you and the monsters. It wasn't about my past at all. I was just a bit of luck. An easy way to get to you."

I step aside as he pulls up another name. "Ganfrey's still alive—or they haven't found his body yet."

"They've gotten it down to a two-four imbalance. They don't have to kill him."

"Unless they know Luthiel isn't actually on their side. He'll tie any vote as long as the two of us are alive. And a tied vote is an automatic failure."

He puts through a call to Richter and Trench, and I read through Ganfrey's information as he fills the two brothers in.

The only other remaining member of the council who *doesn't* want to eradicate a species lives on the close end of town. He's unmated. He doesn't even have an application in with the Agency—

"I'm going to go warn him."

"*We* are going to go." I correct him as I go to the closet and pull my boots out. "Don't even think about trying to leave me behind."

"Of course not." He holds out a long-sleeved shirt, made of the same fabric as the suits they wear when they go out hunting monsters. "Put this on."

As far as I know, it's the equivalent of a bullet-proof vest.

I pull it on, yank my normal shirt back over top, and he hands me a gun. "You know how to use that?"

"It's been a while, but yes."

"Good. Let's hope you don't have to."

CHAPTER
SEVENTEEN

DRIFT

GANFREY LIVES IN A SMALL, historic community.

There are no gates, no security. Just centuries old architecture, and neighbors who actually talk to each other.

It's the middle of the week, and he might not be home, but I don't have another address. I don't even know if he has a job.

His door is frosted glass, and when I ring the bell, there's movement beyond the milky pane. Thank the saints.

"Drift?" His smile is laced with amused astonishment, until his gaze shifts behind me, then it contorts in confusion. "And Kimba?"

He looks like he's just gotten up. Robe belted, slippers on. It makes him look a lot older than I know he is.

"Can we come in?" I ask, while he's still distracted by her.

She might still be getting used to being famous, but I don't feel the same confusion she does at his awe.

Ganfrey recovers quickly, shaking the confusion away

238

and sweeps his hand toward the living room I can see from where we stand. "Of course. Anything for the brotherhood."

He steps aside and I let Kimba precede me. He watches her like he can't quite believe she's here.

He'll get over it.

A quick scan of Ganfrey's house is all I need to know he has no regard for his own safety.

It's all windows at the back.

There's not a curtain to be seen and the vast expanse of the grass, seemingly unending until it hits the foothills and the mountains that rim the exterior caldera.

"It's a beautiful view of the place you call home," he says, stopping beside me and smiling out at it. "If we could get the cavrinskh under control, I'd have already inquired about one of the empty outposts. The Zone is so beautiful, it is a shame it is relegated to the domain of monsters."

I don't know Ganfrey well enough to decide if he includes me in his grouping of monsters.

"To what do I owe this visit?" he asks, moving to stand behind his counter—close to the knives.

"Have you seen the news? Mada and the others are all dead."

"What?" Ganfrey's smile fades like melting ice and he blinks, too quickly. "Please tell me this is some sick joke."

"I wish I could. Someone tried to contract Kimba to kill me eleven days ago."

Ganfrey looks at Kimba, bewilderment on his face. "They thought she would kill you?"

Nodding, I look around the house, trying to see if anything is out of place. "You could be next."

"They asked your bondmate to kill you?"

"I wasn't his bondmate when this started." Kimba has

moved to the far end of the room, looking at the strange collection of things he has on display.

"But you've been seeing her at Margot's for—" His voice trails off and he looks away like he's doing math.

"How do you know that?" Kimba has turned back to him, fully and I don't know if he's seen her rest her hand on the gun.

"I try to keep track of everyone on the council—clearly I'm not doing a good job of it—and knowing what women they prefer at Margot's is part of that."

"But you didn't know we weren't bonded?"

"I don't go digging into files. I just observe what is presented to me."

I should have paid more attention too. "She's the only one I've let get close to me in the last six years. It could have worked... had circumstances been different and if she'd wanted the payment they offered her."

"I see..."

"I don't doubt they're coming for you, too."

"Unless," Kimba says, still studying him from the other side of the room. "You're the one who put out the hit."

"The *hit*." Ganfrey looks like she'd hit him with a handful of zurgle shit.

"What century do you think this is?" He catches himself and dips his head. "I apologize, you do not deserve the anger of my bewilderment. But I would never..."

"I've lived here long enough, I know that there are some things that span galaxies. A lot of you play at being more evolved than humans, but at the end of the day, our species are more similar than simply being able to mate."

While he doesn't look happy about it, Ganfrey doesn't argue any further. "I swear on my life that I am not behind this."

Kimba might still be suspicious, but I believe him.

"How is it possible no one's made the connection between those three?" He asks, scratching at the skin above his brow ridge.

Stalking around the room, I start to check the too-many windows. "How many people would know the link between the five of us?"

"Only the other members of the council and any CSS officials who have access to the databases."

"That narrows down your suspect pool, doesn't it?" Kimba asks, squinting out the window, like she might see something. But before I can follow her gaze, movement in Ganfrey's garage catches my attention.

Someone is moving around on the other side of the wall, trying to be as quiet as possible.

"Who else is here?"

"No one. I live alone…" Ganfrey's voice trails off, and I follow his narrowed gaze out the window. "That gate wasn't open when I got home."

The back of his property might be open to the field, but the sides are lined with panels of interwoven metal, the floral and vine design is broken.

Closed, the lines would blend seamlessly to the normal eye, open…

Whoever is in Ganfrey's garage, he's not good at sneaking around.

He's probably like Kimba, opportunistically set up to perform the task. I'd be amazed if Ganfrey doesn't know him.

"Your garage has access from the back yard?"

"Of course."

The door that leads out from this room is half-hidden behind a bushy red palm. When I get to it, watching the man move in the darkness on the other side, it's clear he's not there for a simple theft.

I spare a glance for Kimba. She's got the gun drawn. It's at her side, and I doubt that Ganfrey has noticed it.

"Turn off the lights."

Ganfrey shoots a confused glance at me, but he doesn't hesitate. And neither do I.

It takes two seconds to slip through into a corner of the garage. To wait and watch.

They work quietly, but with no attempt to hide themselves. Darkness always feels like safety to those intent on causing harm.

Too bad for him, I can see perfectly.

He's unfamiliar to me, but that doesn't mean anything. The ugly brick of a device in his hand when he turns, however, is something every boy old enough to watch an action flick has seen.

I let him get on his back, let him half shimmy under the car, then I grab him.

One hand on his neck. One on the wrist holding the bomb.

The man makes a sharp noise, but he doesn't speak. His eyes are so wide, I can only imagine what he thinks of me, a looming figure in the dark of the garage.

I'll let him keep thinking I am whatever creature he's come up with that has kept him silent.

I twist the brick out of his hand and drag him to his feet, hauling him back through the door into Ganfrey's house.

Kimba immediately lowers the gun she'd had raised and steps out from in front of Ganfrey.

"Do you know him?" She asks, not bothering to look at the man who would have tried to kill him.

"No. Wait, yes." Ganfrey leans forward on his counter,

studying the man. "You came to my office weeks ago, wanting to buy this house…"

Ganfrey looks from me to him and out to his garage. "This place isn't worth killing me over."

"I don't think that's why he was here." Kimba says, looking at Ganfrey instead of me when she asks. "Do you?"

"You think he was hired, the way they tried to hire you?"

"We could always ask." She's watching him, and I wonder if they can see the faint silver light behind her pupils.

She is changing. But that is a concern for another time.

"Why are you trying to kill me?" Ganfrey asks. "Were you hired?"

He nods, jerkily. "They told me I had to place that on the underside of your car, or else." Swallowing, the man looks between the three of us. "They were going to kill us."

"Us?"

"My partner and I."

"Chances are they were going to kill you either way." Kimba says, reholstering her gun.

"I sent him to Lasiana for a week, just in case."

I drop the brick on the counter—it's inert. "He was planting a bomb under your car. "

"Would it arm when he hit fifty?" Kimba asks, her snort of a laugh draws all our attention. But she waved us away. "Nevermind."

The man's pulse still throbs in his neck. He's frantic. Panic makes his tongue looser than it probably should be.

"I don't know how it was supposed to work or what it was supposed to do. I was just told to put it on the car."

"By who?"

"I don't know." He shakes his head, "I don't have a name. All I can give you is a description. But he knew things about me... things not even my partner does."

I see the movement, too late—too focused on what's inside, instead of what's out. I only hear the shot a second before it knocks him back into me and throws both of us to the ground.

KIMBA

As soon as the window shatters, I hit the ground. The second D's back touches the tiles, I scramble across the floor to him, using the furniture to block me from view.

The harsh "what the fuck" from behind the counter tells me Ganfrey was smart enough to take cover too.

Pressed against the cabinetry, he looks up, as if he's trying to see over the counter.

There's nothing to see.

No one outside... and I would see them.

Ganfrey whispers harshly. "I already called for the CSS when D told me he was in the garage. Do you think they'll get here in time?"

D is hurt, but not badly. It's the man laying over top of him that's the problem.

He's dead.

A limp weight on top of D, watching me with a death stare.

Underneath him, D is perfectly still, but that's because he's looking for the shooter, his clear pupils narrow and widen like a camera aperture.

When he relaxes, I relax.

"They're already gone. Help me get him off me."

I stand, and Ganfrey comes too, pulling the man away

and lowering him to the tiles in the same pool of blood that covers D.

The bullet went clean through the middle of the guy's chest, leaving him a glassy-eyed mess. But it didn't make it through the material beneath D's shirt. It embedded itself dead center.

Dead.

He should be too.

"I think I like this stuff," I say, plucking the mangled metal from where it was embedded. "If it keeps you alive, I'm a big fan."

He smiles, but it's not real. All of his focus is trained on the windows outside. He doesn't trust that we're safe yet.

"You *should* be dead." Ganfrey says, glaring at D's chest.

"Hurts like fuck, but it's not serious."

D draws me to him, turning us so he blocks me from the door when the CSS personnel kick it down and flood in.

Ganfrey glares at the officers. "I already have to replace a window and now my door. Knock next time, assholes."

"They tend to get over excited when someone calls in a murder. Especially when the caller says the murderer is still on the property." Riann doesn't look happy to see us. "Especially right now."

"I didn't say there was a murderer on the premises." Ganfrey pulls his phone from his pocket, scouring the alert he sent in.

"Actually, we got two calls." Riann looks between all three of us, stopping on Ganfrey. "Yours, of course, that's why *I'm* here, but they're here because someone reported three murders and a suicide."

"What?"

"An anonymous witness—we still don't know who he

was or how he called it in without his location being logged—told us an altercation had taken place."

"They thought they killed me and you two were next." D looks out the window again. "I'd guess they realized they didn't finish me off *after* they made that call."

"Is this related to the other thing?" Riann asks.

"I don't know."

"Why did they think they could sell this as a murder suicide?"

D glances at me, giving me the option to tell or not.

I pull Riann aside, and briefly explain. He looks disturbed, but accepts it and then says, "Maybe he hoped to paint the three of you in a similar light?"

"How?"

"Ganfrey is one of the many men who frequents Margots… that only goes when you dance."

Ganfrey looks at him, wide-eyed, and Riann shrugs.

It's D who says, "But they don't know that you're not there because you want her."

Riann scrolls through his device. "Even if your bank records try to tell a different story?"

"I appreciate the way you move," he says to me, before turning to glare at Riann. "Those records will also show that I don't use the facilities. I pay my membership fee, I tip for the dances, and I occasionally have a meal. There is no jealousy to stoke."

"No?" Riann asks.

Ganfrey looks at me. "You're beautiful, but not the kind of beauty I covet."

I think I understand.

While D and Riann argue over something else, I step closer to Ganfrey. "Do you want me to teach you some of the moves sometime?"

His eyes widen, just the smallest amount. "I would, thank you. If you have the time."

"Talk to Margot about ordering a pole for a guest room, if you'd rather do it here than there." I glance at the others before I say, "Or ask Margot to set you up with one of the other dancers if you'd be more comfortable. Several of them teach."

He nods, and I go to D's side.

"He's not going to like that." Riann says.

"I don't care what he likes." D nods toward Ganfrey. "I don't care what any of them like. *All* of the members of the council should have CSS details until we figure out what's going on."

"Even you?" Riann can't feel the irritation, but he can see it on D's face. "Look, I can warn them and offer. That's it."

"Let me know which ones don't take you up on it."

Riann gives him a curt nod, but I don't think he wants to agree to it.

"Thank you," I say, not sure D has remembered to in the midst of all this chaos.

"You're welcome. I haven't had a chance to get in touch with Kilo."

"He has some interesting insight. And he might be willing to tell you some of the less savory things." D glances at me. "He censored large parts of it for the women present."

I roll my eyes and that, at least, makes Riann smile.

"I'll call him as soon as we're done here," he says.

"Do." D's voice is brusque.

CHAPTER
EIGHTEEN

DRIFT

"WHAT DO you mean you can't get a hold of him?" It's been hours since we saw Riann at Ganfrey's, and the man doesn't look any happier.

"He hasn't answered or returned any of my comms."

When I don't answer him right away, Riann asks, "Do you need me to explain it in a different language?"

"He shouldn't be unreachable," I say, pulling up his outpost data.

"Well, when you get in touch with him, tell him I'm waiting on his call. I just had to explain to my boss why I haven't mentioned the cavrinskh connection yet and he spent an hour yelling at me like he hasn't been avoiding every other problem under him for the last month and a half." Riann hangs up and I immediately dial Kilo's comm.

No answer.

When I override the comm, there's no one to greet me but his zurgle.

It lounges on his couch, tail twitching as I call out Kilo's name.

Again, no response.

"What's going on?" Kimba asks, coming up the stairs, her hair still wet.

"Kilo isn't answering his comm and he doesn't seem to be at home." Through the comm video I can't see the things I would be able to if I was there.

"I'll see if he's at Margot's." She goes to make the call, toweling her hair.

I check the schedules. Fault *is* at Margot's, which means we're the closest.

Pulling out Kimba's coat and boots again, I grab my things. I already know what Margot is going to say.

"He's not there."

I hold out a hat. "It's quicker to get to his outpost by crossing the Zone."

There's a fizzle of uncertainty and I offer what I already know she'll refuse. "I can go alone."

"No way." She snatches the hat and pulls it down tight. "Let's go."

Once we both have our cold gear on and make our way to the lowest level, I start to worry.

Kimba doesn't.

"Front or back," she asks.

"Front." If a cavrinskh comes at us, I don't want it tearing her off of me.

But no cavrinskh attack. I don't see another living thing until we get inside Kilo's outpost and his powder blue zurgle watches us with contempt.

Kilo's outpost is meticulously clean, and he isn't here.

The only movement is the twitching tail of that zurgle that watches both of us with its star-filled eyes.

Perched on top of the kitchen island, it glares at us like a sentry. The low whistle of its disapproval tickles a nerve cluster at the base of my spine, telling me to get out.

"We'll leave in just a minute." I tell it, before going to the screen beside the door. "He's gone."

Kimba doesn't argue that we need to check the other levels of the outpost. "His car is here. Is he out in the Zone?"

"Bike's still here. He wouldn't have gone out on foot." I pull up the recordings and watch as Kilo leaves, hurrying down the drive and hopping into someone's car. But before he gets in, he turns back, as if inspecting the outpost. His lips…

"I might need help." I repeat what I see.

"What?" Kimba looks at the screen, glaring at Kilo's face when I replay it. "I don't see anything."

"Safe to say he knew I was going to be the one who saw this." I take the registration number from the car and shoot it over to Riann. "He'll get me the address before we get to town."

Kimba nods and turns to go. I pause, looking at Kilo's zurgle. "We're gonna go get him. Don't worry."

"Does it understand you?" Kimba asks.

"I've been told they might be able to. And if it can, I'd rather set it at ease, wouldn't you?"

The zurgle lets out a chirp and I tell myself I'm being ridiculous when I think, for a moment, that it's the creature's way of saying thank you.

"We'll take his car." I say, grabbing his neural link from a square dish by the door. "It'll be faster."

I don't get more than three steps before Kilo's zurgle hops onto my shoulder, claws digging in.

It lets out a low yowl before hopping down and going to paw at a tablet on the couch.

When I open it, I curse. "Nevermind.

Kilo was doing more than following and observing. He was tracking movements and keeping notes… and planting the cameras that now show him tied to a chair, having the shit beaten out of him.

"*Saints,*" Kimba whispers. "Where is this?"

Kilo has that marked on a map as well. "Remember those abandoned outposts I told you about?"

She nods.

"It looks like someone is squatting."

The car won't be faster after all.

KIMBA

"There's no way I'm going to convince you to go home, is there?" D asks for the fifth time as Shock and Risk join us. The cold boys blend into the icy landscape better than D does.

"No chance." I manage not to shiver.

"Arc is going to be so pissed off," Shock says as he slips off his bike and joins us. "He's all the way up in Ward's territory."

"Do I know him?" I ask. The name sounds familiar.

"No." D glares up at the outpost. "Someone's been making changes. There's a lot of Lasap paneling that wasn't there before."

I don't ask how they managed a renovation under the brotherhood's noses.

"What do you think they're hiding?" Risk asks. But he doesn't look up.

He's watching the Zone. We should probably all be paying more attention to it than we are.

I don't know which direction holds the least savory monsters, out or up.

All four of us know what D found the last time the Company was involved and Lasap was used.

D grimaces. "Whatever it is, I don't think we're going

to like it."

The lower entrance to the outpost is half iced over and very clearly hasn't been used in a while. Risk tosses Shock a blowtorch and the man gets to work melting.

"I can code it so that the sensors don't note that it's opened," D says as we stand in the cavern-like space that hides us from the outpost far overhead. "But the power isn't on, so it shouldn't anyway. We're going to have to manually open it and take the stairs."

"I haven't done my cardio yet today," I say, still trying to ignore the sinking ache in my gut.

Pulling up a map that projects over his hand, D points out Kilo's location, where the Lasap is. Two places where the hallways have been blocked off. They've encased a few hallways and bedrooms in Lasap.

I don't know how many people are on site. Including Kilo, I count six, but who knows how many are hidden behind that metal.

"Sure is nice to have someone who can do recon from outside." Shock says with a low whistle. "So how are we doing this?"

D looks at me, a question…

I don't have to answer Shock's if I don't want to.

He's giving me the choice.

I turn to the other two. "You two are *actually* cold, right?" I ask. "Like… won't trigger the thermal sensors up top cold?"

Risk nods, still watching the Zone. "And we have a knack for sneaking into places people don't want us to be."

"D and I should go in here. The two of you should circle around and go in from the side. That way if we run into trouble, they don't nab us all at once."

"Nab?" Shock asks, head tilting to the side as he kills

the torch.

It's the only word I didn't translate.

"Sorry, so they don't *catch us* all at once."

He tips his head in a curt motion.

D checks his guns' charge, and then mine. "Our first goal right now is to get Kilo out. We know he's there. I know we're all assuming they have something to hide behind that Lasap, but Kilo first. Then, depending on the state of him, we'll see how much more we can do right now."

The other two nod and go to their bikes, pulling climbing gear from the myriad of supplies strapped to the sides.

"I go first," D says.

"I know." I tap my chest and then his. "Even with this shirt on... you can bounce back from a harder hit than I can."

D opens a panel beside the door, connecting wires that don't look like they've seen electricity in a decade and when he's satisfied, Shock comes over and helps him pry the door open.

It lets out a horrific shriek. We all go still.

But Drift looks up, watching the things none of the rest of us can see and after a moment, he nods. "No one heard us."

"Good." Shock steps aside and helps me over the hatch, and once we're inside, he wishes us good luck and helps close it again.

The lowest level of this outpost is pitch dark and I hesitate.

"How well can you see?" He asks.

"Everything is pale gray lines..." Everything is vectors and grids.

"Welcome to my world."

"This is what you see?"

"It is right now." He starts for the far wall and the open doorway there.

More darkness, but the stairs that zig zag back and forth, leading upward. It feels like I'm in an old, low-res video game, but I don't say a word as we climb. Up and up… until we get to a door with no markings.

D pauses at it, pressing his hand flat against the panel and I catch his wrist, stilling him.

"Make me a promise, okay?"

He dips his head until our foreheads touch. "Anything."

"Don't make me a widow twice over."

"We will both walk away from this, Kimba." He kisses me, so sweetly… "Do you think anything in this universe would stop me before I've had the opportunity to breed you in truth?"

He takes a deep breath and his exhale is a growl. "We have our futures to live for. The saints know what I would do to them if they took me to meet them before I was done with you."

He kisses me once more and then releases me.

I stay back as he eases the door open. There's light on the other side… but it's a distant light, creeping into the hallway he leads me out into.

"The walls are lined with Lasap," he says quietly. "I can't see around corners here."

I look down the hallway cluttered with crates and drop cloths and discarded Lasap panels. "Okay. We take it slow and we're careful."

Easier said than done.

Before we get to the next corner, two men turn it.

"Hey!" One shouts in surprise and D shoves me to the side as a light flicks on.

The flashlight is blinding, and I stumble, off balance, falling behind the crates.

There's a scuffle and I try to get myself upright but…

FREEZE.

It's not a word, but a feeling that shoots across the bond.

It's a command that I obey without even thinking.

I don't move a muscle as the struggle on the other side of that short wall comes to an end.

I can't hear what D says to the men who have him. But one thing quickly becomes clear.

They don't know I'm here.

The sharp and heavy feeling coming through the bond doesn't ease until silence has fallen once more.

I untangle myself from the trappings of their renovations and get myself upright. The men are gone and so is the light they brought with them, but there are windows on this level and they let the moonbeams in. They wash the metal walls in pastel hues and it's enough that my eyes don't turn everything to those eerie lines.

Hand on my gun, I listen for any sound that might hint they're coming back, and then I make a choice.

I head in the opposite direction of the one they took him.

Kilo first.

I know where he is, and I'm going to want backup when I get to wherever they've taken D.

There's no other artificial light—no one to run into—until I get to the room where they are holding Kilo.

This outpost is massive, and they've got him in one of the myriad bedrooms on the second floor.

Two Sian stand with their guns trained on Kilo and their backs to the door.

They're not worried about a rescue.

There's a fire that paints the room in strange shadows and orange light.

I switch the gun to shoot an electric stun pulse instead of the energy impact bullets and step out of the shadows so that Kilo can see me.

He jerks a little when he notices, and his eyes narrow.

"Think you hit me too hard, boys." Kilo says, rolling his head to the side. "I'm seeing a beautiful woman." He chuckles. "And she certainly wouldn't be here alone.

The one on the left of the door tells him to shut up. The one on the left tells his compatriot that Kilo's just hallucinating again.

Kilo chuckles in the chair he's been tied to. His jaw doesn't look right. It's been dislocated.

"I think I asked too many questions, boss." Kilo looks up at me and winks with the eye that isn't swollen shut.

I think they were reeling him in from the beginning.

"Don't worry about this, I've been hit harder by half dead cavrinskh. These guys have done everything I've wanted them to. Playing right into my hands."

But the two men with guns trained on him smile like they've got everything under control.

They still haven't looked back at me to check whether I am a hallucination or not.

Too bad for them.

I shoot them both, the second man jerking from the impact a moment before the first hits the ground.

"I get that you're not a cold-blooded killer, boss lady, but it would be better for all of us if those ones don't wake up."

"You're lucky they didn't turn around."

He shakes his head. "I got them ready for you. Claudia told me the story of 'the weeun who cried wolf,' and I remembered."

"The point of that story is to stop you from telling lies."

Chuckling, he says, "And yet, I learned the correct lesson."

He rotates and stretches his wrists when I get him untied. "Have you lost feeling anywhere?"

"No, just a little rope burn. I'll be fine." He gets to his feet, but he wobbles a little.

I'll ignore it until I think it's going to cause a problem.

"Who did you bring with you? Or did you actually come to get me by yourself?"

"D and I got separated." I glance out the window at the rocky mountainside, glad I can't see the others. "Risk and Shock are here too."

"If those two are here, then Arc will no doubt turn up at just the wrong time too."

"Then we better have everything ready for him when he decides to crash."

"Crash and burn." He snorts and stretches out his shoulders. They both pop, horrifically, before he picks up both men's guns. He inspects them, checking the safeties and doesn't look at me when he says, "You might want to turn away."

There's something in his tone that tells me I can't argue with him. So I turn toward the door. I don't watch.

Both shots are quiet and I shiver as Kilo passes me and heads for the hall. He checks both directions, signaling the all-clear and then asks, "Where are we headed?"

It should unsettle me that he waits for my direction.

But it's not who I was that makes him do it. It's who I *am*.

I made a choice when I took D for my own. This was part of the package deal.

I lead, I don't linger.

CHAPTER
NINETEEN

DRIFT

THE MEN who caught me shove me to my knees in the middle of what would be this outpost's living room.

There's a fire in the fireplace and four more in places that no fire should ever be. But they're contained… and it means the space isn't freezing.

I already know that Kimba didn't head back downstairs and hope that Shock and Risk could deal with the problem I've gotten myself into.

I didn't actually expect her to.

I feel her irritation and assume she found Kilo. I feel her relief, followed by a brief shock, but not sadness, just determination—someone's dead, and I don't think she meant for them to be.

That tells me Kilo's in good enough shape to squeeze a trigger.

The two of them are going to need surprise on their side.

Four guns are trained on me from a safe distance away. Four men watch me, warily.

One of them stares at me as he speaks into a comm. "We got him. Yeah. The freak you told us about with the eyes."

The freak with the eyes. I laugh at that description.

The man's pulse jumps at the sound.

"Should we blindfold him?"

I don't hear the response, but I see the disappointment.

He won't hold eye contact with me.

Good.

The blindfold wouldn't have changed anything for me. It would simply have set him at ease.

There's a screech behind me, and a door opens from a room they built when they butchered the original floor plan.

I thought I'd be surprised when I finally figured out who was behind this, but I just feel foolish for writing him off so early.

"It's such a pity that shot didn't kill you this afternoon. I didn't think you'd wear body armor for a social call, more the fool me."

I watch Roiban in the reflection of the windows. "Somehow, I thought you were above getting your hands dirty like this."

"Oh I *am*. You've dragged me down to your level." He chuckles. "I had to bring my own power with me to camp out in your backyard. It's disgraceful."

"You should have told me you wanted to move in. I could have warned against it."

He goes to the kitchen, and I see the glow of a small generator that explains the light when he opens the refrigerator.

He doesn't say another word as he makes himself a drink.

259

The other four men keep all of their attention on me, but I don't take mine away from Roiban.

"Why are you so desperate to drop that bomb?" I ask.

"Because Earth is a scourge and the longer we leave ourselves open to them… the more our society will plunge into darkness."

I wonder if that's the line he uses to recruit.

All four of the men with us look like they've heard it before.

Roiban keeps his distance, walking behind the men with their guns trained on me. "Where is that sweet little dancer of yours? Do we need to collect her from your home? Or were you stupid enough to bring her with you."

Like the others, he doesn't meet my eyes. He looks at the pale green liquor in his glass, swirling it and watching the blintz berries bobble about.

"Honestly, I'd written you off as a loss. I was going to deal with Ganfrey and then it would just be you and that spineless Luthiel standing in my way. Then it would be so easy to get rid of the monsters you've all been so protective of."

"A statement like that would get your teeth knocked in if you said it to any of the brotherhood."

"And yet, here you are and all of mine are still in place."

"Untie me. See how long that lasts."

He snorts and sips at his drink. "How did you do it, by the way?"

"How did I do what?"

"How did you train them to hunt my men down?"

My men.

"You're running the Company?"

He grimaces. "I loathe that disgusting word. They want to be here and they can't even choose a word from our language? No. I'm not *running* anything for those Earthly spies. I'm taking advantage of their idiocy. But you still haven't answered my question. How did you do it?"

"I didn't." I look at the flurries starting to swirl out the windows, trying to find Kimba in the reflections. She's close. "No one controls them. They're not pets."

He stares at me, eyes narrowing just a little bit. "You're not lying."

"No, I'm not."

Roiban goes a little pale, tipping the entirety of his glass back and throwing it into the fire. "Well, *that* is terrifying. Isn't it?"

KIMBA

I don't like what I see.

I *do* like that I can see it from all the way back here.

"If I sent you in there to deal with it… how long will your 'you can't see me' thing work?"

Kilo shrugs. "As soon as they register me as a threat… I could probably kill two of them before they realized what was going on."

If direct action voids his "ignore me" privileges, we're going to have to hide him as long as possible.

I watch as the man from my parking garage speaks to D.

They know each other. D's calm. He's not *happy*. But he doesn't feel the threat is imminent.

I don't like being here when he's there.

"I think we're going to need to stall until the other two get here." Handing Kilo my gun, I say, "Stay close, but don't let them know you're here until you have to."

"What are you—"

He doesn't finish his sentence. He bites back a hissed

version of my name as I step out into the firelight with my hands raised. I can still see him in my periphery, but he's haloed in a strange aura.

I ignore that. I can't afford to give him away. If we make it out of here, I'll ask later.

"I heard you were looking for me."

All four guns turn toward me for a split second and then—as the men process me as 'not a threat'—they go back to D.

"*Nadine*," the man says with an ugly smile.

"That's not my name."

He rolls his eyes at me. "How kind of you to join us. At least I can count on you not doing what he's told you to do either. Check her."

The man closest to him hesitantly holsters his gun and makes his way to me. The pat down I receive is thorough, but not because he enjoys it.

I know when men want to touch me. He doesn't.

"Nothing," he says, quickly backing away and pulling his gun once more.

The man glares at me. "Pity, I thought you had a better sense of self preservation."

I go to D's side. He doesn't try to stand, so I place my hand on his shoulder and he rests his head against my hip.

"I still don't know your name," I say as I register this strange sense of peace.

It's faith. D's and mine reflecting through the bond. Faith that the brothers with us won't let this end badly. But more than that... Faith that whatever is about to happen is better, as long as we face it together.

"His name is Roiban." D says. "Not only is he the most vocal about the bomb... he's the one who made the CSS facial recognition software."

That's why the name is familiar. Luthiel mentioned him.

"It ignores me," Roiban says with a too-smug grin. "And I don't show up in any searches. It's quite helpful when you don't want to be found by a woman who can't do anything right."

"I can do quite a few things right."

Roiban sits in an ugly chair and smirks at us both. "To be completely honest, I never expected her to kill you. I expected her to try... but, well, look at you. I thought you'd protect yourself and snap her pretty little neck." He shrugs. "Either way, I would have gotten what I wanted."

"D, out of the way." I don't have to guess. He's not that creative.

"You're ineffectual. You and the rest of your mutated mercenaries." He waves a dismissive hand at the Zone out the window. "You're not protecting us. You're guarding a fence... one that has holes in it. And until we can get rid of the creatures once and for all, we won't be able to get rid of this disgraceful connection with Earth."

Roiban looks at me and lets out an exaggerated sigh. "You're only good for one thing. I hoped you might have more uses, but you're just harmless."

"You might think differently if I had a gun."

D's grip tightens on my leg and a warmth-like warning sizzles through the bond.

But I've already said it. I'm not going to back down.

"You're not a killer, sweet little *Kimba*." Roiban pouts at me like I'm a child. "I should have known that from the beginning. But my research had some unfortunate holes."

He studies me like he's looking for something he hasn't seen before. "We both know you wouldn't have actually hurt Jax if he hadn't put you into that broken bond blood fury, so don't pretend like you'd be able to shoot me now."

D drops his head and I can feel him grimace.

"Give me a gun and find out."

D is eerily calm in the bond. I don't know what he's thinking. I don't know if he's seen something, and I can't risk trying to find it if he has.

Roiban tips his head to the side, amused disbelief in his smile. "Why not?" He motions to one of his goons. "Give her your gun."

The other man looks at him like he's lost it, but after a moment's hesitation, he pulls the clip from his gun. There's still one in the chamber.

"Looks like your guy thinks I'll do it. He doesn't want the second one to have his name on it."

Roiban smiles so widely, it makes *my* jaw hurt. "Do it."

The man backs away, quickly.

The safety release issues a loud snap and I level it at him. He's wearing the same material we are. A body shot isn't going to do anything but knock him backward.

Whether I pull this trigger or not, we're not walking out of here. Might as well make it count.

Maybe I didn't want to kill the men Kilo dealt with… but they weren't actively trying to kill the man I love.

It's been so long since I've been at a shooting range, but the basics never change.

Exhale, squeeze the trigger.

Roiban takes my preparation for uncertainty. "Harmless, just like I sa—"

Roiban curses so loudly it echoes off the window

He moved at the last moment, but I still hit him.

I throw the gun to the floor, it's useless now. And Roiban is sadly still standing, only missing a chunk of his ear.

The blood flows freely and I watch him clutch at his head, struggling to staunch it.

"You little bitch!" His furious shouts make me wince. "You shot me! How fucking dare you."

It never ceases to amaze me how hypocritical murderers are.

The men with their guns move nervously, almost as if they've been told *not* to do more than contain us.

Roiban runs through more curses than I can translate and for a moment, D actually seems worried.

Still raving, he looks down at me, glaring darkly. "This would have been so much easier if you'd just died like you were supposed to. Now there are inquiries and questions will be asked when you disappear... but don't worry. They'll never find your bodies."

He drops his hand, and the gory remains still drip onto his shoulder.

He picks up the gun, and one of the others tries to tell him, but he tells them to fuck off, all of his anger is focused on me.

"Don't worry. I'll bury you together, in the traditional way. I can't begrudge a couple in love." He says the last word with such contempt...

A cold slither makes its way across the bond.

"At least I know how to deal with you both at once." He levels the gun at me and I wait for the click of the empty chamber.

I don't hear it.

A pale green blur knocks me off my feet.

CHAPTER
TWENTY

DRIFT

SEEING Arc before anyone else didn't prepare me for what he was about to do.

Still covered in ice, he darts from a dark hallway, vaulting over Kimba. I barely have time to throw myself to the side to cushion her fall before she hits the ground.

No one catches Roiban.

His head hits the ground with a sickening crack. For a moment, the four men watch, unmoving, guns held ineffectually in front of them as Arc gets him on his belly.

They didn't see Risk and Shock enter right behind him, or Kilo step out of the shadows.

Arc kicks the gun to Kimba as she rolls off of me, but she doesn't reach for it. She unties me with hasty fingers, trusting the others to deal with the larger problem.

By the time I'm freed, the others have them contained and Arc drags Roiban's unconscious body to the center where the rest have been gathered.

Shock makes them kneel the way they made me, I ignore the reversal.

"The CSS will be here shortly," I tell the ones who are still conscious. "Better get your stories straight before they do."

"Assuming you make it that long." Kilo looks down at them with a glower that makes me think *maybe* he shouldn't be left alone with them.

The way Kimba watches him, I know she's not leaving him unsupervised.

The men who guarded him are definitely dead

There's a phantom of a movement... not a threat. Something else.

Shock lunges for Arc and I drag Kimba away from them.

Shock grabs Arc by the throat and slams him against the wall. "Do you have a death wish?"

Arc stares at him for a moment and I almost step in, but Kimba places her hand on mine and gently shakes her head.

When Arc speaks, it starts with a scoff. "The correct response is 'Thank you—'"

Shock lets him go so quickly Arc actually yelps as he slides to the ground. Cursing, Shock walks away. And still, Kimba doesn't want me to get involved.

Still on the ground, Arc looks up at us all, an annoyed scowl carving lines around his lips. "Even if he'd shot me, the gun would never have gotten to a place it could do damage."

"The gun wasn't loaded." Kimba says.

Arc looks at Kimba and then up at Shock, "Then why the hell are you so mad at me."

"Because you didn't know it wasn't loaded, asshole."

"And," Risk says, calmly, "There were four others that were."

I leave Risk to play referee between the two of them and go to the door Roiban emerged from.

I expect an office... I find more crates. More construction materials.

"What's in the crates?" Shock asks.

He still looks pissed. Maybe getting him away from Arc is a good idea.

There's a pry bar beside the table stacked with fasteners, and it takes less than a minute to pop the top. We place the lid to the side, and I snatch Shock's wrist before he can dig through the packing.

"Don't."

Shock cautiously takes his hand back. "What is it?"

A contingency plan.

Stepping back out into the room, I count the crates.

Too many.

And I don't remember how many more we passed on the way up here.

Kilo stares down at the tied up quintet, flicking his gun's safety on and off again.

I go to the man on the floor that looks the *most* freaked out, the one who looks the most likely to talk.

"How many bombs are on site?"

I ignore the curses from behind me.

"Bombs?" The man looks frantically toward the others. "I don't know what you're talking about."

"He's lying," Kilo says what I already know. "Let me shoot one of them. That should get the others talking."

"We don't know, okay." The one with his back to me says it, exasperated. "Roiban told us to be careful with all of the crates, but they can't *all* have bombs in them."

"Why not?" Kimba asks, looking down at him with her own gun drawn.

Four pairs of very wide eyes watch her. They're terrified.

I don't set them at ease.

He swallows and stammers. "Th-there's over three hundred crates here."

"And what else is in the crates?"

"I didn't ask."

"It's supplies." The one next to him shifts and Kilo stills him with a boot to his groin. "I swear! We needed supplies for them until we moved them."

"You're going to need to get more specific," Kilo says, flicking the safety again.

"The women."

"Shut up!" The first guy who lied shoves him with his shoulder, but he doesn't stop.

"There are cells downstairs. We converted the bedrooms. We needed food, supplies. Even though we weren't keeping them here long. They were going to—"

"I said, shut up!"

Throwing himself into the other man, the first tries to... Honestly? I don't know what he's trying to do.

Muttering under her breath, Kimba shoots him. The electric pulse knocks him unconscious. Then, she shoots the others. Even Roiban for good measure. "Hopefully a little time out will get us better answers when they wake up."

"Should we fold them up, put them in crates and get a drone to take them to CSS headquarters?" Shock asks.

"No. I don't trust them to make it there."

Kimba purses her lips and looks at the crates scattered around the room. "So now, we have to check them all, or play crate roulette."

"What is roulette?" Risk asks.

From the looks on the others' faces, none of us know.

"Earth gambling game with a wheel… I'll explain it later." She waves the question away.

"When the CSS officials get here, we need to make sure they are *very* careful." I tell them. "You start opening these ones to see what we have. Kimba and I will head downstairs and see if we can find the cells."

"Kilo, too," she says.

"Don't trust me?" He grins at her.

"Until you get checked out, I don't plan on letting you out of my sight."

"She doesn't want you to find a corner where you can curl up for a nap and never wake up again." Arc says, popping the top off of the first crate and gently moving the packing aside.

He grimaces as he pulls a can of spray paint from his belt and marks it with an ugly orange X.

Kimba nods toward the hallway and Kilo doesn't argue. He goes, almost meekly.

Maybe he is in worse shape than I thought.

We find the cells on the third level down.

Interior bedrooms, "converted" to cells with new locking mechanisms.

"Physical keys again?" Kimba asks. And when I confirm, she runs back upstairs to search Roiban and the others for keys.

Once we're alone, I glance at Kilo. "You okay?"

"I'm pissed off, but I'm in one piece." He glances up at the ceiling. "Those assholes didn't do anything worse than the cavrinskh have. It was almost a treat."

I can't appreciate the sarcasm, but Kimba rejoins us, four sets of keys in her hands.

"One of these has to work, right?"

All four rings have the right key. I only take one set to

pull the correct one from the tangle and then hand it back to her.

"They'll be less scared if you're the one opening the door."

She nods. "Stand out of sight for me?"

Kilo moves before I do, and she turns the key. We all hear the lock disengage. But she hesitates.

Suspicion and a matching scowl...

She steps to the side as she opens it and a shoe flies out, smacking the opposite wall.

It was aimed for a Sian head, so it wouldn't have hit her. But she cautiously peeks her head around the frame.

"I promise we're not here to hurt you."

The collective sigh of relief is loud enough I can almost *feel* it. She steps inside. I listen as she lets them know Kilo and I are out here. She explains the situation and then hands one of them the key.

"We're not going to trap you here, but it will be safer if you stay here until the CSS gets here."

The women agree, and Kilo hands the one her shoe back.

I'm not surprised when they test the key to see if she's lying, but they don't venture out.

We repeat the process twice more.

Five, five, and six. Sixteen women who should be with mates who would care for and protect them... not in the hands of someone like Roiban.

With that information, I step aside and call Riann.

"We're on our way," he says as he answers. *Irritation* isn't the right word for the tone in his voice.

"There are some developments you need to know before your men get here."

"Go ahead."

"Firstly, I have five men in custody."

271

"Alive?" he asks.

"Yes." I glance toward Kilo. "Several others are not."

"Okay." He exhales. "What else am I walking into?"

"You're going to want to call for bomb disposal."

There's a hesitation on the line and then a curse, "Do I need to hold my men back?"

"I don't think so. The man in charge wouldn't have risked being inside the blast." I hear him relaying information to someone else. "And we have sixteen women in makeshift cells."

"Have him get ahold of Rose." Kimba says and I nod.

"I'll give you the information for a woman who works with a foundation in Gongii. She might be able to help with Agency efforts to re-place them."

"Anything else?"

"Not yet."

"We'll be there soon." Riann hangs up so I turn back to Kimba.

"Can we leave Kilo here for five minutes to update the others?"

She looks at him—sitting on a crate that was open before we got here which has towels instead of bombs. "Only if he promises not to wander off."

"I promise." He looks at the doors. "If they need something, I'll be here."

Kimba leads the way back upstairs, and I don't like the amount of paint I see.

Risk draws an X on the last crate. "Did you find them?"

"Yes. They're safe and in one piece."

"Good." He shoves his paint can back into his belt. "How long before the CSS gets here and can get them out of here."

"I don't know, but—"

"*Saints.*"

There's a low growl, and we all turn toward the shadow of the hallway…

Eyes glowing gold in the firelight, the cavrinskh stalks out of the darkness.

Staggering backward, Risk pulls his gun, and I have to knock his hand down. "We can't risk hitting a crate."

"How the hell did it get in here?" Risk asks, still gripping his gun.

Cursing, Arc holsters his and pulls a knife. "I may have left the door open in my haste."

The creature stalks around the room, keeping close to those crates, as if it knows…

KIMBA

I can't take my eyes off the monster in front of me.

It clacks its beak-like mouth at us, its jaw separating in three places to manage it.

"What do we do?" I ask, quietly.

None of us move.

"Don't let it get behind you." Shock says.

"Right, but what do we do?" I ease my grip on my gun. "Would a stun pulse set off the contents of one of those crates?"

"No, but it would also just make the thing mad," Arc says.

The hair on its back rises and the firelight shifts… changing the color. But its black claws don't change.

It stalks forward on six ugly legs that could probably tear any and all of us to pieces.

"We need to get it in front of the window." There aren't any crates there.

Arc gestures toward the unconscious men in the

middle of the room. "Or I could throw one of them at it so the rest of us could get away."

The thing paces, watching us like it doesn't really want to advance.

The dark spot on its forehead seems to glow and it turns as if someone's called its name.

But there's no one in the shadows.

I see the movement a moment before one of the men in the center of the room wakes. Before the screaming starts.

The one that's woken struggles at his bindings, screaming and thrashing... the cavrinskh pounces.

I lurch backward, straight into D's arms and he lifts me, turning us both as he bolts for the hallway.

I don't see that man die, but I *hear* it. The sickening sound races after us.

D doesn't let me go until we're down the stairs.

"We just left them?"

"I, for one, am not upset that they turned into a snack." Arc says, checking his guns again.

"Even four to one, the likelihood that all of us made it out of there in one piece and without setting off a bomb that killed all of us..." D looks back up the stairs. "We don't stand a chance against them in close quarters."

"And if it's us, or people who deserve to be eaten," Arc says, pausing in front of a door and touching the metal as if he's checking for a fire. "I'd much rather it be them."

He pushes the door open to an empty bedroom with a wide window, kicking a crate inside. "We've got to take advantage of its dinner break."

The cold boys start moving crates out of the way. D shifts Lasap panels over the corridor openings. Setting up the only path the monster will have to get to us.

I know a killbox when I see one.

Shivering, I step into the room with its stacked crates,

keeping out of the way. This room isn't lined with Lasap… it looks like it might have been next on the list though.

But when I step fully inside and turn around, back to the wall of windows, it's my turn to curse.

I don't know how D missed it. I don't know why Roiban broke through to this room… but I can see up into the level above… and the crates of explosives aren't the only things up there.

"We have a problem!"

I barely manage to get the words out and scramble backward from the hole in the ceiling before the shadows shift, and the thing falls from it like a sack of bricks.

The cavrinskh rises from where it's fallen. Roiban is underneath it, whimpering as his head lolls on the floor.

Blood slicks the monster's beak, its claws, even part of its tail… the cavrinskh latches one set of its claws into Roiban's chest as it stalks toward me, dragging him along too.

"Wait." D shouts, though not at me. And I can't focus on the argument that ensues.

The cavrinskh backs me into a corner, jaws snapping. The low rumble of its growl ghosts heat across my skin.

Window to my left, hard rock at my back, there's nowhere to go.

"Stay still, Kimba. You're not going to enjoy this."

Arc takes aim, but Shock grabs his hand at the last minute, shouting "No."

The window explodes beside me and the scream of the wind is so loud, I don't hear what they shout at each other this time either.

Shivering, I lock eyes with the creature. It should have lashed out or pounced. Hell, it should have flinched with the glass burst.

But it stares at me, tail twitching and beak chattering.

The dark spot at the center of its forehead pulses.

If I raise my gun to shoot it, it will snap my arm clean off.

If I don't…

It jerks its head away, as if it's been slapped.

Huffing and gruffing, it's almost like it's arguing with itself. And then, it goes startlingly still.

Roiban mutters something and I don't breathe as the cavrinskh raises him up between us.

The creature studies him for a moment, and then snaps his neck. I draw in a sharp breath covering my eyes and trying to squeeze even further back into the corner. But I can still see it through the spaces between my fingers. It drops Roiban to the floor and with a disgusted sound, it leaps out the window.

The tension that had held me disappears and the only reason I don't drop to the ground is because D catches me.

I take a few deep breaths and remind myself that it's gone.

D's eyes trace over me, looking for any sign… "You're okay?"

"I'm okay." I nod and he releases me. He'd know if I was lying.

Swallowing back the ugly coil of panic, I turn to the window and look out at the crater left behind in the snow.

The cavrinskh isn't dead. It struggles to its feet, shakes itself off, and sprints back for the interior caldera.

"Do you think there are others?"

"No." He says, glancing at the cold boys. "But we won't be taking any chances, either."

Arc and Risk pull their guns and start a sweep of the lower levels. Shock goes up to let the CSS contingent in.

Kilo joins us a few minutes later. "Arc took over and sent me up."

He sits on a crate and groans. "Am I going to get a few days off to recover?" He asks. "Or are you going to take those away from me because I went poking around after you told me not to?"

"Get your strength back." D says. "But you are definitely on my shit list."

The last words—said in English—makes me laugh. Laughing makes me cry.

D picks me up, rocking me and whispering gentle words I barely hear as the stress and fear leaves me in streams of salty tears.

I feel puffy and gross when I ask him to let me down, but I also feel better.

"*Saints and sorrows.*" Riann's curse turns our attention.

All three of us look to the door as he steps through and stops dead in his tracks.

He covers his mouth with his hand and looks around the room, unblinking. "How in the everliving fuck am I going to clean up this mess?"

"I'd suggest starting with a mop?" Kilo says, laughing and then grabbing his ribs with a groan.

Riann goes to his side and catches him before he can actually fall. Still listing to the side, Kilo smiles, but it flickers with pain. "My hero."

Riann does not look amused. "The power's not on, I assume the medfac won't be working either?"

"There are generators…" D looks at Kilo. "Are you actually that bad off, or are you being an asshole?"

Kilo sits up, chuckling. "If he had taken my calls, I might not have met so many fists today, so excuse me if I feel like he deserves to take care of me a little."

Riann lets him go, stepping back, and Kilo falls to the floor.

"Ow," he winces, not getting up. "I might need a medic."

Riann calls up for one and I look past him to see human CSS officers following Shock downstairs.

"Roiban's dead." I look down at the mangled remains. "We aren't going to find any more answers in this room."

And I don't want to be here anymore.

CHAPTER
TWENTY-ONE

DRIFT

THE SUNS HAVE ALREADY RISEN by the time we get home. Everything that can be taken care of has been. And Kimba needs to sleep.

"We both do," she says, yawning as she slips off her boots. "That's what you were thinking right? That *I* need to sleep."

I nod and help her out of her coat. "A lot happened yesterday."

"True. And there is some of it that I would prefer to never think about again. But the part you seem to be missing is that *we* need to sleep."

"There's going to be pandemonium in the council." I can already imagine the reactions to the truth.

"But that's not our problem until after we've woken up." She takes my hand and tugs me downstairs.

"We still don't know why the cavrinskh knew to go after the Company men."

"I really want another name for them." She doesn't hesitate on the threshold of our room. "And we aren't going to come up with any answers while we're exhausted."

She pulls off her clothes and goes into the bathroom, moving through the room in complete darkness...

"You can still see?"

She nods as she turns on the water. "It's lasting longer."

Stepping under the spray, she beckons for me, and I go to her.

"We almost died today."

I pick her up, my teeth going to her throat. "We did."

"Let's stop doing that, okay?"

I huff a little laugh against her skin. "I will do everything I can to make sure it doesn't happen again."

"I'm going to hold you to that."

We clean up, dry off, and when we lay down, Kimba nestles beside me, letting out a long sigh. I let the contentment I feel in her weigh me down. That peace drags me under, so quickly... and when I wake, Kimba's not there.

I reach out for her in the bond and follow the teasing sensation that I get in return. She's on the floor in the living room, stretched into an odd shape. I know how it *feels*, but that doesn't change how it looks.

"Good afternoon," she says, unfolding and then hopping into my arms. Once she's kissed me, she gently nudges my chin, pointing out into the Zone. "Look, the world didn't end, just because you got a good night's sleep."

"I haven't looked south yet."

She snorts, and I kiss her, holding her close.

"I've scheduled another meeting tonight."

I almost joke with her about stepping into dangerous territory, but if she's willing to help me with this problem I think we've only just seen the start of... I'm not going to complain.

"Fault said he wouldn't be able to come. When I asked why, he told me that was something I should ask you."

"He and I agreed a long time ago that it was better if he abstained from the meetings."

She looks at me oddly, and I know we're going to have to have that conversation at some point... but not yet.

We have visitors.

Kimba can see the same signs of it that I can, and she pulls a chunky sweater over the workout clothing she put on to turn herself into a human pretzel.

"This one's for me." She pats my hand and leads the way upstairs.

The car is unfamiliar. The people who climb out of it are not.

Kimba opens the door for Rose and Kylan and greets them like they're old friends.

We'd agreed that Rose would be the best one to know how to advocate for the women who weren't like Laurel... the ones who did end up in the path of Roiban and whoever else was behind the schemes. She's more prepared to consider their traumas.

She leads Rose away to the couches and Kylan... Kylan looks a little sick as he stares out at the Zone. It's a clear day today. The inner caldera's peaks are visible and I know he's heard plenty of the stories about our monsters and the evils beyond them.

"No one really prepares you for the scale." He says, glancing back at me with a worried smile. "How many of you are there?"

"Thirteen." I point to the map of the Zone and he goes to it, eyes wide.

"That's a lot of responsibility for thirteen..."

281

"Some say it's what we were made for."

He nods and blows out a long breath. "Don't get me wrong. I'm grateful she found you... but I wish, just once, she could fall into something that would keep her out of the spotlight."

"I think the spotlight would fall on her wherever she went." Looking over to where the two women sit making plans, I can't help but smile. Kimba shines brighter than any light could.

KIMBA

When Cindy bursts through the door before the meeting, I'm eternally grateful that I've already put my lenses in. She still glows.

"Look!" She wriggles out of her coat and sweeps her shirt close to her body. "I've popped!"

Cindy still has a while to go yet, but she is showing. "Finally!" She cheers, doing a jiggly little dance before hugging me. "Is Andrea here yet?"

"She is now," Andrea says as she comes in, unwrapping her coat. "What's going on?"

Once again, Cindy does a little presentation, wielding her—very small—bump like a weapon.

"Congratulations!" Andrea hugs her and says, "You won."

"What did we win?" Core asks having put their things aside.

"Pride!" Cindy says, smiling up at him.

"I have nothing but pride when I look at you, keruun." Core picks her up and carries her away and Andrea says hello while Strike gets their things put away too.

I ignore the way Andrea hides her own bump beneath her plaid shirt and the scarf she leaves on.

"Oh my God, what happened to you?" She goes straight to Kilo, who reacts like his mother has started fussing over him.

"I'm fine." He swats at her ineffectually. "Leave it alone or I'll stop teaching you how to beat him at bakat."

I watch Strike as he joins them and gently pulls Andrea away from mothering the other man.

They all file in, but Laurel is the only one who stays with me as the rest get settled, even though every question she asks is one I tell her to ask again when we're getting this mess sorted out. She glances at D who is far enough away that I know he can't hear us.

"I'm sure D has told you that I'm not 'qualified' to be Richter's mate."

"He's said nothing of the sort and if he had, I would have set him right in a heartbeat."

"Oh, well… Richter was supposed to have been matched to a weapons specialist or something? I'm not really sure. But what I was going to say was, I think I *can* pull my weight."

"That's not a *requirement* of being here, Laurel. No one's going to kick you out."

"I know, but… Cindy's a nurse, Andrea does her data analysis and Trench says you're some kind of strategist… I felt very much like the odd man out. Until I realized… what's the plan for preschool? What's the plan for school at all?"

I don't know. "Are you volunteering to put something together?"

"I would happily put together a proposal."

"I think that would be great."

Nodding, Laurel glances at D and grimaces—it's the tiniest of movements, but I see it. "I'll go sit down now and save the rest of my questions for when they're appropriate."

She squeezes my hand and goes straight to Richter, slipping into the conversation with Trench like she's been party to it all along.

The cold boys aren't sitting next to each other this time, but Shock hasn't done much other than glare at Arc the entire time they've been here.

Things aren't settled.

But they're going to be. I'll make sure of it.

EPILOGUE

DRIFT

KIMBA HOLDS the attention of every eye in the room. Her skin glitters in ways they can't comprehend, and I let my retinas burn, just a little, to see her better.

Her routine has changed in subtle ways.

No more big drops, no moves that hit her stomach against the pole... eventually the others will see the evidence of what I already know.

"Congratulations," Ganfrey says, leaning on the bar beside me. "It seems that the saints are in a mood to give you everything you've ever wanted."

"It seems they are."

"Change is good." He says, nodding as he takes a sip and I wonder if he means the changes to the council.

Kimba took my seat. Rose travels from Gongii to fill Roiban's and the other new members have proven to be reasonable.

I get to enjoy the feeling of arguing with Lutheil without any of the headache.

Margot taps Ganfrey on the shoulder from behind the bar. "She's ready for you."

He chose to get his lessons from a different dancer. Wishing me well, he heads downstairs to learn from her.

I watch as Kimba finishes her performance, trying to ignore the neon painted woman leaning over the bar beside me.

But Margot won't be ignored.

Kimba spirals down the pole and into the floor, blowing a kiss to me before she disappears. Only *then* do I give a shred of attention to her boss.

"What can I do for you, Margot?"

She snorts. "You can't do anything for me, *brother*."

Again, the way she calls me that leaves me unsettled.

"I'm feeling nice tonight," she says sliding a drink my way. "You can both leave out the same door. Since I know you've got 'better' places to be."

"I'll follow the rules." I tip the drink back. "I already owe you too much."

"Yes, you do." She chuckles. "Remember that when I finally come to collect my favor."

"That sounds like a threat."

"It might be. I haven't decided yet."

I wait another ten minutes before I leave through the door for patrons. I wait in the parking lot at our car, watching the employee entrance all the while.

My heart lifts when I see her, and it lifts again when she sees me.

She runs across the pavement to me and hops into my arms.

"Hi." She kisses me. "Take me home?"

"Always."

Kimba still dances five nights a week. She needs the

286

energy release and several of her friends refuse to come to the outpost to visit. I don't blame them.

And once a week… on my night off, I still come to her.

But we leave after her second dance, instead of going downstairs.

After we've parked in her garage and she's done her override trick to send the elevator straight to the seventy-third floor, we take our time getting from the front door and up to the bed, but once we're there…

Sitting at the foot of the bed, Kimba angles her hips, and her hand grips my cock, stroking me to steel. "Do you know what today is?" she asks.

"How could I forget?" Three years ago, she came to me for the first time.

"I spent that first night, terrified. Frozen, just staring up at the mirrored ceiling."

"I know."

"I think I was already aware of *why* you terrified me."

"There are a lot of reasons you should have been."

"I think I knew from the moment I saw you that there was no chance I *wouldn't* fall in love with you." She draws her thumbs along my lip. "I'd be lying if I said you didn't still terrify me a little."

"Three years is too short a time to know much with certainty." I hold her back against me, chin resting on her shoulder as we both watch the glittering lights outside. "I've made many mistakes. But loving you… waiting for you… Is the one thing that I know I will never regret."

I hold her open as I gently rock into her. With the lights off, we're not really on display, but I press a kiss to the crook of her neck and say, "I would fuck you for the whole world to see. Just so they know I'm yours."

"We're going to have to take a break soon." She kisses

me and sweeps my hand over her stomach to place my fingers on her clit. "The consequences of your actions."

I chuckle as I toy with her clit.

"Consequences I will gladly face, whenever you're ready for me to do so again." I kiss her shoulder and drink in the rush of desire that floods through our bond as my hand and cock work in tandem.

I want every part of her... even the so-called consequences.

I want her past, her present and her future.

Good or bad.

She'd asked if we should sell this place and get something new, but I don't want that.

She has started calling it our *ojuin*—our love nest—a private place where the responsibilities of the Zone can't touch us. It faces south, so we can't even see the mountains.

The faint light from the building exterior makes it so that I can see her though. She is utterly beautiful. She's mine.

And I'm never going to let her go.

ABOUT DALIA

Dalia Davies came up with the title for "Railed by the Easter Bunny" as a joke. But that joke grew legs and hopped right out of her brain and onto the page for you to read and enjoy with her. She writes fantasy romance that pairs old gods and monsters with mortal women who get exactly what they want and maybe a little more than they came for. Living in the southwestern US, she's let the outside heat permeate her stories and hopes they leave you panting.

Find more info and sign up for the newsletter at www.daliadavies.com

BECOME A PATRON

For early access, exclusive stories, sneak peeks at art, and book mail, at patreon.com/daliadavies

CORE INSTINCTS, a novella about Core & Cindy's first days is available to Patrons

MORE BOOKS BY DALIA DAVIES

SHADOW ZONE BROTHERHOOD

Richter Scale

Seismic Drift

Trench Tactics

VALLEY OF THE OLD GODS

Railed by the Easter Bunny

Banging the Easter Bunny

Railed by the Krampus

Railed at the Bacchanal

Railed by the Reaper

Railed by the Tooth Fairy

Railed by the Yule Cat

Railed by the Leprechaun

THE DEVIL'S DANCE

The Dame & The Devil

The Flame & The Fallen

The Halo & The Heathen

CONTEMPORARY ROMANCE AS ANDI SIMMS

A TASTE OF SOMETHING WICKED

Fate at Fault

Fair Bargain

With This Vow

All Fun & Games

At Summer's End

Like & Sub

Nine Two Five

Gifted & Talented

A Taste of Something Wicked Print Omnibus Vol 1

A Taste of Something Wicked Print Omnibus Vol 2

SPICE MENU

Kimba gets her first taste of D's cock
(Chapter 5, pg 72)

Drift makes up for lost time (with his tongue)
(Chapter 5, pg 83)

Drift uses one of Kimba's many toys to get her hers
(Chapter 6, pg 100)

Kimba & Drift seal their bond
(Chapter 9, pg 145)

Kimba wakes Drift up with her pussy
(Chapter 10, pg 153)

Kimba dances for Drift and he takes everything she'll give him
(Chapter 12, pg 173)

They have a little hotel honeymoon

With the help of three dildos to size up, Drift fucks her ass like she wants.

Soft epilogue sex